Lee Stuart Evans was born a
up in north Nottinghamshi
writer for fifteen years, he's
television and radio shows
Cats and *8 Out of 10 Cats Does*
Ross Show, The Frank Skinner Show, A League of Their
Own, and *Live At The Apollo.*

He mostly likes trains, books, guitars and his family.

WORDS BEST SUNG

Lee Stuart Evans

ARUNDEL
BOOKS

First published in Great Britain in 2017 by
Arundel Books
www.arundelbooks.co.uk

ISBN 978-0-9558133-9-9

Typeset in Garamond 11pt

Acknowledgements

Thanks to my family and friends who very kindly read and offered much helpful feedback during the writing of this book.

Double thanks to Antoinette Cecilia Kelly for not only reading it, but then also designing the brilliant cover.

Big thanks to my publisher, Alan Dance of Arundel Books, and his wife Carol, for their always generous support, advice and enthusiasm throughout the publishing process.

And especially big thanks to Nina, Alfie and George for their constant encouragement and belief, and for putting up with my frequent disappearances (either in mind or body) for hours, days, weeks at a time. I promise the book is now finally finished.

This book is dedicated to The Mowbrays.

Though one moment's pleasure
In one moment flies
Though the passion's treasure
In one moment dies

Yet it has not passed
Think how near, how near
And while it doth last
Think how dear, how dear

John Keats – *Hither Hither Love*

Yeah, I get up
And I see the sun up
And I feel good, yeah
'Cause my life has begun

Ray Davies – *Till The End Of The Day*

PROLOGUE
November 1963

'You'd better get a move on, Alastair, hadn't you?' said Gladys Braymoor as she burst from the pantry cuddling a loaf. 'At this rate them engines'll be turning out black as they went in.'

His mother looked like somebody else in the mornings, in her old dressing gown and with her fiery gingerbread curls clamped wonkily about her head in big thick rollers. But she sounded the same as always.

'And what have you got on your feet?'

'Socks,' said Alastair. 'You wear them inside your shoes, Mother.'

'I can see they're socks, you daft sod, but *cream*?' Gladys shook her head. 'Of all the bloody colours to choose! Now hurry up and finish your breakfast.'

Alastair gulped his tea before perching himself on the arm of the sofa to tie on his boots, warm from the hearth. Although it was practically the middle of the night, he'd been awake the best part of an hour already, partly with excitement but also with worry about the bike. Having spent all Saturday morning bringing it back to life he now regretted skimping on a new inner tube, instead adding yet another layer to the lumpen patchwork of the old. Serve him right if it were flat as a pancake when he went out to it.

'And you don't need that on, now,' his mother said, swooping on the portable radio he'd left burbling away on the table and carrying it off, along with his empty breakfast plate, into the kitchen. 'Your dad won't want wakening up with that racket at five o'clock, I do know. Now look sharp, or you'll be late.'

'Stop whittling, Mam. It's only five past,' said Alastair, checking his reflection in the mirror over the fireplace. 'Takes me half-hour at most to get to Langbrook.'

Smoothing his hair where it stuck out over his ears, he thought perhaps he should have shaved again after all. A floorboard creaked

1

overhead. Alastair gazed at himself, one ear cocked towards the ceiling. He'd wondered if his father might be up to see him off, but hadn't really expected it. Since moving up to the pit top with skin trouble Jock no longer needed to set off before about half past six, so you could hardly blame him if he chose to stay in bed and enjoy his extra hour of oblivion.

'I shouldn't bother preening and titivating yersen up too much,' said Gladys, smiling up at her son as she held out a clear plastic lunchbox, heavy with sandwiches, an apple and a chocolate biscuit. 'You're being set on at the railway, not The London Palladium.'

Alastair smiled, still not quite able to believe it himself. He stuffed the snap tin into his rucksack and buttoned up his grey duffle coat, the one that made him feel and, or so he hoped, look like a cool young poet, some West Coast hip cat troubadour. 'See you later then, Mam,' he said, making towards the back door.

'Don't go without these!' Gladys swivelled round, prising open the cuff of a navy blue glove. 'I've been warming 'em up on the stove while you had your breakfast.' Alastair slid his hands into the hot wool, bending to kiss his mother's cheek only for her to outmanoeuvre him and land him one smack on the lips.

'Mam!' he protested, wiping his mouth on his sleeve.

'Won't hurt you! And don't you go telling me to stop whittling, neither. Just cos you're at work now doesn't mean you're too big for a bit of *this* round your tab-hole.' As his mother held her palm inches from his cheek, Alastair wondered if they weren't tears gathering at the corners of her eyes.

'I'll get off then, Mam,' he said, pulling on his hood. 'Toodle-oo!'

Outside, the waiting November morning was as black as the fire back, but it was not half as cold as his mother had shiveringly forecast. And finding the worrisome tyre hard as stone beneath his thumb Alastair even found himself whistling a jaunty tune as he manoeuvred the bike out of the outside toilet and rolled it down the gennel, just like a proper grown-up man would on setting out for work. Meanwhile, above, in the front bedroom of number 7 Welgrove Terrace, Jock Braymoor stood at the dark window, scratching the thick hairs that flowed from the neck of his vest, watching as his son threw his leg over the crossbar and coasted silently down the hill towards town.

Despite the creeping day and the fuzzy haloes of floodlights, as Alastair neared Langbrook Shed the sky became suddenly darker than ever. Heavy grey clouds hung low and sinister in an air thick with the smells of industry. He pulled up on the bridge, balancing on his pedals to peer over the parapet. It was a sight he'd seen countless times before, although never at quite such an unsocial hour. In the sprawling yard, beyond the sloping roofs of the engine sheds, Alastair traced the outlines of perhaps fifty or sixty steam locomotives, huge shadowy beasts standing buffer-to-buffer along the two dozen roads that ran into and alongside the various buildings, water towers, coaling plants and workshops, and fanned out around the turntable. In the patches of light between, silhouettes of men flitted and crawled about, their voices echoing in the lulls between the whoosh and hiss of waking engines.

The doors of the main engine shed were flung wide open and in the light that poured out a small group in filthy overalls, clutching steaming mugs, gathered round a large diesel locomotive, little more than a box on wheels, really, but smart-looking in its coat of fresh green paint.

Alastair had found a space in the bike shed and was trying to remember the way to the foreman's office when a chubby man about his father's age appeared from the shadows and, rubbing his hands noisily together, said, 'How do, I'm Shep. Alastair, is it?'

'Yes.'

'Ah, thought so. Well then, young Alastair, we'd better get thi set on at summat, hadn't we?' And just like that, Shep strode purposefully off along a cinder path towards a series of low red-brick buildings huddled around the engine sheds. These, according to the neat hand-painted lettering on the doors, housed the various workshops, stores and offices needed to run a busy railway yard, though none seemed especially busy just at that moment. But as they drew closer towards the noise – the hammering of metal, the ratcheting of cranes and the clank and rumble of crawling steam engines – the darkness faded and more figures could be seen moving about behind the narrow, brightly lit windows.

'Thi dun't want to be wearing tha best coat, lad,' Shep said, watching as Alastair carefully hung his duffle in the locker he'd been assigned. 'Not if thi wants to keep it nice.'

Shep kitted him out with a pair of grubby overalls and a jacket to slip on over his own clothes, as well as a pair of large and loose-fingered gloves which appeared to have been knitted entirely from coal dust. 'And thi'll need some good thick jumpers and long johns on under them, this time o' year, or thi'll freeze to death. If we ay a winter like the last one, phew-by-crikey!' The foreman clapped his hands and rubbed them together, rough as two sheets of sandpaper. 'Rate then, we'll see about getting yer 'ands dirty shall we?'

'Awight then, Shep? Say, it's enaff to nip yer knackers off this morning, ain't it?'

'Aye, it's a fresh un, Terry, tha's not wrong there, lad,' Shep said, his booming voice warm and friendly as it rattled the frosted glass of the office windows.

'Cam on then! Let us parrst. Oim in a 'array, 'ere, ent I?'

'Go on then, Terry. I'll let thi past. But just this once, mind – you hear?'

Alastair peered round Shep's massive shoulder, intrigued to put a face to the unfortunately voiced Terry. Clad in a dark smock coat which reached almost down to its ankles, a hunched figure rustled towards them from the gloom, driving along a large sweeping brush with such brightly grinning enthusiasm Alastair wondered if the lad were quite the full shilling.

'Fank you, Shep. Gentleman you are,' Terry said. Terry was about twenty, and an unexpectedly pleasant-looking lad who, Alastair noted, had it not been for the round shoulders and pronounced stoop would have been about the same height as himself. As he drew level, Terry, without pausing for even a second in his duty, beamed delightedly up at Alastair. 'Awight, mate! Am Terry. Arr spect we'll be seein' lot of each ather. Snice-a-meet-you.'

As he made his way past, sweeping nineteen to the dozen, Alastair saw that not only did Terry have a very bad limp, but that he also seemed to be dragging a heavy right foot.

Alastair turned and plunged smack into Shep's vast, low-slung belly. 'Oops! Sorry, Shep.'

4

Shep neither budged nor smiled. 'That there's Terry,' he said carefully. 'You'll see a lot on 'im about the place. He's a nice lad, do owt for yer. And he's not shy when it comes to mekkin' tea, neither, so...' Shep hesitated, resettled his cap on his huge head. 'But he's, er, not, er...' Shep pursed his lips, apparently unable to find the right words to explain what it was that Terry was not. 'He's not, er... well, he's from Kent, in't he? Look, tha knows worram gerrin' at. He's a nice lad. And if I catch thi tekkin' piss out on 'im, I'll be down on thi like a ton o' bricks.'

Alastair, laden with brushes, rags and paraffin, had a job keeping up with Shep as he skipped nimbly between the rails and wound along the avenues of locomotives and tenders which rose up darkly on all sides, hissing, woofing and clanking The Junction's dawn chorus. The East Yard, which ran right alongside the mainline, was the largest of three and where, apart from the workshops, most of the noise and activity seemed to be centred that morning. Smudged figures of men, armed with brushes and shovels, oil cans and grease guns, scurried between the ranks of patient engines or hung from the boilers and footplates of others as they barked along beneath clouds of thick, spark-lit smoke. Shep laughed at one or two comments that came from the shadows as they passed by, and at one point he rubbed Alastair's head as if he were the new boy in school, but they might have spoken in a foreign language for what sense they made to Alastair.

In the distance a train worked hard against the steep gradient on the approach into Langbrook. Alastair's first instinct was to blurt out the type of locomotive, like he and his pals had always done since they were boys, but he decided against it. As Shep halted between the buffers of a shabby-looking engine, he seemed about to say something when suddenly, very dramatically, he raised a finger and waited while the world fell silent. Seconds later a long train of coal empties burst from the sooty mouth of the road bridge, a raucous cacophony of smoke and squealing steel. They watched as the driver shut off and coasted towards the old station, Shep smiling as the din faded and the last wisps of smoke dissolved in the pale morning air.

'Enthusiast, are we?'

'No,' said Alastair, defensively, not wanting to appear childish before his foreman. 'Well, yes – a bit. More when I was younger, you know, not so much now.'

Shep smiled, yellow teeth almost white in his grubby face. 'Ah, me an' all. Followed engines all over t'place when I wor a lad. Derby, Donny, Crewe. Swindon once; missed last train home and had to sleep in t'waiting room till morning. Marvellous! Thi'll soon change tha tune though, when tha's up to thee eyes in muck and mess all day. At least that's what my old foreman told me, when I started.' Shep winked. 'Course, it'll be nowt but them, soon,' he said, nodding towards the shiny green diesel, at the steps of which a gang of drivers, fitters and firemen waited their turn to climb up into the cab for a glimpse of the future. 'We've a dozen of them "Brushes" now. And ten of them little single-cab jobs. But that's a fresh un, on trial. Gerrin' on three thousand hosspower, that is, and ready to go at touch of a button.'

They wandered a little further until Shep, with surprising athleticism, suddenly leapt up onto the buffer beam of a filthy black engine and pulled Alastair up beside him. As they stood before the yawning hole of the open smokebox Alastair could almost taste the ashes on his tongue. The smell, for some reason, reminded him of home. The diesel's air horn gave a sharp blast and then, as if to demonstrate Shep's earlier point, its engine fired up and roared effortlessly into life.

'They do look smart in that two-tone green, mind.'

'Suppose so,' Alastair nodded begrudgingly.

'Bloody boring though. Not a patch on these.' Shep turned his back on the yard. 'Right then. This, as tha probably knows, is an 8F, ex-War Department job. As thi can see, it's bloody filthy. So tha first job, young Alastair, is to see if thi can get the bogger summat like sparkling again. Now, watch and listen...'

As the weeks passed Alastair was delighted to find that being an engine cleaner was just as filthy and backbreaking a business as he'd always dreamed it would be, if not more so. The variety of tasks was so varied, so interesting and enjoyable – to him, anyway – it seemed unimaginable that the job could ever become tedious or routine. The first time he climbed through the hole into the firebox of a steam engine he actually laughed out loud. And from sweeping the footplate and lubricating the countless bearings, joints, links and other intricate mechanisms located along the length and breadth of an engine, to the driver's controls – regulator, brake valve, reversing handle, firebox door – to the ashes which constantly piled up, forever needing to be dropped or shovelled out (sometimes when they were still hot, but which in winter you were often glad of, despite the risk of being scalded if you weren't careful), Alastair loved every single minute. He took great pride in being able to raise a good fire, or properly wash out a boiler; in making sure tenders were adequately descaled and promptly filled up ready with coal and water. And he didn't mind one bit that he nearly always came home after a shift with axle grease in his hair and soot in his underpants. The cream socks had probably not been his brightest idea. But then they hadn't remained cream for very long.

'You'll never remember everything,' Norm Allison, one of the Passed Cleaners, said as they cycled out of the yard at the end of Alastair's first week. 'Just do the best you can, and give us a shout if you get stuck or break summat. We're nearly all heavy coal traffic here. So mek sure the sandboxes are always topped up and the gear well maintained, especially this weather. Otherwise they slip like bastards and we get our arses kicked. If sand bunker's low, tell Terry. Terry's the sandman.'

PART ONE

A CLEVER LAD LIKE YOU

CHAPTER ONE

September 1964

'Alastair? Alastair? *Alastair*!!!'

Alastair struck a vicious open G Major and let it ring out until the speaker began to squeal and the windows almost rattled out of their sash frames.

'Alastair!!!'

He laid the guitar on the bed and flicked off the amplifier, securing the towel around his waist as he went to call over the banister. 'What're you bawling at, woman?'

'Mam says you're to stop that horrible noise,' said Sarah, peering up the stairs, one wing of her jet-black bob tucked behind her ear, her face made up with its usual spidery dark eyelashes, deep red lips and heavy black eyeliner that terminated in sharp feline points around the side of her face.

'Horrible noise? Bloody cheek. That was The Rolling Stones, tell her.'

'Didn't sound like them. Well, you're to stop it anyway. Mary's here.'

'Sarah,' Alastair, leaning precariously forward, whispered. 'Send her up, will you?'

Suddenly Sarah's face was gone, wrenched away from the stairfoot door and replaced by his fuming mother's. 'She'll do nothing of the sort!' Gladys said, outraged. 'Send her up? I ask you!'

Alastair drew back, watched his mother in the stairwell mirror, smart and furious in her brown twin-set and pearls beneath a floral pinny.

'What do you think this is? Some sort of dosshouse?' Gladys did not, as some parents do, become someone entirely different when in company, rather a larger and considerably less relaxed version of her usual not especially relaxed self. 'And *you* can behave yourself tonight, young lady,' she said, edging away from the stairs and turning her fire on Sarah. 'I'm not having you boozing it up at your age.' Gladys's voice rose and fell as she went about the living room, fussing and tidying. 'If I hear tales you've been carryin' on, you wain't go n'more.'

Alastair heard Sarah say goodbye and a moment later the sound of her clip-clopping footsteps echoed up to his bedroom window from the pavement.

'And I hardly think Mary's the sort of girl who goes up to lads' bedrooms, Alastair. I don't know where he gets it from, Mary, really I don't. He wants to look sharp and get himself down these stairs.'

Alastair stole a palmful of his father's aftershave, listening while his mother launched into a monologue of apology for his shameful vulgarity, the blame for which apparently lay at the door of, among other things, long-haired pop singers, a play on the BBC about abortion, and Christine Keeler's dubious taste in men. 'Bald as a bloomin' coot, he was, and no spring chicken. Worse than lads now they are, some o' the lasses,' Gladys went on. 'Send her upstairs! I don't know what you must think on us, Mary.'

'Gladys, will yi let it go, woman?' Jock said, his Lanarkshire burr rising gently but firmly from behind his *Daily Mirror*. 'Mary's nae more interested in going upstairs than I am.'

'I know she isn't,' said Gladys, glancing up at the ceiling. 'But he would, the – '

'Alastair will be down in a minute. And until then, Mary will wait for him here, *ideally* in peace.' Jock peered over the top of his reading glasses. 'Och, woman, I don't know what yi think'll happen.'

'Whatullappen? Whatull – ' Gladys paused briefly to refill her lungs. 'You don't know the half of it. Young folks nowadays. Why, Peg Marlowe – Alwyn Sheppard's sister, works at Co-op – said only the other day Alastair was seen reading filthy books at work.'

'Filthy books!' Jock began, pointlessly. 'It was – '

'Not *Lady Floosit's Wotnot*; that other one he did. I forget now. Mind you, they're all about the same thing aren't they, all of his?'

'*Sons and Lovers*,' Jock said, knowing that while a second voice was not always necessary for Gladys to hold a conversation, she much preferred it when there was at least one other for her to trample all over.

'Brazen as anything, he was.' Gladys shook her head. '*Sons and*

Lovers! Fancy reading one o' that filthy sod's books, excuse my language, and in front of the whole of British Railways!'

'*Filthy book*?' Jock's eyebrows rose into thick black arches.

'No shame they haven't, nowadays. Sex on the brain, they have, all on 'em.'

'Sex on the brain?' Alastair leapt the bottom two stairs into the living room, tossing his dark green tweed sports jacket over the back of the sofa. 'Who has, mi dad? You should hear what he says when you're not in, Mam. It's enough to mek your eyes water.'

Alastair greeted Mary with a cocky wink and a full-on Nottinghamshire 'Ey up, mi duck', before standing with his feet wide apart in the hearth while he fastened his black knitted tie in the mirror.

'*You*, I meant!' said his mother. 'Young uns! Sex mad, all on yer. You know perfectly well I didn't mean your dad. Your dad's hardly sex mad, but then *he* was in the army.' Jock's eyebrows sprang all the way up his forehead as he looked between his wife, son, and Mary, confused as to the link Gladys had made between military service and his implied lack of libido. 'Not an ounce of shame, they haven't. Not like when we were their age.'

'Och, we were never their age,' said Jock, sending Mary a friendly wink from behind his paper. Mary smiled.

Gladys, rising from the armchair in which she'd fleetingly settled, took her son by the elbow and yanked him from the hearth. She was a little woman, barely five foot, but if the mood took her she could summon up the grip of a navvy. 'Come out that bloody hearth, will you?' she said. 'Can't you get a good enough look at yourself without standing on top of that mirror? It's no wonder the carpet looks like it does, your great boots paddling soot all through the house.' Gladys snatched his jacket from where he'd flung it over the back of the sofa and set about straightening the antimacassars. 'You won't even hang your coat up like any normal lad would. God help the woman that ends up with you to run about after. *Here*!' she said, holding out his jacket. But instead of taking it, like any normal lad would, Alastair spun around and backed towards his mother, his arms outstretched behind him.

'Ah, Wilson, my coat!' he barked in his best Old Colonial

Officer's voice. 'Thank you, my good man. Now Wilson, as you know I shall be dining out this evening, so might I suggest that after you've walked my underpants and ironed the dogs, you kick back with the bootboy here and take the rest of the night orf.' Jock looked at Mary, shaking his head at his son's idiotic tomfoolery. Gladys couldn't help a little smile as she swung for Alastair's ear. He gave her a gentle peck on the cheek. 'And mind you keep that to yourself, Wilson. I don't kiss all the staff, you know, and if the others find out they'll all be wanting one.'

'Yer cheeky-daft! I don't know where you get it from. Now go on, *get*! Mary duck, take him out of my sight.'

Mary bent to kiss Gladys and said goodbye to Jock who, as he always did whenever Mary arrived or departed, put down his newspaper and rose from his chair, smiling politely as he nodded and straightened his tie.

* * *

Nigel Wells had been in love with Sarah Braymoor ever since he saw her swimming in her underwear, in the river, during the summer holidays. She was fourteen; he sixteen. Yet no matter how high he built his quiff, or how tight he wore his jeans, Sarah had never, in the three years since, shown even the slightest sign of having any such feelings for him in return. Sure, she was always very friendly towards him, she enjoyed his company and he often made her laugh. She liked him. He was sweet. But Sarah could say that about a lot of her friends. Yet Nigel was not deterred. He understood that girls – *nice* girls – were supposed to be difficult, and he remained confident that with a bit of patience, kindness and charm, Sarah would one day be his.

'I'll take you for a ride one Sunday, if you like,' Nigel said. 'I often go to Matlock on Sundays. All the bikers do. There's nowt to be frightened of wi' me, I'm as safe as houses. Not one of these madheads, racing about out of control.' Sarah's lips split like an overripe tomato as she let out a girlish giggle. It thrilled Nigel to make Sarah laugh, even when he hadn't meant to.

'Oh, Nigel!' Sarah sipped the last of her bitter lemon. 'You know it's not about you or your driving. I just don't like motorbikes, that's all. I think they're dangerous.'

'Well, I make a point of not being dangerous. And you *ride* motorbikes, not drive them. Anyway, I can't afford to come off it, I need it for work.' Nigel did something with insurance. He said very little about it, but it must have paid well because he was always well dressed and never seemed short of money.

'Well, you won't be getting me on the back of one. If you want to go smashing your head against a tree, good luck to you,' Sarah said. 'Not that there's much in there to damage, mind,' she added, playfully ruffling his hair.

'All right Miss Clever Clogs, suit yourself. Drink?'

Nigel rose before Sarah could answer, taking their empty glasses and leaning across the table of friends where for the last ten minutes a riot or a wild sex orgy might have broken out and he been none the wiser. 'What you having Ally, pint of Best?'

Alastair, hearing his name, reclaimed his hand from where it had lain clamped and sweating between both of Mary's. He could barely grip the glass to finish his pint. Licking his lips, he revived his Old Colonial officer. 'How terribly sporting of you, old man! I'd be *delighted*!'

Alastair wasn't really in the mood for silly voices. They weren't so much fun when Trevor wasn't there to play along. Also, there had always been something about Nigel Wells that niggled Alastair, invited gentle ridicule, and not only the way he persisted in calling him "Ally", knowing full well how he hated it.

'No Trev tonight, Ally?' Alastair feigned deafness until Mary nudged him.

'Trev? *Trev*? Oh, you mean Parkes, old chap? Grandfather did frightfully well out of the old East India business? Yes, yes, Parkes! Quite a fellow. Did you ever meet him?' Bored, Alastair dropped the voice. '*Trevor* has gone to fetch his dad from Chesterfield. Motor's in at Cole's. Starter motor.'

'Why's he taken it all the way to Chesterfield?' Nigel's lip curled incomprehension. 'What's up with – '

'How should I know?' Alastair interrupted sharply. 'He's not *my* father.'

'He said he might call in for a drink, if he's not too late,' offered

Sarah, not that anyone noticed.

'Keep your hair on, Ally,' said Nigel. 'What about the lovely Mary?'

Mary was busy rummaging through her handbag and humming along to the jukebox. 'Hmm?'

'Said do you want a drink, duck?' Nigel jabbed his thumb in the direction of the bar. 'My round.'

He was certainly handsome, Sarah was right, thought Mary, despite the greasy rocker outfit and the slyness she had always suspected lurked in men with green eyes.

'No. I'm fine with this one, thank you, Nigel,' Mary said, sliding her hands once more around Alastair's. 'I've had two already.'

Nigel opened his eyes wide, his square jaw swinging open in mock horror. 'Two tomato juices! You want to watch her, Ally. You'll end up carrying her home at this rate.' Nigel slapped Alastair manfully on the back. 'What is it with these two, eh?' he said, nodding between the two girls. 'Bitter lemon. Tomato juice. They make a cheap date if nowt else!'

A few strides and Nigel was leaning against the bar. The taproom was filling up with the usual Friday night crowd; familiar faces who traded nods and winks over cries of *'How do?'* and *'Ey up, mi duck!'* as they looked about for their pals, despite knowing they'd be at the same tables where they always sat, week in, week out.

Sarah pulled her chair around to sit beside Mary. 'You are awful to him sometimes, Alastair,' she said, glancing across to see Nigel watching her thoughtfully from the bar. 'What have you got against him?'

Alastair drained the last of his pint and pursed his lips. 'I've not got anything against him,' he said. 'I like anybody that buys me a pint – even Nigel. You want to be careful that's all, and keep off that bloody motorbike. They're deathtraps.'

Suddenly, as if his ear had been hooked by an invisible fishing line, Alastair looked over and scowled at the jukebox. 'Who keeps putting Adam bloody Faith on?' Mary nudged Sarah's elbow, the pair of them struggling to stifle their giggles.

Nigel settled the tray of drinks on the table and drew his stool up beside Sarah. You had to admire the daft sod's persistence, thought

Alastair. He caught his sister's eye; smiling, she looked away.

They'd all been friends since infant school. But recently, since she'd been allowed to go to the pub, Nigel had begun behaving like a wasp round a seaside bin with Sarah. It was a blessing she hadn't yet taken to alcohol, but it could only be a matter of time, especially if Nigel Wells had anything to do with it. Alastair was naturally protective of his sister, and, being a young man about the same age, he had every reason to be wary of Nigel's motives. He knew exactly what Nigel saw when he looked at Sarah; it was what he saw himself now, when he looked at practically every woman in the street. Yet he also knew from the occasional flippant conversations they'd had regarding their love lives, such as they were, that Sarah was far from a silly girl. Much to Alastair's discomfort, Sarah had not so long ago admitted that she was in no rush to lose her virginity, that it would happen when it was meant to and not before. Besides, she'd added, the only man she'd ever seriously considered going all the way with so far was Adam Faith, and he was hardly likely to turn up in Warinstowe to take her up on her offer, was he?

In his heart, Alastair understood it would take a lot more than a lantern-jawed insurance man with a leather jacket and a throbbing Triumph to sweep Sarah off her feet. Just because she'd brains enough for two didn't mean she'd settle for somebody without one.

'Leave off it, Ally, will you? They're not as bad as all that, y'know.'

'Adam Faith tunes? They bloody well are!' Alastair said, shaking a pantomime fist at his sister. It was the third time in half an hour he'd suffered *What Do You Want?* What Alastair wanted was for the whining shortarse to shut up.

'*Motorbikes!*' stressed Nigel. 'I heard you – "Deathtraps". Give over saying that. Bad as mi mother, you are. Like I say to her, bikes are like guns – they're only dangerous in the wrong hands, and I haven't got wrong hands, Ally. I've passed my test, haven't I? And, touch wood...' While Nigel touched the fingers of one of his presumably *correct* hands against the table, Sarah rapped her knuckles on the side of his skull. But Nigel's eyes remained on Alastair.

'I haven't come off it yet, and I don't mean to, neither. Safe as houses, I am.' Nigel lifted his glass and took a long, slow mouthful of bitter before placing it down heavily on the table. 'Safe as houses.' he repeated.

'Even houses fall down sometimes, Nige,' said Alastair.

Nigel ignored the comment, shrugged and took another pull at his beer. As he drank he peered over his glass at Sarah, drinking her in with the sour ale. Beneath her face powder Sarah's cheeks were burning. She pulled self-consciously at the hem of her dog-tooth patterned mini-dress, as if realising for the first time how much of her shapely legs were on display. She folded her hands primly over her knees.

Mary sensed a feminine voice was needed amid the tension. 'That's a lovely dress, Sarah. Where did you get it?' she asked, not considering that her dress might be the last thing Sarah wished to draw attention to just at that moment.

'From Simpson's. But don't you think it's a bit too short?'

'No! I think it's smashing.'

Alcohol had begun to lighten Alastair's mood. A cheeky smirk crept across his face, pinched the corners of his eyes and made them sparkle. 'You'd get some wind up your knickers wearing that on the back of a motorbike,' he grinned. 'That is if you've remembered to put a pair on.'

Nigel choked into his pint, sending a spray of beer out through his nose and spattering his jeans. A little splashed into Mary's glass and on her fingers, for which Nigel apologised effusively. Mary laughed, waved away the incident through a grim smile.

'It's not you that should be sorry, Nigel,' she said. 'It's Alastair and his filthy mouth. Fancy saying that about your own sister!' Alastair felt a crack across the back of his head and then Mary taking his chin between her thumb and forefinger. 'Kiss to say sorry?'

He gave her a noisy peck on the lips and then, excusing himself, rose and marched across to the jukebox to give Adam Faith what he'd been asking for all evening.

CHAPTER TWO

'You don't seem at all yourself tonight, Alastair,' Mary sighed. 'What's the matter?'

'There's note-a-matter wi' me, duck,' Alastair said as they walked slowly away from the town, their hands joined and swinging gently between them. Away from the pubs there was hardly a soul about, though traffic on the main road was steady as always.

'And what are you talking like that for? It's silly.'

'What y'on about? Am talkin' rate enough.' Alastair walked along on the outside of the pavement, nearest the road. He did so partly because he felt it was important to at least try to behave like a gentleman when it suited, but mainly because there were times – now for instance – when he had a sudden urge to walk with one foot in the road and the other on the pavement, causing his body to rise and fall in clumsy, spastic jerks and making it seem as if his left leg was a good five or six inches shorter than his right. The fun was in seeing how far he could travel like this before either a car hooted its horn or Mary self-combusted with rage.

Clump! *Down goes the left foot – ahh! And u-u-u-p comes the body!* an internal voice urged him on. He was Douglas Bader, taking his first steps on tin legs. *Now swing rou-ou-ou-nd with the right hurr-urr-gahhrrr! And d-o-o-w-w-n it goes again, down, down, down to the dusty road.* Clump! *And again! U-u-u-up with the leftahh! And swing – aahhrr!* Clump!

This will soon get her goat, he thought, enjoying himself. Alastair loved to be silly, to make himself laugh. Liked the way it made you feel light as a feather, like you were the nicest bit drunk, which to be fair, at that moment, he was.

Beneath the amber glow of the last street lamp, at the point where the town ended and the park began, Alastair saw that Mary's face was seething, that she was fighting hard to keep her composure, to hold her humourless dead-ahead gaze, determined she should not give in and acknowledge his childish, idiotic games.

Alastair clumped on, watching her out of the corner of his eye. How gorgeous she looked! She really was like a young goddess. She had the sort of beauty that grabbed you instantly, smacked you between the eyes and left you breathless. Even her simplest gestures, made at the right moment, had the power to set his whole innards aflame.

But there was also something a little unfair about Mary's beauty. The way it sometimes made him feel so utterly sick and helpless that all he wanted to do was to annoy the hell out of her. Alastair decided his interior monologue was far too amusing to keep all to himself. He would share it with Mary.

'*U-u-u-p comes the body,*' he said in a big, determined voice. '*Ahhh! And then e-e-easy from the hip-ahh!*'

'Alastair!'

'*A-a-a-nd swing the leg* – Ouch!'

'Come out of the road, will you?' Mary screeched, sounding like his mother as she wrenched him from the gutter. 'You're worse than a baby sometimes. How old are you?'

'Never mind how old I am. That bloody hurt, you beastly girl!' Alastair leaned against the lamp post rubbing his dislocated shoulder.

'Alastair!'

'What? I should jolly well report you, Mary Windale,' Alastair whined in his best *Brideshead* voice, though he dared not risk a smile in case it should send Mary completely over the edge. She'd something on her mind, he'd sensed as much at the Fox & Hounds. But then there always was something on Mary's mind.

'You're a bully, Mary. That's all you are, just a rotten bully.'

'That's better.'

'It most certainly is *not* better!'

'I mean *you*. You're speaking nicely again – *properly*. You know I don't like it when you act silly and deliberately try to sound all...'

'All what?'

'*Common* – like one of the rough lads off the estate.'

It was one of the ways Alastair most painfully wounded Mary, his selfish transgressions into the Common. And he knew exactly where it would lead them if he weren't careful. The worst thing he could do now would be to antagonize her...

'I work on t'railway, Mary. Dost tha find *that* common an' all then, mi little duck egg?'

'*Don't*! I know you work on the railway, Alastair, but that doesn't mean you have to talk like that. And anyway, you might not always work on the railway, will you?'

As she spoke these last words, Mary's delicious features seemed to crumple inwards towards their centre, revealing more than a trace of the little girl she had been not so very long ago – mardy, stroppy, and just a little bit spoilt. Somewhere beyond the park, across the distant fields that stretched darkly towards Langbrook, a train blew its whistle, unaware of the quiet amusement it would bring to Alastair just at that moment.

'Why won't I? I love the railway, Mary. There's nothing I'd rather do, you know that.' In the jaundiced light he could see the fine dusting of powder that covered her sharp-edged cheeks, darkening towards the hollows. He noted how expertly it had been applied, unlike that of a lot of young girls whose make-up skills were enough to land them a job as a council plasterer. As he looked at her he wondered if all women were at their most beautiful when men made them angry.

'It's just that it's not really you, is it, *the railway*?' Mary pronounced it as though it were a profession a young man should be ashamed of, as though he were a backstreet abortionist or a male hairdresser. 'All that hard work, those filthy engines, it's not... You know what I mean, Alastair. You don't *have* to do it, do you?' She moved close and gently straightened his tie.

'No, Mary, I don't *have* to do it,' he said, stepping away. 'I do it because I enjoy it. Because it's all I ever wanted to do. And I'll not always be a cleaner. I'll be passed for firing soon, and then I'll be...'

'An engine driver, I know.' She didn't know. Rising through the ranks on the railway was a slow old business and it could take years to become a driver. But that was irrelevant; as Mary saw it, he'd wasted quite enough time already messing about on trains.

'You're a clever lad, Alastair. You've got brains. All those books you're forever reading – what's it all for?'

'Bright people drive trains, Mary! They don't just round up village idiots and set them off at ninety miles an hour, you know.'

19

Alastair hated it when Mary criticised his work. He was well aware he was throwing his life away at Langbrook Shed, had heard it more times than he could be bothered to argue – how he was blowing the chance he'd been given by grammar school, how he could do anything he wanted, if only he'd set his mind to it. Why couldn't they see he was already doing what he wanted to do, had spent the best part of a year doing it and loving every moment?

'I just think you deserve better, Alastair, that's all. Who knows what you might achieve if... Well, look at my dad; he's nowhere near as clever as you and – '

'He's a Pit Deputy. And don't I know it! And what makes you – and your dad – think the pit is any better than the railway? It's still the same shovelling muck and shit all day, only there you're underground, trapped like a filthy rat, scratting about for your money until the roof comes in or your lungs get so choked up with dust you may as well stay down there for what life you'll have left when you get out. You call that better?'

'You wouldn't have to go underground. You could train as a draughtsman, dad says, drawing plans and surveys, that sort of thing. They need clever lads for that, Alastair.'

Alastair felt the anger rising inside him. He had a slow temper, but on the rare occasions when it had been roused he had once or twice frightened himself. He knew that if he didn't walk away sharpish he was liable to say or do something he'd immediately regret.

Mary saw the fury she'd stoked in him. The muscles that twitched at the corners of his jaw like little irregular heartbeats. His glare stung like a palm across her cheek.

'I only thought...' she said calmly in what she hoped was a voice of irresistibly sweet appeal, 'that a little more money would be nice. For when, one day, we might think about... a house and... You could save up for a car. Wouldn't – '

'Forget it! House! Car! All of it!' He pushed his face so close she could smell the beer on his warm breath. She found this as reassuring in its own way as the spicy tang of his aftershave, which she had always cherished as being *Alastair's* fragrance, even though, strictly speaking, it was his father's.

'Where are you going?' she said, gripping the sleeve of his jacket.

'Where am I going? I'll tell you where I'm going – anywhere but down the pit, above the pit or anywhere bloody near it!'

Alastair turned away, angrily kicking a loose stone into the path of an approaching single-decker. He was disappointed when the driver neither blasted his horn nor made an obscene gesture. God, how he wished to be away from her!

After a short while staring at his back, Mary spoke softly to it. 'Shall you still come for tea tomorrow?'

'*Tea*? You can stick your tea, along with your car and your bloody saving. Anyway, I'd only embarrass you in front of your family – what with me being so common an' all.'

Alastair walked Mary to the gate of her parents' house in Glade Road in silence. Half an hour earlier than usual. When she kissed him softly on the cheek and turned and walked away up the path, he cursed himself for the stupid waste of an evening.

* * *

For a few months between leaving school and starting at the shed, Alastair worked on the fruit & veg stall on Shireworth market. Towards the end of one summer Saturday afternoon, Mary had been left to buy the last of the groceries while her mother collected her weekly ammunition from the Wool Shop. At first she'd taken no more notice of him than she would any other market trader (none at all), and it was only after she was forced to cough pathetically and call '*Excuse me!*' twice before he pulled his head out of the paperback he was reading that she realised they'd met before.

It was his pale blue eyes. The way they'd peered up at her from under their heavy black brows as if to say, '*This better be worth me putting down Graham Greene*' (or whoever it had been). They seemed to set something off inside her right there, a ticking clock, a time bomb, and which she had been unable to switch off ever since. And she'd behaved like such a fool, blushing and stumbling over her words as she tried to give him her order. Luckily when he took it from her fingers he'd been able to decipher it for himself, humming some little tune as his eyes slid down the list.

He was Sarah Braymoor's brother. Of course! She'd last seen him rehearsing with a skiffle group at the Miners' Welfare, two or three years before. He'd have been about fifteen or sixteen. Mary remembered how when it came to his turn to sing (Buddy Holly, was it?) he'd seemed embarrassed and gone all moody in front of her and her friends.

'Soap?' he said, frowning up at her. 'Talcum parder?!' She hadn't remembered him speaking broad Cockney, though you can't always tell from someone's singing voice.

'They're not – ' she stuttered.

'Oim 'fraid oi 'ave no soap milady, nor any talcum parder. But if it's your skin you be wantin' to look arfter, moight I rec-a-mend a delicious English apple?' Mary smiled as Alastair tossed a Granny Smith into the air, caught it and bit out a huge chunk before returning to her list. Nodding, he settled what was left of his apple in a crate among two dozen unblemished sisters and in a frenzy of activity began to skip about the stall agile as a boxer, bending in and out of crumpled sacks, holding fruit up to the light, sniffing suspect matter before tossing it into a steel dustbin. With a final clang of scales and the conjuror's flourish with which he twisted and sealed the brown paper bags, Alastair lined up the peas, carrots, parsnips and tomatoes for which she'd been unable to find the words to ask. 'Will that be all today, madam?' he said with a pleased-with-himself smile.

'Yes, thank you,' Mary had said. 'That's everything.' Alastair passed the bags one at a time, watched her settle them in her basket. Mary looked up. 'It's Alastair, isn't it? Sarah's brother?'

'Course it's me! How are you, Mary?'

On the bus home Mrs Windale, as usual, went through her shopping, ticking off the items on her list against those in the bags between her feet. 'What's this, Mary?' she said, taking a single green apple from a paper bag on which had been pencilled "*For Mary. X*". It might have been a pair of guilty knickers, the way Mrs Windale held it up, frowning.

'It's a delicious English apple, Mummy,' Mary said, putting the fruit back in its bag and reading the message once more. 'I was told they're very good for a lady's skin.'

Mrs Windale shook her head, peered outside and said it looked like rain.

When Mary returned to the market the following Saturday, Alastair asked her if she'd like to go to the pictures with him, to see *The Pink Panther* at the Tuxfield ABC. She thought the film very silly, but not in quite the same way Alastair did. Afterwards, in Café Milano, they drank milky coffee and talked about records and friends and television, marvelling at how in a place so small as Warinstowe they'd managed to see so little of each other since their schooldays.

'I hope it won't be like that from now on,' Mary said on the bus home.

Alastair took her hand and smiled. 'What're you doing tomorrow night?'

CHAPTER THREE

Saturday, like Friday, was market day in Warinstowe. By nine o'clock when Alastair and Trevor stopped off for crisps and lemonade at the newsagent's, the market square was already a shambolic bustle of chirpy traders and the town's early birds, who, armed with trolleys, baskets and bags, scurried about the sprawling maze of stalls and barrows.

'Crafty sotl!' said Alastair, spotting his father puffing a sheepish cigarette at the second-hand bookstall to which he often paid a visit Saturday mornings while out fetching his paper and doing a few errands for Gladys. Alastair waved.

'What would your mam say if she caught him?' asked Trevor, smiling as Jock nodded and held the finger of secrecy across his lips.

'She wouldn't *say* anything. She'd murder him.'

Heads down, they'd covered a little over half the sixteen miles along the road to Gamston when Alastair, hearing Trevor calling his name, looked back to see his friend limping his bike onto the grass verge.

'I'm shit at mending punctures,' Trevor said, staring hard at the inner tube he held an inch from his nose. 'Where are you, you bleeder?'

Alastair polished off a Cox's Pippin and overarm bowled the core into the back of a passing builder's lorry, blinking against the gritty whirlwind whipped along in its wake. 'Giz it 'ere!' he said, snatching the inner tube. 'Right – you pump.'

Alastair fed the rubber ring carefully through his fingers, squeezing, stretching; holding it against his top lip until he tasted the tiny, fetid jet of escaping air. 'Bingo!' Alastair chalked the spot, dabbed the glue tacky. 'Get that patch on, quick.'

'Christ, that seat doesn't half make your arse sore.'

'You've been pampered, driving that little shagging-wagon of yours.'

The shagging-wagon was a blue, four-year-old Morris Mini. Sadly not the Cooper, or better still, Cooper S, Trevor coveted, but it was nippy enough, and he'd made it smart with its wide rims, bucket seats and steering wheel his father said was the size of a Two Shilling piece.

'Shagging? Chance'd be a fine thing, lad, nah that it would!' Trevor laughed, slipping into his affable northerner. 'Tha'd 'ave all on shagging in t'back o' that even if thee wor a pair o' dwarf contortionists. By 'eck! I tell yer nah, serry, I think me father wor right. Ah'd a bin better off wi' a bigger car. Not that he wor thinking in terms o' me gerrin me leg over, mind.'

'Expect he wor sick on thee doing it in t'back of 'is Cambridge, yer filthy bogger,' returned Alastair. 'Eh, by gum! We 'ad some fun in that motor, din't we?'

Like so many young lads of their generation Alastair and Trevor had been captivated by The Goons, and within days of hearing it for the first time they found it increasingly difficult to speak in anything other than silly voices from the show. Then after seeing Tom Courtenay's *Billy Liar* at the pictures they'd soon created their own cast of characters, from the daft and lecherous to the queer and pompous, which, along with some very variable impersonations of one or two famous folk, they unleashed at every possible opportunity with the sole purpose of making one another laugh. But the voices occasionally also served a practical purpose. Alastair and Trevor found they could be very useful when it came to discussing matters of a sensitive or personal nature – sex and girls mostly, but other more boring stuff too, stuff which would otherwise be too ridiculous to tackle with a straight face, such as work and health, and if it was all right to cry when the family cat was poisoned and had to be put down.

'Ey up,' said Alastair when they were back on the road, riding two abreast beneath the browning canopy of oaks. 'I heard there's a Mini just like yours been seen parked up, late at night, in the bushes at Clumber Park. You been taking Jean Britchardsley badger-watching again?'

'Giyovver! Tha knows I'm always tucked up in bed by nine

o'clock for work. And why – does Jean reckon to like badgers then?'

'Thee should know!' With a sly wink Alastair dropped a couple of gears and sprinted off into the distance. Trevor had no idea if Jean Britchardsley had feelings for badgers one way or the other, though he knew a great deal more about her than he often cared to let on. Cashier Miss Britchardsley, as he professionally knew her, was the bank beauty, sharp, teasingly pretty and physically upholstered very much in the Monroe – Mansfield style. Soon after Trevor joined as Junior Clerk, a mildly flirtatious relationship had developed between them based around the usual office pleasantries and his not so discreet enjoyment of her wiggling about the office and reaching up to high shelves in a skirt so short the Branch Manager would be forced to loosen his tie and reach for a glass of water.

As he was leaving one evening Trevor had almost knocked Jean down the steps when she stopped abruptly to open her umbrella. By way of apology he invited her to go for a drink at the Greenwood Inn. Three gins and orange later Trevor found himself back at the big stone cottage where, after checking her parents were fast asleep, Jean hitched up her skirt, just like that, and demanded he "make love" to her in front of the crackling fire. The memory was enough to arouse him even now, riding along on his bike.

But Alastair's information had been only half correct. It was Trevor's car that had been seen in Clumber Park. But it was not with Jean Britchardsley he'd shared those tender hours beneath the limes as the night deepened from blue to black; nor between whose limbs he twisted uncomfortably in the bucket seats while Radio Luxembourg tinkled through the single speaker and the windows fogged with the heat of young love. It was with Sarah Braymoor. Alastair's sister.

* * *

It was to be just the two of them. On Saturdays Frank worked till lunchtime, delivering fresh bread and cakes from Parson's Bakery to shops and cafés around Nottingham, after which he usually fell asleep on his mother's sofa until opening time at the Fox & Hounds. And Jumbo had arranged to "*meet this bird*" in Lincoln and then had rehearsal with the rhythm & blues group he'd joined a year or so ago, out Mablethorpe way. It had long been the source of much teasing, how as soon as he came off shift at the pit Jumbo would set off, pop-popping along the seventy-odd miles to the coast on his little white Vespa, its tiny engine grumbling beneath the seventeen stones that had earned Kenneth Moorhouse his elephantine nickname.

Alastair lay on the tartan blanket staring up at the sparse white clouds that made their unhurried way across a sky of faded denim. It was just as it had always been when they were kids, the tough grass poking through the blanket into his shoulder blades, the distant ringing of church bells. With a tranquillity that was sometimes ripped apart only a dozen times an hour by expresses hammering breathlessly north and south, it was the perfect spot, a bespoke vantage point hewn from the sprawling fields of wheat, turnips and sugar beet by long dead navvies just so that young (and not so young) boys might watch trains. 'Gamston?' his mother had said the night before, as she set down matching suppers of crumpets and hot milk before Alastair and his father. 'You don't mean to spot engines?'

'I'd have thought he'd see enough trains at work, nae mind riding all the way to see them on his day off as well,' Jock said, folding a crumpet into his mouth as he squinted into the dust and helicopters of the ten o'clock news.

'Train daft, he is. Always has been.' Gladys had been studying a heavy catalogue rested across her knees. 'What about an electric blanket, Alastair?' she said without looking up from the displays of brightly coloured comfort payable over forty weeks.

'Eh?'

'For your bottom drawer. Would Mary like an electric blanket?'

* * *

'I'll try and take some decent pictures today,' said Trevor, biting into a sandwich with greedy impatience.

'Instead of shit ones, you mean?'

'Funny bugger, aren't yer? I mean, I wouldn't mind getting into it a bit more – photography. Properly, like. Saying that, I can't remember the last time I put a film in this.' Trevor's words struggled against the bread and corned beef that filled his mouth.

'I've gone and forgotten mine,' said Alastair, double-checking his rucksack. 'My bloody mother's fault, mithering me before I've woken up. And I bought film especially.'

Alastair pictured the camera on the dining table, where he'd left it after loading the new film, his mind perhaps distracted by the other film he'd had developed at the chemist the week before, the film he'd even forgotten lay in his bedside drawer until he was reminded of it by Charlotte's letter. Fifteen colour exposures of that bright summer afternoon, almost three years ago, were now secreted in his bedroom, within the sleeve of his *Out Of The Shadows* LP.

'Do you ever think about Charlotte?' said Alastair, the thoughtful tone of his question masked by his immediately tearing open a packet of crisps.

'Charlotte? You mean Charley Bloomsberry?'

'Hmm.'

'Thought she'd run away to join the circus. Why? You don't still...'

'Don't be daft. Only I had another letter from her last week. From London.'

'She's still there then. What kind of letter?'

'Just a letter – asking how everyone is, what we've all been up to, you know.'

'I'd no idea you still enjoyed correspondence with the young lady,' said Trevor, briefly slipping into the clipped tones of the Squadron Leader. 'You should ask her to take some photos of engines down there. I always fancied a day at Paddington. Only ever seen one "Castle". Or was it a "Hall"? Remember – Nottingham Vic?'

Alastair rose and went to stand at the edge of the embankment, staring intently up the line, his hands deep in his trouser pockets. 'It was a "City",' he said. "*City of Truro*".

'Was it?' Trevor frowned. 'Does Mary know?'

'Difference between a "City" and a "Castle"? Probably. She's not as dim as you.'

Trevor swung a sharp kick at his friend's ankles. 'About the letter, you arse.'

'Course not. She'd go bananas. She's working in a jazz club...
Charlotte. In Soho.'

'No! Well, I can see her fitting right in there, matey. Late night
grooves in a smoky basement and all that. Imagine! Lucky cow.'

'Some big names played there, she says. Course she couldn't
remember any, not really her thing, jazz.'

'I suppose she was never going to stay in Warinstowe a minute
longer than she had to, was she?'

Alastair gazed up at the telegraph wires that ran parallel to the
railway line, blurring his eyes until thirty strands became six became
one, became thirty again. He wondered about the messages tingling
through them at that moment, the joy, the havoc, the routine
humdrum they carried along their silently humming lengths.

'Remember how we used to ride up to Retford Station when we
were kids?' Trevor said, shielding his eyes as he made an anticipatory
glance northward. 'How Charlotte would sometimes get on a train
and close the door, pretend she wasn't going to get off? Then, as
the train was starting to pull away, she'd jump off, laughing like a
lunatic? I always thought one day she'd stay on it.'

'She did. Only we weren't there to see her off.'

'We would have been if she'd bothered to tell us she was going.'
Trevor twisted the top off the lemonade. Well shaken by the journey,
it leaped out in an impatient sticky fizz.

'Watch the Douglas, you clumsy sod!'

'The *what?*'

'The Douglas!' said Alastair, indicating the rug. 'Mi mam's
favourite tartan.'

'Sorry, Gladys, I'd no idea,' said Trevor, hastily brushing away a
few bubbles of pop. 'You sure it's Douglas?'

'Oh, aye! As worn by the pipers of the Cameronian Scottish
Rifles.' Alastair smiled. 'You know mi mam and the Bonnie
Country.'

'I suppose it's only natural, what with your dad being one of
them.'

Alastair aimed Trevor's Kodak just in time to capture his friend
belch his appreciation of the lemonade.

'Mam's the only person I know who actually likes the sound of bagpipes. Dad hates it.'

'Poor Jock,' Trevor frowned. 'Moving all the way down here thinking he was getting away from that racket. Still, any nation that can produce *Kidnapped* and shortbread fingers deserves to be revered, in my book.'

'Aye, there's a lot to be said for the homeland,' Alastair nodded, exaggerating the voice of his father.

The line began to tingle and *tiss*. There followed a deep droning sound, far off and faint at first, but which grew louder and deeper as it rushed towards them.

'Non-stopper,' said Alastair, raising his voice against the gathering din. Stepping back at the last moment from the edge of the embankment, they watched as an immaculate green diesel hummed deafeningly past, whipping behind it thirteen coaches as if they were made of tissue paper. The train swept through the steady curve on the approach into Retford Station, its drone rising to an echoing crescendo as it sliced between the platforms at seventy miles an hour before dying away once more.

'Too quick to read the bloody numbers!' Trevor jeered.

'D9016,' Alastair winked. 'Or 018.'

'Better eyes than me.'

'Her mam's not very well,' Alastair said, when they'd resettled on the Douglas. 'That's really why Charlotte wrote.' He stuffed a piece of fruitcake into his mouth and wound on the film in Trevor's camera.

'I heard. She's a tough old girl, though, Monica. She'll be right as rain again in no time, I bet.'

'Yeah. She asked if I'd go up and see her. Make sure she's all right, let her know.'

'Can't Charlotte write herself? Or come up?'

'I don't know. They've a strange going-on. It must get lonely for her though, on her own. Monica, I mean.'

'Mmm. She never used to be short of visitors, from what I remember.'

It was only what had been said about Monica many times before, and Alastair knew Trevor meant no offence by it, either to him or to

Monica. A few minutes passed before Trevor broke the silence. 'But you're still all right with Mary? This Charlotte business?'

'Mary's all right,' Alastair said. 'She isn't half bossy though. Think it must be her being an only child, you know how highly strung they can be.'

'Piss off.'

Trevor, moving to kneel at the edge of the embankment, aimed his camera at an approaching freight train, a slow untidy snake of work-blackened wagons, vans and tankers. It would make a good snap with all those wisps of steam, fluttering like dirty white ribbons, leaking from the seams of the dilapidated engine's boiler. The guard, leaning against the balustrade of his brake van, waved as he flicked his cigarette end down among the ballast.

'You'd be hard pushed to land one better than Mary, Alastair.'

'I don't want to,' Alastair said, thoughtfully. 'But sometimes, I just wish she'd slow down a bit, that's all.'

Trevor nodded in agreement as he casually flicked through the *Melody Maker* he'd spotted in Alastair's rucksack.

'It shouldn't have to be like that nowadays, Trev. Rushing to settle down at the first opportunity like it's a bloody race. Congratulations! First up the aisle, first with a house, first up the duff with not one, but two bouncing babies! But be careful and make sure it's one of each, mind, otherwise you'll have to go back and have another go, and this time try a bit bloody harder! You know what I mean, don't you?'

'They do seem to see it like that, don't they, girls?' said Trevor to the back of his friend's head, which was once again teetering over the edge, a detective ear cocked towards a distant rumble.

'Just shut off at Markham Moor,' said Alastair, referring to the summit from which enginemen would begin their three-and-a-half-mile descent into Retford. Trevor wound on, lifted the viewfinder to his eye.

On the way home, Alastair and Trevor stopped off at The Duke of Newcastle Hotel, on the edge of Clumber Park. After serving them with two halves of bitter, the barman, a chubby youth who sported a mop-top so precise it might have been a wig, whistled along behind them as they made their way out to the beer garden.

They seated themselves at a table while the barman stood with his back to them, smoking a cigarette and gazing out across the car park to the busy road beyond.

'Funny in't it?' the barman said, sighing a thick cloud of smoke into the air above his big glossy head. 'All them cars and lorries. You'd think one of 'em would fancy a pint, or a bit o' summat to eat, wouldn't you?'

'Been quiet, has it?' Trevor said, addressing the broad back.

'*Quiet?* Chuffin' dead'd be more like it.' In his voice the barman carried all the knowing, world-weariness of a lifelong innkeeper, yet he was probably no more than twenty-three at most. 'And I've gorra lovely pork pie on that bar,' he said. 'Best *Bird's* an' all, it is. Still, it'll not go to waste.'

From the way his suit concertinaed tightly about his middle, like cling film around an armadillo, Trevor and Alastair saw there was little chance of a pork pie, or anything else of an edible nature, going to waste if this lad had much to do with it.

'These your bikes?' the barman asked without turning round.

'Yes,' said Alastair, swallowing the last of his half pint and immediately fancying another. 'Not in the way, are they?'

'No, no! Put 'em where you like. As you can see, we're hardly pushed for space.'

Then suddenly, and with some ceremony reminiscent of a Far Eastern martial art, the barman sprang stiffly to attention and very slowly stretched out his arms to an angle of what in any regular body shape would have been ninety degrees to the trunk. The pose was held for a few seconds before, bending his arms at the elbow, he now carefully lowered his hands until they came to rest on the fleshy ledge of his hips. A thick cloud of smoke appeared above the mop-top, adding to the sense of sacred ritual. Then, with what appeared to be some considerable physical effort, the barman leaned back, arching himself to the limits of his clothing and physique, and broke wind with such ferocity that for a brief moment afterwards the world seemed to fall silent, as it does following an almighty thunderstorm.

The barman swung round, a look of shameful horror stretching wide his features so that he resembled a child's drawing of Paul

McCartney. 'Pardon me, lads!' he spluttered. 'I'm ever so sorry. You see, I've got so used to being on mi own. You know how some folks talk to themsens?' The barman looked earnestly from one to the other, like a dog who, fouling the best carpet, anxiously awaits his master's response, uncertain if he's just earned himself a pat on the head or a boot up the arse. Alastair and Trevor exchanged glances and immediately both fell about in hysterical laughter.

'I do apologise, lads. For doing that in front on yer – mi *customers* – it's not right, I'm ever so sorry.'

'No need to apologise,' said Trevor slipping into his Noel Coward. 'I found it *most* entertaining.'

'Did you?' the barman said, surprised.

'You have a most effective arse, my friend,' rasped Alastair, following Trevor's lead. 'You should never keep an arse like that hidden under a bushel.' Alastair giggled at himself and set Trevor off again. The barman too now began to laugh, though he did so through eyes half-suspicious, as if waiting for the catch, for some rug to be pulled from under him.

'Never keep a fine arse hidden under a bushel! Who was it said that, Alastair?'

'Princess Margaret, I think,' Alastair replied, wrinkling his nose. 'And she knows a fine arse when she sees one. You must never be ashamed. Tis a young man's duty to share his arse with the world!' Alastair clapped his hands flamboyantly.

'What're you two playing at?' the barman said, his confused features darkening in an instant from docile pup to lethal attack-dog. 'Are you taking the rise out of me?'

'Oh no! We're not taking the rise, pal,' said Alastair, glancing towards the bikes as he plotted a swift route of escape. 'We enjoyed your performance so much we simply wanted to pay tribute to it in the manner it deserved.'

'Eh?'

'We're only having a bit of fun. That, my friend, was bloody funny.'

'That was some arse-cracker,' Trevor said. 'I thought a wagon had blown its tyres.'

The barman chuckled, regained his affable smile. 'Aye, I thought so,' he nodded. 'You had me for a minute, though. I didn't know if you were mekkin' fun on me or what.'

'Not at all,' said Alastair, shaking his head. 'It's just how we are. Daft as a pair of brushes.'

'Idiots,' said Trevor. 'Can we buy you a drink?'

'Er, cheers! I'll just have a cola, thanks. I don't reckon to drink on duty. And what can I get you two?'

They ordered two more halves.

'Ey up. You're not actors, are you?' the barman said, as if a thought had suddenly dawned.

'Christ, no!' said Alastair.

The barman dropped his dead fag and carefully buried it in the gravel.

'Only we get one or two staying here from time to time, queers most on 'em – not that that bothers me, live and let live, I say. But they aren't half tight-fisted bastards. Unless somebody else's paying, they'll mek a gin and tonic last all night. Now that *is* unnatural behaviour.'

As the barman strode purposefully towards the corridor lined with prints of game birds, beagles and other assorted hunting paraphernalia that led to the empty bar, there came from the road a familiar a-brum-boppa-boppa stutter of a slowing two-stroke engine.

'Scooter boys!' said the barman, rushing back to his post overlooking the car park. 'Well, one of 'em, anyroad.' Alastair and Trevor exchanged a look of happy surprise.

'Found you, you boggers!' Jumbo bellowed as he burst from the corridor with a tray laden with pints – three bitters, one cola – and a small feast's worth of assorted bar snacks, including a pickled egg that rolled about its tin perimeter like a wonky roulette ball.

'You hungry by any chance, Jumbo?' Alastair grinned as Jumbo kicked his white crash helmet under the table and began setting out his banquet. His big round face was flushed, his hair a shock of sweat-darkened stalactites that dripped moist beads across his brow.

'It's not all for me, you cheeky bastard. It's for all on us – a few nibbles. It's gone teatime.'

'A few nibbles?' Trevor said, taking a bag of pork scratchings. 'Here you are, lads!'

Struggling to contain his excitement, the barman now came scuttling across the lawn, a plate covered with a large glass cloche held stiffly out before him as if it were a bomb ticking perilously towards its time, and set it down among the spoils. Inside was a large pork pie, from which a generous wedge had been cut and placed seductively at its side.

'Trust me,' the barman panted, 'you won't be disappointed. It's best *Bird's*.'

'See owt special at Gamston?' Jumbo asked, brushing shards of pastry from his chest into his hand before tipping them into his mouth.

'Not really.'

'Cracking pork pie.'

Alastair and Trevor, cheeks bulging, nodded. The barman, feeling all of a sudden awkward at the edge of the group of friends, now turned and made his way back towards the bar.

'Ey up!' Jumbo called after him. 'You've been gooin' on about how nice this pie is. Don't you want a bit?'

'I'd love a bit, if you don't mind?' the barman said, returning to the table. 'Ta very much, er – ?'

'Kenny. But I'm mostly known as Jumbo.'

Jumbo bit the pickled egg in half and stared appreciatively at what remained between his fingers.

'Thanks, Jumbo. I'm Barry,' said the barman, seating himself at an adjacent table and tucking into a thick piece of crust.

'How's the group, Jumbo?' asked Trevor, taking a long swig of his pint.

'All right. We played Lincoln last night, went down a storm. There again tomorrow – bit of a bugger, cos I'm on day shift Monday. We're getting quite a following.'

'And I bet you still can't keep time for toffee,' Alastair teased.

'Balls!'

Barry looked up. 'You in a group?' he said, smacking his lips. 'Must be marvellous. What do you play?'

'Drums. We've gorra big gig coming up end of March, if you

fancy coming along.'

'Thought you'd never ask,' said Trevor. 'Where at, Warinstowe Welfare?'

Jumbo put away the rest of the pickled egg, washing it down with half a pint of bitter. 'Skeggy! We're booked for this big weekender, "Seaside Beat" or summat it's called. Four or five groups and – '

'You topping the bill?' joked Alastair.

'No. We're bottom! But guess who're the headliners? Godfrey Payne and The Comforters, *and* The Berries!'

Alastair made a doubtful face. 'Giyovver!'

'At Skeggy? With your lot?' said Trevor. 'You're having us on!'

'Thought you'd like that,' said Jumbo, eyes twinkling in his otherwise ever-calm features. 'Brian reckons it should get us some proper gigs, being on the same bill as them two. Personally, I'll be chuffed just to see Godfrey Payne for nowt.'

'So would I!' said Alastair.

'Count us in, Jumbo,' Trevor said, decisively. 'You'll go, won't you?'

'Try and keep me away,' Alastair said. 'Is it all right if I throw my frilly panties at you, Jumbo? Hey, think of all the birds he'll have after him now!'

Trevor wolf-whistled.

Jumbo laughed shyly. 'Talking of birds,' he said, typically shifting the focus from himself, 'guess who I saw at Retford?'

'Who?'

'When?'

Jumbo looked at his watch and shrugged. 'Half-hour ago. When you weren't at Gamston I had a ride up the station. Thought you might have gone for summat to eat.'

'We took sandwiches today, and one of his mam's fruitcakes.'

'Is that where you reckon to go for your dinner? Refreshment Room?' Barry said, his interest stirred. 'Bet they don't serve pork pies like this.'

The slamming of doors and the crunch of gravel drew the barman's attention to a young couple who'd just climbed out of a white Ford Consul. 'Excuse me, lads,' he said, wiping his mouth and making his way inside.

'Who?' repeated Alastair across the crumpled packets that now littered the table.

'Charlotte Bloomsberry,' said Jumbo.

Trevor looked at Alastair. 'But she's in London, Jumbo.'

Alastair frowned. 'Are you sure? That it was her?'

'Looked just like her. I didn't see her properly, mind. She was already half on the bus when I pulled up. Probably weren't her. Her mam's been badly, hasn't she?'

'Yes,' said Alastair.

Daylight was fading fast, and it was getting cold to be sitting out in a beer garden. From the busy road a car sounded an impatient horn.

'Race home, Jumbo?' said Trevor. 'Reckon I could beat that hairdryer of yours.'

'You probably could an' all. Looks sharp though, dun't it? You can hardly call yourself a proper Mod if you haven't got a sharp scooter, can you?'

Alastair and Trevor made admiring glances at the much be-mirrored machine gleaming at the edge of the car park.

'No, I don't suppose you can,' Trevor said with a sly smile across at Alastair.

Alastair tried to think of something witty to say, a cheeky little jibe about Jumbo's laughably slow and inappropriate mode of transport, but nothing came. His thoughts were elsewhere.

CHAPTER FOUR

Charlotte Bloomsberry was the first girl Alastair ever met. It was the first October of the new peace, and he'd been dozing in the crook of his father's arm, in the little porch at the front of number 7. Jock had taken his son out for an hour, along with his carefully folded newspaper and a small flask of tea, a situation that was as new and unusual to him as it was to the tiny, nine-day-old bundle he held onto so carefully.

It could have been anyone, but it just so happened that the first person Jock should see coming down the hill on that fine late morning was Monica Bloomsberry, on her way to work at one of the rowdier pubs at Tuxfield.

'Now then, Jock,' said Monica, as she kicked the brake on the shiny red pushchair and turned it towards him. 'How y'all gerrin on, then? Stop that, Charlotte, you'll give yerself headache.' Jock smiled as the pretty two-year-old girl took no notice and continued to nod and shake her head so that her golden-yellow hair flicked wildly about her face.

'How do, Monica?' Jock said, scrunching his eyes against the light. Alastair was wide awake, but Jock kept his voice to almost a whisper, hoping Monica would perhaps get the message and so avoid waking Gladys. The baby had come as rather a shock to his wife. Somehow Gladys had not bargained for the sudden and total domination of her time and strength the child would bring, and for the first three or four months after Alastair was born she would hardly leave the house, other than to peg out her washing, or maybe to sit a while on the low garden wall, singing quietly to the little thing that clung so tightly to her breast. But Jock never once complained. It seemed the least he could do for the girl he'd patiently courted for three years before they were married, the promise of whose kisses had kept him safe from the bullets and shells which hounded him among the deathly hedgerows and shattered cities of Europe.

'Nice morning we've had si far,' Jock said, nodding up at the clouds.

'As long as it keeps like it, Jock,' Monica said, through a heavily painted pout. Monica Bloomsberry was a lively, striking woman then. The sort who knew precisely who she was, a vivacious chatterbox to her friends and a tittle-tattling busybody to those who frowned upon her brash unconventionality. But Monica pleased herself, and if by doing so she failed to please others, then, well, they knew where they could go. Jock though, always had time for her. There was something very admirable about the way she managed all by herself, with the kiddie and all.

'What yi up to then, Charlotte, eh?' Jock said, his eyes brightening beneath their heavy brows. The little girl hid behind her mittens.

'Don't you want to see the baby, Charlotte?' said Monica. 'Charlotte? Bogger you then! So she finally had it then, did she, Jock? A boy? Let's have a look at him... Ooh, he's a smasher, in't he?'

Jock nodded proudly as Monica stroked the baby's cheek with her plump fingers.

'Doesn't half look like you, Jock. And do you know, I'd have had a pound on 'im 'aving red hair like 'is mam. But look at him! Black as the ace o' spades, it is. Ooh, he's a smasher, Jock.'

'To be honest, I was expecting a bald one,' Jock said, only half joking. He felt a little annoyed at himself suddenly for coming out without a jacket. Sitting holding a newborn baby, you were bound to end up talking to a woman.

'Gladys doin' all right, is she?'

Jock said Gladys was doing very well, thank you. A bit tired, but that was only to be expected. Monica smiled. 'What've you called him, Jock? I never asked – too busy gabbing, as usual.'

'Alastair – same as me.'

'I always forget you're an Alastair. But then I've forgotten plenty of chaps' names before now.' Monica cackled, ran her fingers through her mousy curls. 'Remember them blackouts, Jock, eh? Ooh we did have some fun, din't we? I don't think half o' the time chaps told us their real names. I bet you were t'same, though – all you soldiers were!'

Jock smiled, gave a knowing lift of his eyebrows.

'Baby's name's *Alastair*, Charlotte. You'll about end up playing together when he's a bit bigger.' Charlotte peered at the baby then, catching its father's eye, covered her own again with her mittens. Before Jock could ask her how she was herself, with a glance at the gent's silver watch she wore on her wrist, Monica blew out her cheeks and kicked off the pushchair brake.

'Ta-ra then, Jock. If I don't get a move on they'll all be dying o' thirst on the pavement. Send my love to Gladys, wain't you? I'll come and see her in the week, tell her.'

'Will do, Monica,' Jock said. 'Ta-ta now, lassie,' he added, waving his fingers at the little girl.

'Say bye-bye to the baby, Charlotte,' said Monica.

'Bye-bye, baby,' said Charlotte.

* * *

An orange silk headscarf shone like a beacon of reassurance among the lonely hats and caps on the upper deck of the night bus. Not that Charlotte was by any means a timid sort of girl. In fact, she believed that to temper your behaviour for fear of what would probably never happen was a weak and foolish thing to do. Yet she had also lived in London long enough to know that it always paid a girl to keep her wits about her, especially when travelling alone, late at night.

Through the haze of cigarette smoke, the ghosts of a faded evening, she made her way to the front seat, her favourite spot. With those great big windows it was like being at the pictures, you had this incredible view all to yourself. And also, at night, when the lights were on, the glass, at a certain angle, became a mirror in which you could keep an eye on the whole deck behind you without having to turn around.

It was a little after two as the bus jolted across Cambridge Circus and turned into Charing Cross Road. Charlotte took a cigarette from her handbag, lit it with a match and took a long, deep drag. Her legs ached and her feet burned like her shoes were lined with hot coals, but she was happy, filled with the lightness of spirit that always comes at the end of a long shift. In the daytime, when traffic was bad, Charlotte always read a book. But at night, after eight hours at The Hot Foot Club (it lived up to its name all right), she preferred to look out at the sleeping streets and enjoy a private, unhurried smoke. It was all part of her nightly ritual of winding down, of becoming herself again. She lit another as they passed the Houses of Parliament and crossed the river, black and shimmering.

Of course, "NOTTINGHAM" was written on every packet of John Player's. She just hadn't remembered ever noticing it before, not until she moved down south. Funny. It was only a word, but every now and then, when it caught her eye, she suddenly found herself thinking of... No, not of home exactly. And it was not as though she could ever have felt any great attachment to the place, otherwise why had she upped and left as soon as she was able?

Charlotte crushed her fag end into the floor. As soon as I get home, she decided, after I've made my tea and toast, I'm going to sit down and write to Alastair. She regretted not having kept his last letter in her handbag, so that she could read it again now, and instead made do with trying to picture his face and remember some of the silly voices he always did. She began to rehearse what she might write, the news she had to share. *Dear Alastair...*

She rang the bell as the bus neared the end of her street, a wide avenue of tall, once-elegant Victorian villas. A brown lump of a man, stinking cigar hanging from the corner of his mouth, followed her with piercing eyes as she walked down the gangway towards him and the stairs. Thinking he looked the sort to make trouble, Charlotte averted her gaze just as he took the damp stub from his lips. 'Goodnight, Miss,' the man said with a gentle bow from the neck. 'God bless you.'

'Goodnight,' said Charlotte as the bus squealed to a halt. That was the thing about London, she laughed, skipping down the stairs. Nothing was ever what you expected.

CHAPTER FIVE

'I'm such a bloody idiot sometimes!'

'You always say Minis hate water,' Sarah giggled from where she sat, smoking a cigarette on the gate overlooking the ford. The water was no more than a few inches deep where it trickled across the road, but it had been enough to bring them to a spluttering halt within a dozen or so yards of hurtling through it at forty miles an hour. 'Is the distributor sodden?' she enquired, thoughtfully.

'How did you know that?' Trevor called from under the bonnet.

'That was the trouble last time, I seem to remember.'

'Ouch, you bleeder!' With a jolt Trevor sprang up, smashing his shoulder against the bonnet catch, the point of impact marked by a greasy black smudge on his crisp white shirt.

Sarah leapt from the gate, tossed her half-smoked cigarette into the grass. 'Are you hurt?'

'Burnt my knuckles on the engine.'

Sarah took Trevor's hand, examined his filthy fingers. 'Hmm. I don't think it'll have to come off,' she said. 'Dip it in the water then I might kiss it better for you.' Sarah gave a cartoon flutter of her long dark lashes, smiled up at him in a way that seemed at once both shy and suggestive.

'You are funny,' she said while Trevor washed his hands in the cold stream. It was dusk and the gaps between the trees that surrounded the old Duke's estate had begun to close, the crumbling house beyond already no more than a blurred, melancholy hulk.

'You won't think it funny when it won't start, and we have to walk home in the dark.'

Trevor flicked his wet fingers at Sarah. She stuck out her tongue.

'Ah, but it will start. Just like it did last time. And the time before. You're not quite as silly as you look, Trevor Parkes, even if you do always insist on driving us into the river.'

The engine fired first turn, shattering the silence and scrambling a squadron of starlings from the telegraph wires and up into a swirling dogfight over the damp fields. Trevor swung the car off the verge and floored the accelerator. He smiled at the roar of the little engine, the throaty echo of the exhaust as they ducked under the railway bridge and turned into the main road.

'Pictures?'

'I don't really fancy the pictures now,' Sarah said, lazily. 'Can we just go for a drive instead?'

They drove for almost an hour, chatting and listening to the radio, Sarah occasionally being forced to grip on to her seat in a mixture of terror and admiration as Trevor flung the little car through the twisting lanes of the old Sherwood Forest. Eventually they turned into Clumber Park. In the pitch dark Trevor was able to make out just enough of Sarah's shadowy outline to find her spearmint-flavoured lips, and for his hands to discover that her coat was not only already unbuttoned, but that her skirt had risen indecently, invitingly, high up her thighs. Against the steady tick-tick of the cooling engine, Trevor recognised the sound of her dress being unzipped, felt his hand being drawn towards her young warmth. He knew from previous adventures such as this that sometimes the only way to stop Sarah from giggling was to kiss her.

CHAPTER SIX

'Balls!' said Alastair, waving a match at the gas ring. 'Tea bags!' He knew he'd forgotten something the moment he walked out of Edmund's. The excitable little shopkeeper was such an old gossip he very often talked whatever it was folks went in for clean out of their heads. Alastair shook the caddy – enough for another day or two.

Tea had always figured prominently in visits to Monica's. Even as kids, when he and Charlotte played tea parties, they'd nearly always served up the real thing, the two of them happily swallowing the dollies' and teddy bears' untouched cupsful, as well as their own. Ever since she was a baby, Charlotte, so her mother liked to say, had always 'been one more for the tea than the tit'. It was the sort of comment that made some people think Monica vulgar and common. But not Alastair.

'You remembered my bits? You are a good lad,' Monica said, coming up behind Alastair as he emptied bread, cheese, corned beef, tinned soup and four bottles of stout onto the sideboard from his rucksack. There were also sausages, eggs, tins of baked beans and some tomatoes, but these he made clear were for his tea, when he got home.

'Have you come straight from work, duck?'

'Yes.'

'Well, mek it and 'ave it 'ere, if you want. You must be hungry, working hard all day. Go on, you know where everything is. And it'll save your mam the bother later on.'

'Will you have a bit with me?' Alastair asked, knowing already what her answer would be.

'No, duck, I shan't. I'm fat as a porky pig as it is.'

The floorboards of the converted railway carriage groaned as Monica crossed into the living room, but this probably revealed more about the structural condition of the vehicle than of Monica herself. Before becoming her home, "1, Ridgetop Allotments" had once been a pair of teak-bodied express coaches built for the Great Northern Railway. Now, sixty years on, spliced end to end at an angle of ninety degrees, and with a neat three-bar fence mirroring the two internal walls to enclose a small garden, they made a quirky little domestic plot among the potting sheds and rows of peas, cabbages and rhubarb. And apart from the narrow aspect of the rooms – kitchen and living room in one coach, two bedrooms and bathroom in the other – and the minimal light let in by the narrow windows, Monica, with the help of variously skilled men friends she'd known over the years, had made it so practical and homely that once inside it was easy to forget you weren't actually in a proper house at all.

'You enjoy your tea, duck.' Monica settled into her chair and lit a cigarette. 'Ooh, I'm glad of a bit o' company. It doesn't suit me, this. I'm used to allus having folks about me, day and night.'

'You'll be back at work soon enough,' Alastair shouted over the spitting frying pan. 'You should enjoy the rest, while you can.'

'You're never without friends in a pub,' he heard Monica say from the far end of the coach. 'And a right bloody sample they can be an' all, some of 'em!' Monica chuckled to herself as if she were savouring a treasured moment; a face, a joke, one of the numberless fights she'd broken up in her professional capacity as barmaid-cum-referee.

'Sure you won't have a bit, Monica?' said Alastair, setting his steaming plate on the table. After retracing his steps back to the kitchen he returned with the big brown teapot and topped up Monica's cup. 'There's plenty left. Shame to waste it.'

Monica shook her head. 'No, duck, I'm not bothered.' After a moment she leaned forward in her chair and peered over the top of her glasses. The thick lenses and sharp, upward-curving frames lent her a stern, owlish appearance perfectly suited to the perma-dusk gloom of the old coaches. 'So what's she had to say, then – Charlotte? Does she think I'm ready for the knacker's yard?'

'She didn't say very much this time. Asked how you were. Sends her love. She works all hours, by the sounds of it.'

Alastair noticed how Monica's eyes followed each forkful of

food he lifted to his mouth. He put down his knife and fork and returned to the kitchen.

'Yes, she's a hard worker, Charlotte,' she called after him. 'It's about the only decent habit she'll have got from me, duck, I'm sure.'

'Well, you have got some very bad habits, Mrs B.' Monica looked up sharply from stubbing out her cigarette in the ashtray to find Alastair standing before her, holding out a second plate of food he'd been keeping warm under the grill. 'Like not eating properly, for a start. Good job I made too much again, isn't it?'

Reseated at the table, he turned to find her grinning sheepishly.

'Is it any good?' she asked, dubious.

'*Awful*. I'd be ashamed to serve such slop to a lady of your refined tastes, Monica. Pigeons'll have it though, if you haven't got room.' Alastair gave her a wink, cheeky-daft as his father's. Yes, he was Jock's son all right, Monica smiled as she watched him carefully mop up the last of his bean and tomato juice with a thick toasted crust.

'Down to mi last two Gingers,' Monica said after they'd washed up and made a fresh pot of tea. 'You have 'em, duck. I know how partial you are to a Ginger.'

Monica sat back in her chair, remained silent for a few moments as if she were in deep thought.

'It's good of you to do this, Alastair,' she said in a quiet and unusually serious (for her) tone of voice. 'Coming to see me.'

'S'all right. I wasn't doing anything else.' Alastair picked up the *Evening Post*. A photograph on the front page showed the Mayor with his arm around a toothy schoolboy who, for reasons Alastair decided he did not care to discover, was grinning as he held an incredibly fat cat above his head.

'Well, I do appreciate it. Must be hard work on them engines. You'll be ready for a rest when you get home, or for seeing your pals, not wasting your leisure suppin' tea wi' an old fart like me.'

'Don't talk so daft. I like coming up. And you let me have more biscuits than mi mam does.'

From her strained expression and unusually prolonged

silences (usually you struggled to get a word in edgeways), Alastair knew something was not quite right, that something was afoot. He was about to ask when she leaned forward and placed her hand softly on his wrist. 'You don't have to go puttin' yersen out for me, duck. I can manage. I've allus had to before, so I don't see how that should change just cos I've gone arse-over-tit down a pub cellar. It were only a little heart attack. I'm not a bed-ridden old fart, just yet, even if I do pissing well look like one.'

Alastair smiled. 'You've gorra gob like a brickie's labourer, sometimes, Monica, you really have.'

'What do you mean?' Monica laughed, revealing dark caves where once there'd been teeth. 'Well, you're not the first to say so.' She looked at him steadily for a moment. 'I mean it though, duck. Don't bother coming no more, if you don't want to. Putting yersen out. I can manage.'

'If you say it again I'll start to think you really don't want me to come. Either that or you're expecting a fancy man and you're worried I might frighten him off.'

'Yer cheeky bogger! Chance'd be a fine thing! You never know, it might do me the world o' good, a quick knee-trembler wi' some nice young chap!'

A further twenty minutes passed until, as Alastair stepped out onto the dark allotment, Monica finally got around to asking the question she'd been avoiding for the last hour.

'I don't think you can ever tell, properly, what folks mean to say in letters,' she said at the kitchen door, cigarette glowing between her fingers. 'You can hear the truth in a voice, or see it in a face, but... I've never been much of a letter writer.'

Alastair glanced along the body of the coach. In a faded sign-written hand, he made out the letters THIRD, just below the window of what was now the master bedroom.

'I know you write to her and let me know what she says. But I wondered if you might be able to go and see her for me. I'd feel a lot happier knowing that she's all right. That she's *settled*.'

Across the allotments, the quarry, and the woods beyond, the headstocks of Warinstowe Main and Shireworth collieries twirled dark silhouettes on the horizon.

'I know it's a lot to ask,' Monica said. 'I'd go myself only... Well, I can't really, not at the moment, what with me being...'

'A bed-ridden old fart?'

'Well, yes,' Monica nodded, her eyes moist and twinkling. Speaking through the open carriage window like that, Alastair was reminded of *Brief Encounter* and he was almost tempted to say, 'Well, cheerio till Thursday!' in the plummy voice of Trevor Howard. Only they weren't hopeless lovers. Just two people standing on a damp allotment worrying about a girl whom they'd both used to know, in their different ways, but who were now no longer sure that they did.

'She'd probably be more pleased to see you than me, anyroad, Alastair duck. Will you at least have a think about it?'

'Yes, Monica. I will,' Alastair nodded, his mind flooding with postcard images of Charlotte draped across the capital. 'Shame we can't put the wheels back on these coaches,' he said, turning towards the lane. 'Get one of the Langbrook drivers to pull you to King's Cross.'

'Alastair?' Monica called after him.

'Yes?'

'Remember mi tea bags next time. And some more Ginger biscuits. Some greedy bogger's gone and eaten all mine.'

* * *

Alastair was incapable of walking anywhere slowly. Head down, shoulders hunched, hands pushed deep into the corners of his coat pockets, he looked as if he were walking into a gale even on the brightest summer's day. Usually this annoyed Mary almost as much as the Douglas Bader business, and more than once while walking along together he'd turned to find she was no longer beside him but fifty yards behind, arms folded in a pose of stubborn immovability and with a face like bloody thunder. Other times, though, when the mood took her, he'd find her smiling sweetly, shaking her head in mock exasperation while he retraced his steps to give her a big kiss. He much preferred the latter.

Mary! The thought of her, and what (with any luck) might

lie in store for him after the pictures, warmed him from his very middle, so that he barely noticed the bitter wind that blew in off the allotments and savaged his left ear. He recalled with tingling, lustful wonder how last Thursday, on the riverbank, she'd taken him completely by surprise when she'd pulled her dress up over her head and laid herself before him, on his duffle coat, in just her knickers and knee-length socks, that inflaming look of shy challenge on her face. It was an incredible (and most welcome) development in their relationship. Especially as it had been a night almost as chilly as this.

Alastair was luxuriating in these thoughts, and others less wholesome, when he heard a familiar voice calling his name.

'Yi away oot, then?' Alastair turned to see his father clambering over the stile from the allotments, waited while he crossed the street. 'Yiv had yer tea?' Jock asked from behind the turned up collar of his donkey jacket.

'All right, Dad? Yes, I had something earlier.'

Jock took a step back. Having to peer up so steeply – so *obviously* – to meet his son's eyes always made him feel a bit of a fool, as well as a shortarse. 'Your mother wis wondering after yi. Ah said he'll have had something oot, or at his work. He'll nae go without, ah telled her.'

Alastair nodded. 'I'm just off to meet Mary. Going to the pictures.'

'Not ti Tuxfield, eh?'

'No, just down here.'

'Even so,' said Jock, a quietly amused expression coming over his face as he looked his son up and down. His eyebrows leaped up into the peak of his cap. 'I know the Empire's not si grand the-noo, but... You're never takin' the lassie oot dressed like that, are yi?'

Alastair looked down to see what his father found so amusing. 'Oh, balls!' Two filthy great boots stared up at him from the frayed edges of his work jeans. He looked at his hands, ran his fingers through his hair, grits of coal dust sharp against his scalp.

'You'll be daydreaming again, aye?'

'Must've been. I should get a move on or I'll be late.'

'Aye, must nae keep her waiting.'

'My bike! It's at Monica's.'

'The bike's all right.'

Alastair fell in beside his father as they strolled in the direction of Welgrove Terrace. 'How's she doing today – Monica? She's nae been good jis lately.'

'She's all right, I think,' said Alastair. 'But you know Monica, she's...'

'Aye, I know Monica. She's a tough old bird.' The way Jock rolled the "R", with his rumbling Scots purr, could still make Alastair smile, as it had always done, since he was a little boy. 'She managing for coal, is she?'

Alastair frowned at his watch. 'Eh?' he said, impatient at having to keep to his father's leisurely pace.

'*Coal,*' Jock repeated. 'Yi might want ti take her a bag up next time. She'll be getting through it, havin' ti heat that place all day.'

'I suppose.'

'I'll leave one in the coal hoose. Nae need ti mention it ti your mother.' It was too dark to make out his features, but Alastair sensed there was a wink hidden somewhere in the shadows of his father's face.

'And young Charlotte,' Jock went on, thoughtfully. 'She knows all about her mother, does she? How she's been?'

'Charlotte?' Alastair said, sounding as if he'd never heard the name.

'Charlotte, aye. You're in touch wi' her, aren't yi? Ah thought that wis who's been writing yi from London – no?'

Alastair pictured the lights of Piccadilly Circus. Eros. Monica's request. What was he meant to tell her? Of course he'd gladly do anything to help the old girl, but... Well, he could hardly just go swanning off to London at the drop of a hat.

'Ah managed to intercept the last letter and slip it under your door afore your mother had her hands on it. But she knows, aye?'

A fat ginger cat trotted out of a porch, weaving between their legs and getting under their feet for a short way down the hill before tearing off down a black gennel.

'Yes, Charlotte knows. She's been writing to me to ask if I

50

wouldn't mind popping up to Monica's now and again. Take her a few bits of shopping, have ten minutes with her – you know.'

'Aye.'

'Evening, Jock. How do, Alastair,' Mr Whittaker, a neighbour, called as he let himself in, closing the door quickly behind him before too much light or the meaty whiff of his tea could escape into the night air.

'Must be hard for her to get up this way now – Charlotte. Wi' her work and what have yi.' Jock paused at the back door. 'But her mother'd love ti see her if she could manage ti come up.'

Alastair nodded. 'I know.'

'Now away and get yersel' tidied up. I'll keep your mother at bay, otherwise you'll never get oot again the neet.'

'My bike.'

'Don't yi worry about the bike, son. It'll be here for the morning.' Alastair smiled at his father. There was no doubt about the wink this time.

'That you, duck?' Gladys's sharp voice called from the pantry.

'Aye, course it's me,' Jock answered. 'Who'd yi think it was, Tom Jones?'

'What's *he* sneaking about for – our Alastair?' said Gladys, weighing the kettle before taking it over to the sink. 'He's had no dinner again. He'll mek himself badly if he carries on like that.'

'He's had food, love. Dinnae yi worry 'boot him. He's late for his meeting wi' Mary.'

Jock moved towards Gladys where she now leaned against the draining board, folding a tea towel with swift precision. Even at five-foot-seven Jock towered over his wife's neat little figure. It was just one of the many things about her that reminded him how lucky he'd been compared to so many men of his generation. War was a bad time for choosing a wife or a husband. The thought you might be blown to Kingdom Come tomorrow might instil a heady zest for life, but it didn't half bugger up a chap's standards when it came to picking up a bit of what you fancied.

'He can't go to the pictures on an empty stomach,' Gladys began half-heartedly to protest as she felt herself being gathered up in Jock's heavy arms. 'He'll be hungry... out at... at work all day.'

Jock touched his lips softly against his wife's. 'They say when a young man loves a lassie he's nae need for food.' Gladys closed her eyes and, after only briefly wondering what on earth had got into him, lost herself in Jock's kisses.

'Won't be late,' Alastair's voice called as the back door slammed shut.

At the foot of the stairs, Gladys turned and smiled a smile which Jock knew was, and always had been, only for him. After he'd put a shovelful of coal on the living room fire, and washed his hands at the kitchen sink, Jock bolted the back door and followed his wife upstairs.

CHAPTER SEVEN

The sun squatted low over the headstocks of Warinstowe Main colliery, its winding wheels spinning a hypnotic blur against the pale afternoon sky. Alastair, cycling no-handed in the middle of the road while he ate an apple, pictured the miners huddled in their cage, lamps charged and eyes wide as once more they plunged deep into the black earth. Poor bastards. It was no life, especially on a day like this. Alastair could think of few things worse than having to go down the pit, yet he had always felt strangely glad of their existence and took strange comfort from the way Warinstowe and twenty-odd other pits within as many miles kept on turning endlessly, reassuringly, on the horizon.

It was a perfect afternoon for cycling; even the road seemed quieter than usual, but Alastair decided to take the footpath across the fields. He was in no hurry to get home. His back was stiff from crawling about underneath engines all day, and a steady walk usually put him right again in no time. He pushed his bike along the rutted track between early shoots of some crop or other he knew his father would immediately be able to identify, but thinking it looked nothing like the wheat he seemed to remember bowing to the wind the previous summer. Coming across the parched skull of a small bird lying in the middle of the path, he was tempted to take it home with him until he remembered he was neither eight years old nor a witch doctor.

At the river Alastair propped his bike against the bridge and, after relieving himself against a hawthorn hedge, settled on the bank, close by the water's edge. The water was low and surprisingly clear. Tiny fishes cast darting shadows across the pebbles on the riverbed, wildly exaggerating their number. From its secret perch a blackbird called in sweet contrast to the shrieks of children that came from the houses beyond. Emptying his rucksack, Alastair was pleased to find his flask contained enough tea for a tepid half-cup. He took out that week's *Melody Maker*, inside which was a manila envelope addressed in a familiar hand and postmarked "London". Alastair swallowed his tea and then began to read:

Dearest Alastair,

I hope this letter finds you well, and that your Mam & Dad and Sarah are also. And Mary — are you two engaged yet? (Joke!)

Thank you so much for looking in on Mam. She's written back (finally!) and says you've been ever so good to her, fetching her shopping and doing her dinner. I can't imagine you cooking — do you wear a pinny? Ha-ha! I didn't expect you to go to so much trouble, but it's very nice of you and I know how much Mam enjoys your visits. You know, I wouldn't put it past her to be ill for evermore if she thinks you'll keep going to see her.

Alastair, do you think she's all right? Really? I'd like to get up, but it's difficult with my hours. And by the time I've paid my rent I've barely enough left to buy food, never mind train tickets. Please let me know how she is.

Yes, London is very different to Warinstowe. The whole way of life. I'm writing this now after getting home from my shift at the club and it's almost four in the morning. It's ever so funny on the night bus, seeing all the lights on and people still wandering about long after they should be in bed. I do like it though, Alastair. There's something very ALIVE about it. God, that's such a cliché, isn't it? You're always so much better at putting these things than I am. But it's true, ALIVE is the only way I can describe it. At home I always felt so suffocated. As though an elephant or a big fat man was sitting on my chest and I couldn't breathe properly. It's not like that here. There's none of that having to be what you're expected to be, or do what people like us are supposed to do. You feel very FREE in London. Alive and Free! Gosh, you must think I'm out of my mind on booze and drugs! I promise you I'm not — not yet anyway. (Another joke!)

Do you know what reminded me of you tonight? The word NOTTINGHAM written on my packet of John Player's. Isn't that daft? I've just heard the milkman outside. Can you believe he's still got a horse-drawn milk float? London's funny like that. All these big posh shops and flash motors, but at the same time there are lots of people sleeping on the streets and filthy old women selling matches like something out of "Oliver Twist".

I saw Terence Stamp the other day, in a grocery! Do you still like him?

He smiled and let me go in front of him at the till. He was wearing a sheepskin coat and bought milk and carrots. Probably wasn't him after all. You meet all sorts of people in London, especially working in a nightclub. But I haven't met anyone like you, though. So far, Alastair Braymoor, you remain quite unique!

Please tell Mam not to worry about me. I'm looking after myself. I'm managing all right, and I've made some lovely friends who I think you would like too. One reminds me a little bit of Trevor. Remember me to him, won't you?

I should probably go to bed. It's you keeping me up! Thank you again for looking in on Mam. And please do let me know how she is. She's written a few times now, but you know what she is for saying she's all right when she's not. Soon as I've saved enough money, I'll come up and see her – and you. Promise!

Write again soon with all your news.

Lots of love,

Charlotte x

The letter ran to three sheets, though only three sides as Charlotte hated using the reverse side of writing paper, said it ruined all the effort she'd put into the front, made it go all bumpy and ugly, like woodchip wallpaper. But as Alastair read it a second time it was not the texture of the paper that insistently drew his eye, but the dried stain of smudged watery ink beside the words at the top of the final page: *I haven't met anyone like you, though.* A sudden romantic vision formed in his mind's eye of Charlotte banished to a lonely room at the top of countless flights of stairs, some dark, damp hellhole, all cat piss landings and crippled banisters, the sort of place people neither moved in to, nor out of, through choice. After signing her name, Alastair imagined how she'd put down her pen then immediately fallen across her desk utterly inconsolable, her hopeless tears splashing down to form the indigo flowers that now bloomed on the pages he held between his fingers.

'You dozy sod,' he said to himself, carefully refolding the letter. He sat for a while, quietly watching the clouds of tiny fishes flitting about just beneath the water's surface. 'So far, Alastair Braymoor,' he smiled, 'you remain quite unique.'

CHAPTER EIGHT

Ten and a half months after his first shift on that crisp November morning in 1963, Alastair was passed for firing duties. Three days later he worked his first turn on the footplate of a steam locomotive. That this had entailed nothing more glamorous than shunting a quartet of brake vans about the yard for a few hours mattered not, and the delight in his face when he came home at teatime had been so glowingly evident even his father had given him a proud 'Ah telled yi so, son,' wink across the dining table. Gladys had beamed, kissed the top of his head as she slipped two extra potatoes onto his plate.

Jock's reaction surprised Alastair so much he wondered if he hadn't forgotten about the deal they'd both, reluctantly, agreed to a year since. Under the terms laid down he should now have been thinking about leaving the railway, not rejoicing in his longed-for promotion. But of course Jock hadn't forgotten. From the moment Alastair got in to the grammar school he'd been quietly determined his son should *get on* and *make something of himself*; that he should leap up and grab the opportunity he himself could never have dreamt of, growing up in the Lanarkshire slums, destined, aged fifteen, to follow his father and three elder brothers down the pit.

'University! That's what yi should aim yersel' for, son!' As he neared school-leaving age, Alastair heard these words time and again; casually at first, but then soon with increasing regularity and insistence, so that by his final year rarely a week passed when the topic didn't haunt the top of the domestic agenda. 'Wi' a degree from Nottingham, there's nothin' yi widnae be able to do, Alastair.' Jock spoke with such wonder you'd have thought his son had been granted unlimited magical powers and was refusing to sign for them. But the truth was that while Alastair could quite easily see himself turning coppers into frogs, or becoming invisible and sneaking into ladies' bedrooms, the idea of him waltzing about campus in cap and gown, talking jazz and communism through a stinking pipe, seemed utterly absurd.

'Just think of the life yi'd have! The pals yi'd make, the lassies yi'd meet! And all the while yi'd be studyin' great books – *literature*!' A shabby leather-bound copy of *David Copperfield* was produced to illustrate this last, sacred, word, Jock shaking it in the air like some deranged, pit-vested preacher. During these sermons, when Jock would become so animated, so fired-up with the autodidact's passion for knowledge, how you could "learn practically everything for practically nothin' from books, just a wee bit of time and effort," you couldn't help but wonder what he might have achieved himself, had his own start in life been very different.

When the agreed year was almost up, Alastair prepared for a showdown. But it never came. There were arguments, sure. Quite a lot, in fact, and some of them rather heated, but not so as they were ever in danger of coming to blows, not like some of his pals had with their fathers. Not even the cat was kicked in anger. Jock was furious, of course, in his quietly brooding way. That Alastair should be so short-sightedly throwing his life away on a schoolboy fantasy was, well, he was a bloody fool to himself. But Jock could also see very clearly how much the railway meant to his son; saw how hard he worked at it, night and day. What's more, he knew just how stubborn young men could be when they dug their heels in.

As he told his parents about his first day firing, Alastair was reminded of an exchange which had taken place at this same table just over a year before.

'How long has it been there?' his mother had asked, pouring tea.

'What?' said Jock from behind his newspaper.

'Nottingham University.'

'Och, eighteen-eighty or there-a-boots, ah think. Why?'

'Well, if it's managed nearly a hundred years wi'out our Alastair, I'm sure it'll manage one more, won't it?'

Alastair smiled. He couldn't have put it better himself.

CHAPTER NINE

'Bit late for watching trains, isn't it?' said Alastair, climbing up on to the fence beside Trevor. The embankment was eerily dark. In the moonlight the railway lines twinkled like strands of fine silk draped across the open countryside. Trevor hadn't spoken a single word since he screeched up to the kerb beside the post office and ordered Alastair to get in. Thirty seconds later he'd have missed him. Walking back from Mary's, Alastair very often nipped into the bus shelter for a slash, or occasionally something more urgent, depending on how forthcoming Mary had been during the evening. As they raced along the narrow lanes to the embankment, Alastair clinging to his seat and wincing at the twitching speedometer, he rather wished he *had* missed him. Trevor's driving was an acquired taste, and Alastair hadn't acquired it. Trevor drove like a lunatic. How they hadn't ended up embedded in some hedgerow or gone crashing through the parlour of one of the tiny cottages dotted along the roadside was little short of a miracle.

'Since when did you smoke?' said Alastair as Trevor lit up and took a long, deep drag. A pained look on his face, Trevor leaned precariously forwards on the fence, forearms braced across his knees, and began flicking irritably at his lighter. Alastair noticed he was still in his work clothes. He gave him a nudge. 'Hey! What's up with you, you miserable sod? And why have you driven me out here at this time of night? If I'd have known, I'd have brought a picnic.'

Alastair thought a moment. 'I say,' he said in his best Terry Thomas. 'You've not gorn and got that pretty Jean Britchardsley up the duff, have you, you randy little rooster?' Trevor's mouth twitched at the corners. 'Fruity little piece, isn't she? I wouldn't mind having a crack at her mys... Hey, stand by your beds!'

They sat up sharply and watched as a train rushed towards them from the shadows. With a growl it whipped past, a twinkling chain of thunder that left them blinking in a flurry of dust and diesel fumes.

'I hate to say it,' said Alastair. 'But they do make a bloody good racket. Like a Lancaster going over. Now, are you going to tell me what's eating you? You been given the sack or something?'

Trevor leaped down from the fence and walked to the edge of the embankment, juggling his lighter, every now and then tossing it high into the air before catching it again with a snapping fist.

'You're not going to tell me you love me, are you?' Alastair said in a prim, girly voice. 'You know I'm spoken for.'

Trevor took a last drag on his cigarette, tossed it into the ballast. Where to begin? He thought he had all the words. He'd rehearsed them often enough. But now they seemed so inadequate.

'It's Sarah,' Trevor said finally.

'What is?'

'Your sister.'

'I know she's my sister. What about her? *She's* not up the duff is she?'

'Course not!' Trevor snapped. 'I mean; I should hope she isn't. Not that it's any of my business.'

'What's our Sarah done, Trev?'

* * *

It being Thursday and not one of his usual days for seeing her, Trevor wondered if Sarah might be annoyed, perhaps think he was getting a bit too keen a bit too soon. So instead of waiting outside Woolworth's heavy glass doors, as he did on Saturdays, he decided to wait opposite, across the street. On a whim he'd decided to skip his afternoon dentist appointment and surprise her. He would take her to Café Milano for a milkshake. She liked them best there.

The record counter was right at the back of the shop. Trevor imagined Sarah stretching up for that week's Number 1 single, chattering merrily away to her customer as she slipped the disc into a paper bag. He hoped she'd be as pleased to see him as he would be to see her.

The door swung open and Sarah came out. Trevor shouted, but with a glance at her watch she was off, breaking into a run towards the bus station, her unfastened cardigan flapping like a cape behind her. Trevor crossed over and began to chase after her. He was about to call her name when a motorbike pulled up a few feet in front of Sarah. The rider, raising his goggles, twisted in his saddle and beckoned her over with a leather finger. Trevor slipped into the doorway of the Gas Board showroom where, paralysed, all he could do was watch helplessly. She was all smiles. Laughing! Trevor felt he might be sick. Sarah clearly knew this greasy interloper, whoever he was. Or if she didn't, she certainly looked as if she'd like to. The way she touched the tips of her fingers against her lips, self-consciously flicked her hair as she giggled and cocked an ankle towards the road – gestures Trevor knew very well and loved. His fists clenched. His mouth filled with acid that stung his lips. Lips which should right now have been kissing Sarah's. Trevor wondered how much damage he could reasonably hope to do with his fists against someone wearing leathers and a crash helmet. Who the hell was this? Did Sarah have a secret lover? Or was it just some cocky opportunist, trying his luck?

As if to answer Trevor's question, the biker now undid the chinstrap and pulled off his helmet. *Nigel*! Nigel Bloody Wells! Trevor gasped as a pair of invisible claws sank into his guts and began to wring them out like a wet chamois leather. He watched, trembling with impotent rage as Sarah put on Nigel's helmet, Nigel coolly blowing his hair, which hung in an infuriating sweaty fringe across his face, out of his eyes as he helped her with the strap. When Nigel took Sarah's hand and guided her onto the seat behind him, her navy blue mini-dress riding high as she swung her leg over, Trevor felt he was being burned alive by his own furious anger. The thought of her body pushing against the small of Nigel's back was hell.

With Sarah's arms clinging tight around his waist, Nigel pulled back the throttle and off they roared, away into the teatime traffic. In the doorway of the Gas Board showroom Trevor looked on, frozen numb as the staring mannequins in the shop window. For the first time in his life he wished he'd never been born.

* * *

'The times I've told her to keep off that bloody motorbike!' Alastair said when Trevor fell silent. He was as surprised as he was annoyed at his sister's stupidity, for going on the backs of motorbikes as well as gadding about with cocky Herberts like Nigel Wells. He thought Sarah had more sense. As for Trevor's inner turmoil, and the way he'd just poured his heart out and revealed how hopelessly in love he was with Sarah, Alastair said nothing, for the simple reason Trevor had not been able to tell him. In describing what he'd witnessed that afternoon Trevor made no mention of his romance with Sarah, nor of the murderous feelings of jealousy which had been tearing him apart ever since. He dearly wished he could tell his friend how if Sarah herself had cut out his heart in the middle of the street and Nigel Wells crushed it beneath the wheels of his motorbike he could not have felt any worse than he had done just then. But how could he? How would Alastair react on being told that his best and oldest friend had been going out with his sister, behind his back, for months? He knew how protective of Sarah Alastair had always been. Christ, and if he knew he'd been sleeping with her! A punch-up, that he could handle; surely he'd have asked for it. But to tell all now would be to risk losing his best pal as well as the girl he loved more than he had ever imagined was possible – if he hadn't lost her already. It was too big a risk to take.

Alastair meanwhile had for some time suspected his sister was seeing someone. She'd started coming home later in the evenings, and more often than usual. And whereas Sarah had once liked to tell him where she'd been and who she'd met up with, now all she'd say was, 'Oh, just *out*.' or, 'Nowhere special.' Also, she'd recently claimed to have struck up a friendship with a new girl from work (Susie?), and with whom she sometimes went for a coffee after closing. It all made sense now, in the light of what Trevor had witnessed. Yet it was hardly a surprise. Alastair had known Sarah was bound to find herself a boyfriend before very long. But did it really have to be Nigel Wells?

'Well?' Trevor said, sounding as if he'd run half a mile for a bus. 'Aren't you bothered? What are you going to do about it?'

'Course I'm bothered, but what – '

'*Nigel Wells!*' Trevor spluttered, his voice on the edge of cracking. 'Nigel-sodding-Wells! What would Sarah want with *him*?'

Alastair shrugged. 'I dunno, he's a – '

'He's a slimy bastard, that's what he is! She can't go out with him. Wait till I... Urrggh! You slimy... Urrggh!' Alastair looked on curious as Trevor took a running kick and launched a big sod of earth high in to the air and onto the railway line. 'She can't, Alastair! She can't go out with Nigel Wells!'

'I agree. But who says she's going out with him? He may have just been giving her a ride home. Not that she hasn't been told often enough about motorbikes.' Alastair didn't know what to believe. Yet observing his friend's behaviour these last few minutes he'd found himself becoming less concerned with the precise status of Sarah's relationship with Nigel Wells than with Trevor's reaction to it. Close as the two of them were, it seemed unusual for a lad to get himself so steamed up over who his best friend's sister may or may not be going out with. A thought suddenly struck Alastair.

'Course he wasn't just giving her a lift!' Trevor carried on, the whites of his eyes shining like little moons in the darkness. 'I know Nigel, slimy bloody insurance *git*!'

'She was bound to go out with somebody eventually. And it's hardly up to us to – '

'So she *is* going out with him?' Trevor said pointing a damning finger.

'I didn't say that. But what – '

'You don't just do that out of the blue, just turn up at a girl's workplace and offer her a lift home!'

'You seem very annoyed about it, Trev. What were you doing there anyway? Why weren't you at work?'

Trevor looked up to where his friend peered down at him inquisitively from the fence.

'I... I had the afternoon off. I went for a ride.'

He knows, thought Trevor. But what did it matter now, if she was with Nigel.

Alastair's hunch of a few moments ago was starting to emerge like an image on a piece of photographic paper. It was a very different picture to the one he'd started with, Sarah going out with Nigel, but Alastair couldn't honestly say that he liked this new picture a great deal better.

'Probably just a one-off,' Alastair said. 'But it was good of you to tell me. I'll have a word with her, make sure she doesn't do it again.'

'But what if it isn't?' Trevor said, anxiously. 'A one-off, I mean.'

'I'd have noticed,' said Alastair. 'What's got into you tonight?'

Trevor stood at the edge of the embankment. In a careful voice, as if he sensed he might be pushing his luck, he said: 'And haven't you noticed? Has she been getting in late? Expect you'd hear the bike, sleeping in the front bedroom.'

Alastair watched as Trevor lit another cigarette, the flame shaking between his cupped hands. Well, bugger me! If Trevor hasn't gone head over heels for our Sarah, he thought. It was a curious sensation for him at first, picturing them together. Better than Nigel, granted, but still... Of course, knowing Trevor, there was a very good chance Sarah might not even know how Trevor felt about her. He'd nurtured crushes on plenty of girls before and never done anything about them. Just to be certain in his own mind, Alastair decided to have a little bit of fun at his friend's expense.

'I suppose she has been coming home a bit later than usual, now you mention it,' he said. 'Once or twice.'

'When? *When*?'

'Night before last. Tuesday. I had an early night but she woke me up, clattering about. Why don't they buy shoes they can walk in?'

Trevor seemed to make a quick mental calculation. 'You sure it was Tuesday?'

'Not last night, the night before. Tuesday.'

Trevor's heart lightened a fraction. Alastair smiled inwardly.

'What about before Tuesday? You said once or twice?'

'Yes, er, last weekend... Saturday. Giggling and tipsy. It's a good job mi mam didn't catch her.'

'*Saturday*?' A cold shiver ran from the top of Trevor's head and out through the holes in his socks. He'd gone to his cousin's engagement on Saturday. Sarah told him she'd stayed in, had a bath and an early night.

'Hold on!' said Alastair. 'It wasn't Saturday night. It was Sunday.'

'Are you sure? You said Saturday.'

'Yes. I remember saying I'd got to be up for work next morning, so it had to be Sunday. Then another night last week, she came in swinging a dead fish. Hello! What've we got here?'

As Alastair, hearing the distinctive scream of a two-tone chime whistle in the near distance, leapt down excitedly from the fence, Trevor could almost have kissed him. On not one of those evenings could Sarah have been with Nigel Wells, for the simple reason that she had been with him. And it was he who'd won the *half*-dead goldfish, at Southwell Fair. It was like his numbers had come up on the Pools. Of course, there was still the ugly matter of what he'd seen that afternoon to deal with, but it might just be all right. He only hoped it wasn't already too late.

Grinning like idiots, they waved with childish enthusiasm as a streamlined A4 – one of the last few still running – hurtled past at the head of a mail train, dragging a thick grey banner across the night sky. The fireman waved from the glowing footplate, then gave a blast on his whistle that lasted almost until the red tail light vanished in the smoky darkness.

CHAPTER TEN

The drivers and firemen at Langbrook were disappointed when Alastair started to get more and more firing turns. His enthusiasm and hard work had quickly earned him a reputation among the footplate men as a lad who could be relied upon to do a first-rate job, who made sure their engines were always properly turned out and ready on time for duty. It was inevitable, of course. And reluctantly they accepted the move, knowing that a dead-keen engine cleaner would more than likely make a dead-keen fireman, if that's where his heart was set, as they knew Alastair's was.

His first regular driver was Walt Goodman, a railwayman of more than forty years' experience, the majority of it spent on the footplate. Walt too had begun his career as a cleaner, at a long-gone shed near Leeds, working his way up during the 1920s and 30s, the halcyon days of steam, when Britain's railways were still the envy of the world. Alastair took to Walt immediately, and liked nothing better than trying to steer their almost every conversation towards the older man's glory days, belting up and down the East Coast mainline at the controls of gleaming Gresley Pacifics and Streamliners.

'How come you ended up here, then?' Alastair asked on their first big trip out to Tuxfield Concentration Sidings, a huge, sprawling marshalling yard ten miles to the east.

'How'd yer think? A bloody woman, o' course!' Walt sighed, smeared a big black hand across his brow. 'Missis's a Langbrook lass. Met her in a fish and chip shop at Scarborough. She'd been on the excursion I fired that morning from Nottingham. Gettin' on thotty year ago now.'

'So you gave up *The Flying Scotsman* and moved here?'

Walt shook his head. 'I musta bin chuffin' crackers!'

Spindle thin and well over six foot, Walt had the posture of a wilting lamp post. His weathered, inquisitive face looked, like those of most lifelong railwaymen, some years older than the fifty-seven or fifty-eight he must have been then. But he'd lost none of the strength and agility of his youth and could climb about an engine or leap up on to a tender quick and nimble as any young pup at the shed.

'Let's get a bit chucked on then, lad,' said Walt, folding himself to peer into the firebox. 'We're lookin' a bit thin at the back.'

Being able to swing the coal shovel smoothly and accurately from tender to firebox didn't come easily to Alastair. With the constant rattling and jolting as you hammered along, even at twenty-five miles per hour, hitting the target was like trying to thread a needle while standing on the outer edge of a speeding Waltzer. The number of times he'd lost his footing and sent the whole three-stone shovelful scattering across the footplate he didn't like to think.

'Don't worry, lad,' Walt laughed. 'We've all done it. And tha'll do it again a few more times yet. Just tek thi time, and tha'll soon be handling her like you've know her all yer life.'

Alastair liked firing the 9Fs best of all, "Spaceships" as they were sometimes called. He knew these engines inside out, literally, from his cleaning duties. These huge powerful locomotives, with their long, high boilers and ten driving wheels, were easily the most practical engines to work on, as well as being the most reliable, but then so they should be, some of them were barely five years old. Yet already quite a few had been sent off to the scrapyard. Alastair felt this was nothing but mindless vandalism. A steam engine should be good for forty years' service, easy. A couple of the barnacled old beasts at Langbrook were already well into their fifth decade and still going if not strong, then at least doggedly.

'I thought spaceships were meant to be things of the future,' Walt said one time, downing a swift mug of tea while they waited for the signal out of Shireworth Colliery yard.

'They can't scrap them after five years,' Alastair said. 'Mi dad's got socks older than that.'

Walt laughed. 'Madness, lad. It's bloody madness. She's hardly run-in, this one. In need of a damn good clean, mind. Wonder who was down to clean her this morning?'

'Giyyover! It's spotless!'

Walt looked about the cab. 'I suppose it'll do.'

'How long do you reckon they'll keep going, Walt?'

'Steam? Another three, four year, mebbe. Though I can't see as Langbrook will hang on that long, not now the diesel depot's about finished. Gorrit's roof on now, I see.'

This sense of inevitable approaching demise made Alastair feel utterly miserable inside, and not for the first time he cursed himself for being born a generation too late. He envied Walt his decades of steam, knowing they'd all be gone before he was barely into his twenties. It was no wonder his father and Mary thought he was barmy, stubbornly insisting on working at a filthy, laborious job that was already on the cusp of extinction even before he started.

On the way back, as they rattled out an almighty echo against the chalk walls of Pleaswell cutting, Walt twisted in his driver's seat and shouted above the din. 'So what's tha want to do a job like this for, anyway, bright lad like you?'

With perfect aim Alastair swung a good shovelful into the centre of the fire, kicking the door shut with his boot before wiping his face on the sleeve of his overalls. There was no need to answer. The huge smile that split open his sweating, soot-streaked face said it all. Walt laughed and gave a long, shrill blast on the whistle.

CHAPTER ELEVEN

Trailing a bright ting-a-ling, Sarah tottered out of the shop and across the road to the car. Her clinging white trousers and black and white striped tank top made Trevor feel giddy, his mind racing as he wondered if she might let him remove them later on.

He'd hardly slept a wink since Thursday, when he'd watched her ride off with Nigel Wells. In the small hours the thought of them together turned him like a pig on a spit over the fevered fires of his jealous imagination, so that he soon became as entwined in his sweat-sodden bed-sheets as he feared Sarah had been entwined with Nigel.

Sarah slid into the passenger seat, popped a green sports mixture into his mouth and a noisy kiss on his cheek. Just the sight of her was enough to melt him. And as they sped away from town, rather than demand to know what the hell she was playing at with Nigel Wells, he found himself thinking that the only thing that mattered was simply to be with her, to have her sitting close beside him, chattering away and looking as lovely as she smelled while she rustled in a paper bag to find his favourite-coloured sweets. It was like a cork had been removed from his jealous heart and all the rage and humiliation suddenly drained away.

But then, as they halted at a busy junction and Trevor took a glance across at her straining tank top, it all came rushing back. He pictured her breasts, imagined taking them in his hands, gently caressing them. Only they weren't his hands that he saw, but Nigel's. Suddenly all he could see was the cocky git smirking through his stupid moustache while he got his paws all over her, his mouth kissing her, his tongue *licking*. He changed gear with a nasty-sounding crunch. 'Bastard!'

Sarah sniggered. 'Oops-a-daisy!'

It's no good, Trevor thought. But then, just as he was about to open his mouth, Sarah said, 'You'll never guess what happened the other day.' Trevor swallowed his sweet whole and nearly choked. 'I was running to catch my bus, after work, on Thursday, and guess who pulls up at the kerb on his motorbike? Nigel Wells!'

'Oh?' said Trevor trying his best to sound casual. 'What did *he* want?'

'Nothing. He just happened to be passing. Said he thought he'd seen you at Tuxfield, but then he'd lost you at a red light.'

Sarah pushed a red sweet into his mouth, her hair, piled high, brushing against the headlining as she leaned across. All he could think of was her putting on Nigel's helmet. He listened nervously, in fear of what might come next.

'Course I told him. I said it couldn't have been you, because you didn't finish work till half five, same as me. So then he asked me if I fancied a lift home and, well, I don't know why, but I just said Yes!'

Out of the corner of his eye, Trevor saw how, as she spoke, Sarah remained looking straight ahead, smiling and nodding as though he were not sitting beside her but outside, on the bonnet.

'He's a funny lad, Nigel,' Sarah said.

'Is he? Why? What did he have to say that was so funny?'

'He didn't say anything much. In about ten minutes he dropped me at the Fox & Hounds. I clung on with my eyes closed all the way, but I still got grit in them. I didn't like it. I prefer your little Mini any day.' Trevor smiled at this little victory, though suspecting that really she'd probably enjoyed every thrilling minute on the back of Nigel's powerful bike, as he knew he would himself, not that he'd ever admit it. And then he remembered her mini-dress riding up her shapely thighs as she'd straddled the machine, her arms holding tight around Nigel's waist.

'I'm surprised he didn't take a detour. Through the woods or up a quiet lane for a quick...' Trevor bit his tongue, bumped noisily over the cats' eyes onto the wrong side of the road for a tighter line through a sweeping bend. His heart banged like a bass drum somewhere near the back of his throat. He wondered how much force he could hope to get in a running kick at Nigel Wells's balls.

'A quick what?' Sarah said, turning to him wide-eyed and high-browed.

'I know Nigel. I know what he's like. I wouldn't put it past him to have...'

'Well he didn't. And do you really think he'd have got very far if he had? I don't know what you must think I am, Trevor Parkes.'

Trevor smiled in bashful apology.

'Ooh, you are a silly!' said Sarah, shaking her head slowly as she gave his thigh a tender squeeze. 'A silly daft cloth-head, that's what you are.'

There were often times when Trevor wished he could give himself a bloody good slap across the face. This was one of them. It was plain as day Sarah didn't want to be with Nigel Wells, nor anybody else. How could he ever have doubted that she loved him? 'I will not bugger this up,' Trevor said to himself; 'I will not.' Braking sharp, he swung into the next lay-by and leaned over and kissed Sarah for a long time. 'Where to, milady?' he said, suddenly the Cockney chauffeur.

'How about somewhere *stately*?' Sarah played along. 'Might you know of such a place, Parkes?'

'Yes. I think I know just the place, milady.'

* * *

'It's lovely here, isn't it?' Sarah sighed from where she lay among the long grass, staring up at the sky through the puzzle of spring branches. Trevor took a gulp of lemonade, smacked his lips.

'Stately enough for milady?'

'Oh, I think I could get used to it.' Sarah sat up. 'Have you lived here long, my Lord?'

'Actually, no,' Trevor said nonchalantly, *lordly*. And leaning back on his arms he looked across to the crumbling remains of the great house and abbey. 'Of course it's been in the family for generations. But it wasn't until we buried papa – after that little misunderstanding with the goat and the stableboy – that all this,' he said, with a wide sweep of the grounds, 'became mine.'

Sarah laughed as she fell back into the grass and closed her eyes. 'Lucky you!'

'You can have it, if you like,' Trevor said. 'It's all yours.'

'Why, thank you! But is there a record player?' she asked with a thoughtful pout.

'In every room!'

On the expanse of neatly mowed lawn, where the East Wing had once stood, a group of pensioners shuffled about, twisting their old necks up at the ruins. The sun was warm and the lake a racket of wildfowl.

'Is there a law which states old women must only dress in bright colours?' Trevor asked, as he studied the knots of shuffling pastel.

'I think it's nice. They look like pretty flowers.'

Trevor slipped his arm around Sarah's waist and kissed her until they fell gently back into the long grass.

'Let's stay here all night,' Sarah said, blinking when eventually she opened her eyes.

The pensioners twittered by towards their waiting coaches. Trevor thought what he wouldn't give to spend a whole night with Sarah and wake up in an actual bed beside her.

'I think Alastair knows about us,' he said.

Sarah shrugged and stuck out her bottom lip. 'Do you mind? I mean, do you think it will make it awkward between the two of you?'

'I'm not sure. He's your brother, what do you think?'

'I think it'll be all right,' she said. 'But you never can tell with our Alastair. He might just as easily go bananas and murder you.'

'Oh, very reassuring.'

Sarah flung her head back and giggled, her breasts sending a heavenly shiver through her striped tank top. The clock of the old house struck five. Trevor realised he didn't care what Alastair thought, or anybody else. He loved Sarah, and Sarah loved him. How could anything else ever matter?

'Sarah,' he said. 'Will you marry me one day?'

Sarah narrowed her eyes thoughtfully, comically stroked her chin. She sat forward then and slowly pulled her tank top over her head, grinning as she did so. 'Well you don't think I do this just for the fun of it, do you?' she said.

CHAPTER TWELVE

It was in the *New Musical Express*, between the news Gene Vincent had been rushed to London's Royal National Ear, Nose and Throat Hospital, and that Twinkle would be making her debut on BBC Television's *Gadzooks! It's All Happening* a week on Monday:

Godfrey Payne and The Comforters will headline the "Beat Beside the Seaside '65" weekend at The Regency Ballrooms, Skegness (March 20, 21). The Berries and two further groups are also set to appear.

Although there was no actual mention of The Chequered Saracens by name, Sarah knew they were one of the two further groups because she'd seen the flyer Jumbo brought round on Thursday evening, when he'd called to make arrangements with Alastair. Not that it made any difference to her.

'I don't care if you're nearly eighteen or eighty, Sarah,' Gladys said, frothing beneath her rollers. 'A seaside caravan wi' a load of Teddy Boys is no place for a young lass. Now you can sulk all you like, but that's the end on it.'

'But Alastair's going! I wanted to see Jum – '

'I said that's the end on it! You see enough concerts wi'out trailing to Skegness. Now what're you going to have for breakfast?'

'*Teddy Boys!*' scoffed Alastair, slipping Len Deighton between the clean shirts and sandwiches his mother had made for him into his rucksack. 'In *this* sharp clobber?'

'And you needn't start, neither. Now have you remembered a vest? It'll be bitter on that seafront.'

Sarah, in the chair beside the fire, sat with one leg curled beneath her, sulkily drawing long, hairspray-matted strands from a hairbrush before tossing them crackling into the flames. It wasn't fair that Alastair should get to see Jumbo play – plus Godfrey

Payne and The Comforters *and* The Berries, two of her favourite groups, both of whose records she'd bought in recent weeks – just because he was a boy. And of course Trevor was going. Concert or no concert, it would be so nice just to be at the seaside with Trevor. She missed him terribly already.

Knowing how upset his sister was, Alastair had arranged to leave from Trevor's house at nine, rather than him come round, but he hardly helped now, flitting back and forth between his packing and the mirror, humming *We've Gotta Get Out of This Place* with a stupid great grin smeared across his face.

'I say, why don't yi just take that thing away with yi, Alastair?' Jock said, as his son admired his reflection for about the fifteenth time.

'What's that, Father?' Alastair said, smoothing his sideburns.

'The mirror, there,' Jock nodded. 'Why not see if yi cannae slip it into your luggage. Or will I get a chain so's yi can hang it from your neck an' nivver be withoot it?'

Noisily buttering his toast, Jock studied his son with an amused smirk, eyebrows high, shaking his head. He winked across at Sarah. 'If only he could find a lassie he fancies half as much as he fancies himself.'

'Aye, tis a tricky task, Father,' Alastair mocked with incredible accuracy. 'There's so few lassies aboot quite as pretty as maself. I blame you, Father, yi big hairy handsome brute!'

'Bloody fool he is at times,' Jock said.

Gladys came from the kitchen carrying two plates of bacon, eggs, tomatoes and mushrooms.

'Aye, but mi mammy still loves me,' said Alastair, grabbing Gladys from behind and nuzzling childishly against her neck. 'Don't yi, Mammy?'

'These plates's hot, you daft sod.'

Alastair rested a camp hand on his hip and patted his hair. 'Such cruel beauty it is, this which I possess.' He became hunchbacked and wonky-eyed, the voice of Olivier's *Richard III*. 'I once dreamt I was a monster. A man with a face so *drawn*, so *twisted*, so *ugly* it did cause the birds to fall from their nests and the milk to curdle upon the breast of the maiden from whose – '

'Aye, that's quite enough of that, noo, thank yi very much!' Jock brusquely interrupted. 'I'll give you birds and breasts of – '

'Alastair!' Gladys gave Jock a vicious smack across the shoulder.

'*Me*? It's yi fool son, here! Hit him!'

'I don't know where he gets it from, really I don't,' said Gladys. 'Now come and have your breakfasts.'

'I'll just have toast, Mam,' Sarah said. 'I'm not very hungry.'

'I think you get dafter with age, Alastair. It's a wonder you're not the one who's prancing about on stage, never mind young Kenneth. Now leave your hair alone and eat your breakfast before it gets cold.'

'Who's Kenneth?' said Jock, without lifting his eyes from the football reports.

'Kenny Moorhouse,' said Sarah. '*Jumbo*.'

'Aye, Jumbo, aye.' There was a second or two's pause before Jock looked up, astonished. '*Jumbo*? He's nivver goin' up on the stage is he? In the group you're away ti see th' noo?'

'Yes,' said both Alastair and Sarah. Gladys nodded, smiling at her husband.

Jock took a long slurp of his tea. 'God help us!'

PART TWO

DON'T BALLS IT UP!

CHAPTER ONE

From his sky blue billboard a fat yellow sun wearing a trilby hat and bow tie winked a cheery 'Welcome!' as Trevor swung the Mini through the gates of Beachlands Holiday Park. Without too much difficulty they found the peach and white caravan, the key to its front door hidden, as Jumbo had said it would be, in an old gardening glove under the dustbin.

'Toss you for it,' Alastair said, leaping onto the double bed that filled the tiny bedroom at the rear of the van.

'Tails.'

'Unlucky!'

The wind blowing in off the North Sea was a little *too* bracing along the promenade and they soon turned inland towards the flower gardens. Not yet April, the pretty displays famed for their painstaking detail and jolly variety had yet to reveal themselves, so that the job of brightening the place up was for the moment left to the plastic lanterns, stars and crescent moons that swung between the whitewashed lamp posts and flagpoles. Between the spiky roses pensioners smiled, wrapped up like mummies in deckchairs, wondering how they'd ever get out of them again.

'Ey up!' said Alastair. But Trevor had already spotted the tight behind of the dark-haired beauty bending over at the fifth hole of the crazy-golf course. They wandered across to lean against the railing just in time to savour a very skilful putt into the mouth of an oscillating clown's head. Golf might well be all about the swing of the hips, but there was no denying that a tiny pair of corduroy shorts definitely brought something to the game, if only for the spectator.

'It'd be cosy in that end bedroom,' mused Alastair.

'Oh, I dare say I could manage,' Trevor said wistfully. One of the girls smashed her ball into the sails of the windmill, but Alastair and Trevor missed it. They were too busy watching her sister who, standing to one side, was making quite a job of prizing her shorts out from where they'd ridden up between her buttocks.

'Fine weather for shorts.'

'I'll say.'

When what might have been the girls' boyfriends or brothers ran over to join them, Alastair and Trevor turned towards the Pleasure Beach. The rattle and whirr of fairground rides carried on the breeze, along with the smell of fried onions and snatches of fifties rock 'n' roll which sounded as if it were being played under water.

'You know what I could do with now?' Alastair said after a little while.

'Yes, but you can't do that here. Will you settle for a bag of chips?'

* * *

She couldn't half run, Sarah. At school she'd been one of the few girls who actually liked cross-country, preferring always to come home at the head of the pack rather than dawdle round with the fat, lazy and nicotine-partial at the back, despite hearing how much fun they had.

It was just as well. Having hung about until the last minute, hoping that by some miracle she'd be allowed to go with the boys to Skegness after all, she had almost missed her bus and for the first time was glad of her frumpy, flat work shoes as she sprinted the last 400 yards to catch it.

Flicking through that week's *Melody Maker*, hoping to distract herself from the disappointment, Sarah turned immediately to a piece about Godfrey Payne and The Comforters. It was as though the whole world was conspiring in her torment. But what was the point in sulking about it? She wasn't going to Skegness and that was that. She comforted herself by remembering all the lovely things Trevor had said to her the night before, in Clumber Park, the promises they'd made to one another, the dreams they shared for the future. So lost in her happy, private thoughts, Sarah didn't notice the motorbike as it overtook the bus, the goggled face of its rider glancing in at the window. Nor, as she ran down the hill towards Woolworth's, ten minutes later, did she notice the same dark figure, helmet dangling from his handlebars, as he watched her from the edge of the market square.

* * *

A raucous squeal went up as a roadie crept out onto the stage, swiftly dying away again as he scurried about in the shadows fiddling with guitars, amplifiers and cables, and the crowd recognised him as a nobody.

Alastair and Trevor hadn't expected to feel quite so nervously excited on Jumbo's behalf. But once inside the theatre, seeing how the place was filled to bursting and veritably rocking with mostly teenage boys and girls twisting and jiving between the rows of seats, the instruments twinkling beneath the lights on the stage, suddenly the idea that all this, or even a tiny part of it, should be for their pal seemed utterly incredible. Jumbo was going to be playing up there! In front of this lot!

'He must be shitting himself!' Alastair shouted over The Searchers.

Trevor laughed. 'I am, and I'm not even playing. Still, if they're awful, we'll be able to give him plenty of stick about it.'

Needles and Pins faded abruptly and the crowd immediately started to chant like a foundry picket line on helium. 'God-Free-Pain! God-Free-Pain! God-Free-Pain!'

For almost an hour the invisible disc jockey had spun a perfectly pitched set of Pop, Soul and R&B hits which had kept the young crowd dancing merrily. But now they were restless for the concert to start proper. The chanting grew louder and more insistent, and was accompanied at first by rhythmic clapping and then by a dull tribal stomp, which, rising gradually in volume and tempo, swept through the auditorium like a forest fire.

'God-Free-Pain! God-Free-Pain! God-Free-Pain!'

Alastair wondered if the crowd realised there were three other groups due to play before the headliners came on stage, but then they could hardly be expected to chant for The Chequered Saracens or the other group nobody had ever heard of. The screams went up again as an anonymous figure ran on stage and, after mumbling a few indecipherable phrases into the mike, bawled, 'The Cheque-errrrrr-ed Saracens!'

Alastair turned to Trevor and with a look of comic horror on his face pulled his jumper over his head as if to hide from whatever disaster was about to unfold. Trevor turned away and said, 'I can't look.'

Jumbo was first out. Wearing a pale blue suit he strode purposefully towards his drum kit and seated himself without even a glance towards the screaming crowd. The look on his face showed no signs of nerves, in fact he seemed so cool and composed he might have been settling down to practise alone in his bedroom as he went about adjusting his stool and worked the pedals of the hi-hat and bass drum for comfort.

Jumbo's bandmates followed him out, each wearing a smaller version of the same blue, three-button suit. A thin, shortish lad with a floppy blond fringe – the singer, presumably – made for centre stage, where he now stood, back to the audience, his right leg jerking 4/4 time as he fiddled with his mike lead. A guitarist with dark curly hair and a threatening face took up position stage right, legs wide apart as he fixed the crowd with a still, dead-eyed stare. The final member was a very affable-looking, bespectacled bass player, who, kneeling before the altar of his amplifier, spent a moment or two making sure his instrument had just the right amount of throbbing depth to trigger a full front row nosebleed.

As the squeals and screams grew more hysterical, Alastair noticed how Jumbo suddenly looked absolutely terrified. Sick with fear! Beads of sweat glinted beneath the hot lights as they poured down his face and over his big pink cheeks. He fidgeted nervously with his sticks, the cuffs of his jacket already blackening where he'd used them to mop his brow. The big lad seemed unusually vulnerable up there, peering through his glittering cage like a baby bear in a zoo.

Jumbo raised his sticks and with a 'One-Two-Three!' they were off. With an almighty smash his drums collided with the thudding bass and wildly overdriven guitar, blasting an opening trio of crunchy major chords out into the auditorium, a sonic wave of such force that the whole place seemed to lurch to one side as the crowd screamed and began to jump up and down as one. Bolstered by such an ecstatic, unexpected, welcome, The Chequered Saracens tore through their opening number, an original composition with a driving beat and impressively tight stop-start guitar riff which relied upon some rather fancy percussion-work from their sweat-lathered pal. The lyrics were largely indecipherable, but that hardly mattered when they were belted out with such energy the audience was soon swept away on the waves of noise pouring from both the stage and themselves. When Alastair turned to Trevor he was staring back at him, open-mouthed. The Chequered Saracens were good; *bloody* good, in fact. Raw, certainly, but then so were a lot of groups live. They raced through their set of eight equally breathless numbers, including both a Kinks and a Rolling Stones cover, their confidence visibly growing with every tune. Towards the end of their set the singer even started to pick out faces in the crowd, friends he recognised, girls he liked the look of, acknowledging them with a loaded finger or a cocky wink. The guitarist, despite his surly demeanour, also turned out to be quite a showman, and when not pirouetting about, becoming entangled in his own cables, would suddenly throw himself to his knees like some borstal Chuck Berry, or lay on his back firing a volley of angry notes up into the ceiling. At one point, Jumbo removed his sodden jacket, twirling it above his head before tossing it out over his kit so that it came down perfectly positioned for the bassist to then kick it out into the sea of screaming faces. It was a blistering performance for a band no-one outside the pubs of Lincolnshire had ever heard of. They were hardly The Kinks or The Who by a long way, but The Chequered Saracens definitely had *something*. And whatever it was, they'd given every last drop of it during the twenty minutes they played on that stage.

'Jumbo was fantastic! I can't believe it!' said Trevor as the cheering subsided and the DJ quickly faded up *Doo Wah Diddy Diddy*.

'He's a bloody legend! Christ, they didn't half give it some welly!'

'My ears are ringing.'

'And so are the seats,' smirked Alastair, nodding to the widening pool which had formed between the feet of two plain-looking girls in the row in front.

'Dirty little cows!'

Alastair and Trevor's priority now was to somehow find their way backstage and congratulate Jumbo on his phenomenal performance. During The Chequered Saracens' set they had noticed one or two important-looking figures – and a few pretty girls – coming in and out of the double doors at the side of the stage. It seemed as good a place to start as any. They walked across to the steward just as he opened the door and waved through a short man in a suit. Alastair made to follow him.

'A-a-ah!' said the steward, pressing a hot hand into Alastair's chest and pushing him firmly back. The steward himself couldn't have been much above thirty, yet among all those teenagers and the soundtrack of blaring pop music he seemed as ancient and out of place as the old organ pit or the posters advertising the weekly wartime sing-a-long.

'We want to go backstage,' Alastair shouted politely as on the stage the next group, The Moondust Boys, launched into a pretty decent stab at *Eight Days a Week*, setting the place alight once more. Alastair pointed to the doors. '*Backstage*. Our pal was in The Chequered Saracens. Fat lad on drums?' The steward stared back hard, his nostrils flaring as if Alastair had just asked him for a kiss. But he said nothing. Trevor stepped forward, leaning in towards the man's ear, thinking that having to stand beside the stage every day had perhaps made him a little deaf.

'Would you please let us...' But it was now Trevor's turn to feel the hand pushing hard into his ribs.

'Would you let us through please, mate?' Alastair said, as reasonably as he was able, almost shouting. 'We're friends of the *group*.'

After a moment's blank stare the steward leaned forward until his nose almost touched the tip of Alastair's chin. 'If you don't piss off back to yer seats,' he said, his breath reeking of beer and pies, 'the pair on yer'll be out through that door on the end of my boot. You hear?'

They stepped aside into the aisle. 'Let's rush the bastard,' said Trevor.

'Are you mad? If he hasn't already killed today, he bloody well means to, and I'd rather it weren't me.'

'So what shall we do?'

Just then, as a shimmering chord rang out from a 12-string Rickenbacker, the doors burst open and into the dim light strode a very tall and curious-looking figure dressed almost entirely in black. In the gloom it was impossible to say who or what it was. The height and the huge loping strides it took through the jostling crowd strongly suggested a man. The bright pink and yellow-flowered cotton shopping bag that swung gaily from the crook of one arm suggested something else, as did the hair which swung in a heavy dark ponytail halfway down the stiff, broad back.

'Who the bloody hell's that?' said Trevor.

'God knows! But whoever it is we must befriend him – or *her* – immediately.'

CHAPTER TWO

The sunlight was blinding after the sticky gloom of the theatre, and it was a few moments until their eyes had adjusted enough to begin the search among the crowds for their only hope of getting backstage. Not that he was particularly difficult to spot, striding determinedly between the holidaymakers, chin thrust forward, hands deep in the pockets of his battered army greatcoat, tails flapping behind him like the wings of some huge leathery bat.

Alastair and Trevor chased after him, dodging between prams and dogs, wheelchairs and buskers, the crippling handles of spades which dangled treacherously from sandy buckets. They watched as without a care for either the crawling traffic or his own safety the striking youth stepped out into the road, weaving through bumpers and grilles, looking neither left nor right and seemingly oblivious to all around him, including the blaring carful of Rockers who eyed him with a threatening leer as he skirted the front of their scabby open-topped Sunbeam. They seemed particularly fascinated, as did many of the strolling trippers, with the youth's lustrous ponytail which swung in time to his great strides, like a heavy burgundy pendulum, across his broad back. Alastair was about to call after him when he was beaten to it.

'Ooh, *hallo*, darlin'! I like yer handbag!' lisped the driver of the Sunbeam.

'What's up? Lost your boyfriend?' the back seat chipped in, cackling like a machine gun. The one in the passenger seat was less restrained. 'Look! He's a bloody queer!' he shouted, setting his two clones off in fits of jeering laughter and sarcastic wolf whistles. 'Get yer hair cut, you big pansy!'

On the pavement one or two mums, envisaging a bloodbath, tugged discreetly at dad's elbow before steering the kids away towards the park. The long-haired youth didn't miss a single step. And only the smallest of frowns wrinkled his high, intelligent brow as, with a swish of his ponytail, he stepped back into the road and marched determinedly up to the side of the Sunbeam. He towered over the car and its occupants looking like the Grim Reaper, despite his bright and pretty tote bag. Supporting himself with one hand on the windscreen pillar, he glared a moment into the faces of each of the Rockers in turn before then bending down and, so it appeared, whispering for some time into the ear of the mouthiest lad, in the passenger seat. Quite what he might have said is anybody's guess, but suddenly he stepped away, back on to the kerb, and smiling broadly, blew a series of flamboyant, theatrical kisses to his would-be tormentors. The Sunbeam revved its engine so hard that a good six months' rubber was left on the road before traction was eventually gained and the Rockers screeched noisily away and disappeared down the first side street.

'What just happened?' Trevor said.

'Dunno. Looked like he was trying to commit suicide.'

Alastair and Trevor dodged through the traffic, following the intriguing character as he made towards the High Street. After a few hundred yards he turned into a Gentlemen's Outfitter's, which from its tweed-heavy window display looked the sort of place this lad would not likely wish to be seen dead.

Slipping in behind him, Alastair and Trevor made for a revolving rack of socks and ties opposite a long, L-shaped counter. The shop reeked of polish. Its walls were lined floor to ceiling with rows of neatly labelled pine drawers of varying sizes, some with little oblongs of colour as hints as to what lay within. A pair of dismembered torsos bookended the counter in drab short-sleeved formal shirts. The shop was either unaware it was in the middle of the High Street of the East Coast's liveliest seaside resort, or had deliberately chosen to ignore the fact.

'And what might I be able to do for you three gentlemen?' smiled the softly spoken shop assistant, as he trotted out from his stockroom and slipped behind the counter. The long-haired youth, who'd shown no signs of knowing he'd been followed, slowly peered round and threw a casual glance, first at Alastair and then across to Trevor, who was busy clowning before a mirror in a nasty-looking deerstalker. With a flick of his ponytail the youth turned back to the shop assistant. 'I've come for socks,' he said, rather grandly. 'Grey socks. *Wool*.'

He spoke with great confidence and a slight northern accent. A lad of humble origin who'd been schooled up, Alastair decided, rather than a toff attempting, as the times dictated, to play it down, take a bit of the shine off the old silver spoon.

'Socks! Socks! Socks! Well, gentlemen, you are in luck! If there's one thing I can provide you with today, it is socks!' The shop assistant, immaculate in a dark blue three-piece, smiled kindly and with clasped hands tilted his grey head this way and that, wondering what to make of his remarkable customer. 'Such wonderful hair,' he said. 'Is it... all your own?'

'Yes. Twenty pairs.'

'Hmm? Oh, I do beg your pardon.' Beaming, the assistant nodded over to Alastair and Trevor. 'Twenty pairs of socks. How shall you divide them between three, I wonder?'

'Eh? Oh, they're not for us,' said Alastair. 'I quite fancy this tie, though. After you've served this gentleman.'

'Ta,' said the ponytailed youth, with a faint smile. 'Must be wool,' he reminded the assistant who was now scurrying on all fours behind the counter. 'Not terry towelling, makes their feet sweat. And god knows they stink quite enough as it is.'

'Yes, woollen socks are what you boys need. *Pure new wool*. Now let me see...' The assistant sprang up, a shallow drawer in hand, and began counting out in an urgent whisper, 'fourteen, fifteen, sixteen. I won't be a second... the, er, stockroom.' As he trotted across the floor, glasses swinging on a silver chain, the shop assistant's eyes squinted the length of the youth's ponytail, only just reaching its end, just above the waist, before he vanished through a door disguised as a mirror.

'Sorry to hold you chaps up,' the youth said, turning and speaking down his nose at them. 'I'd have insisted you be served first had I known there'd be all this palaver.' He nodded towards the secret mirror.

'Oh, don't mind us, matey,' said Trevor. 'We hadn't come in to buy anything.'

'No?'

'I've been after a burgundy tie for ages,' said Alastair. And then, looking directly at the youth: 'Actually, it's you we were after.'

'Oh?'

'Yes,' said Trevor, coming over. 'We followed you from The Regency Ballrooms. We wanted to have a word with you.'

'I see. Friends of yours, were they?' The youth narrowed his eyes, pursed his full lips. Alastair noticed the size of his winkle-pickers, like silver-buckled canoes.

'Eh?' he said, confused.

'Boneheads in the car,' said the youth, calmly. 'Sent you two chaps after me, did they?' He glanced towards the window before turning back and studying them in turn with an expression somewhere between a smirk and a sneer. He rubbed his strong chin with a huge hand. Yes, he was a bloke all right. Yet there was a certain gentle beauty about his heavy features, beyond the lady-like hair. Something a little bit horsey, too; perhaps it was the steady dark eyes, or the way he tossed his head and flicked his ponytail in a single motion, curling his lip to reveal a set of large and very white teeth.

'Sent us?' Trevor said. 'You mean... *us*? With that bunch of greasy arseholes? No chance, matey! No, our pal's in one of the groups playing at The Regency Ballrooms – The Chequered Saracens.'

'Fat lad on drums,' said Alastair.

'You mean Kenny?' A wide smile spread across the youth's face. 'You're friends of Kenny?'

'Success gentlemen!' clucked the shop assistant as he spread a fan of socks across the counter. 'Sixteen and four makes twenty pairs of grey, pure new wool socks! Now, is there anything else I might help you boys with today?'

The ponytailed youth tilted his head at Alastair. 'Are you having that tie?'

'I think I will. But after you, though.'

'That's all right. I'll get our friend here to ring it all through together. Pay me back later, if you insist, but the boys won't miss it. Anything *you* fancy?' he said, turning to Trevor.

'The deerstalker,' said Alastair. 'I dare you.'

'Actually, I could do with a new tie myself,' said Trevor. 'I mean, if it's all right?'

'And a very good day to you all,' the shop assistant smiled as his customer casually swept his purchases into his floral-patterned bag. A hesitant twitch appeared on his lips. 'I bet it must take some looking after?' he ventured.

'I beg your pardon?'

'Your hair. I think it's absolutely marvellous. But it must take some looking after. Does it?'

'Not really,' the youth said, tossing the ponytail over his shoulder. 'You see my mother washes it for me every Sunday. When she gives me my weekly bath. Good day!'

'I'm Jay,' said the youth, holding out a pair of knitted ties, one burgundy, one navy. 'I have other names, but I'm mostly Jay to those who know me.'

As they walked back towards The Regency Ballrooms, Jay told them he was with Godfrey Payne and The Comforters. Alastair and Trevor were so impressed they immediately forgot all about Jumbo and asked Jay if he might be able to get them backstage.

'I've been friends with Eric – *Handley*, the guitarist – for years. We were at school together. Well, one of the many I attended. And Godfrey I've known since they got the group together, three, four years, maybe.'

'Are you their manager?' asked Alastair.

'Me? No! I just do whatever needs doing, really – roadie, driver, tour manager, cook, press officer, nurse. You name it, I've probably done it by now. I played bass for six nights once, when Clive had his appendix out.'

Alastair and Trevor smiled in awe, keen for Jay to go on.

'What was it like?' said Trevor.

'Must be amazing,' said Alastair.

'*I* was bloody awful. But, fortunately, no-one seemed to notice.'

'Are you their dresser too?' Alastair smiled, nodding at the shopping bag filled with socks.

'Not officially. Though I do mostly choose their stage gear. I'd hate to think what a bunch of scruffy Herberts they'd look like if I didn't. Like that lot, I shouldn't wonder.'

They turned to the road as a black swarm of bikers spluttered up to the roundabout, rowdily circling the clock tower like an unwelcome circus act before roaring off along the seafront. Reminded of an earlier incident, Jay fished about in his coat pocket, eventually bringing out a car radio aerial, which he now casually snapped in two and tossed into a litter bin.

'Is that off that Sunbeam?' said Alastair, turning to Trevor and laughing out loud.

Jay made a sort of thoughtful, smiling frown. 'Cretins,' he said, before continuing. 'I suppose my main thing though, and what I like best of all, is art. I design a lot of their posters, flyers, that sort of thing. Sometimes take the odd photo that might get printed in a paper or a magazine, you know.' There was nothing at all boastful in the way Jay spoke about this very famous group, or of his *designing* and his *art*. In fact, he made it sound as if to be involved in such work was perfectly normal, the sort of job anyone might do, if he were so inclined.

'Is that one of yours?' said Trevor, spotting Jumbo's face peering out, along with those of his fellow Chequered Saracens, from a poster on the side of a bus shelter.

'*That*?' Jay scoffed. 'Piss off! No offence, dear, but no, that most certainly is *not* mine. Theatre had those run up, stuck the damn things all over this god-awful place.'

Neither Alastair nor Trevor could see anything wrong with it. They were impressed enough just to see their friend and his group on the same poster with Godfrey Payne and The Comforters and The Berries.

'It wouldn't do for a pensioners' bingo,' Jay said, shaking his head. 'Fortunately there's one of mine outside the theatre. I'll show you.'

'The big one, with all the ships in the background?' said Alastair.

'The Docks, yes.'

'Wow, that's on the record sleeve!'

'Sounds like a very cool job you've got, Jay,' Trevor said.

'Must be fantastic,' said Alastair, 'all the travel and the concerts and the... birds?'

Trevor had also been wondering about them.

'There's never a dull moment, let's put it that way. As for birds, well!' Jay gave one of his little frowns. 'You should see how the little hussies throw themselves at them, especially this last year since they've become big. And young, a lot of them. Course you can't always tell nowadays, can you? That's one part of the job I'm not so keen on. I can very well do without papa raging at the Stage Door, desperate to give somebody a damn good hiding for ruining his innocent little Jenny.'

Alastair and Trevor laughed, half in wonder at the picture of the life Jay described, half suspecting he might be teasing them, laughing to himself at their naivety.

Two old men looked up from a bench and made suspicious faces at Jay's shopping bag.

'Imagine,' said Alastair, 'having to fight off girls every night of your life. Wonder if Jumbo gets any?'

Trevor nodded. 'Knowing him, yes. But is it really like that, Jay? Different girls every night?'

'No,' said Jay as they sprang up the steps of the theatre. 'Even the biggest rock 'n' roll stars have their lonely nights. Why do you think I had to go out and buy them all new socks again, the dirty bastards.'

* * *

On stage The Berries were whipping the crowd into another sticky frenzy with their most recent hit single, a catchy piece of blues-skewed rock which Alastair reckoned might almost be as good as The Yardbirds, at their best. Trevor disagreed, but either way, and with all respect to Jumbo's lot, these boys were a real top-drawer outfit and Alastair felt disappointed at having missed what must have been a blinding set, until he remembered there was a second show that evening as well as two more again tomorrow. And the highlight of the show, Godfrey Payne and The Comforters, was still to come! Alastair imagined how much Sarah would have loved it, and would have said as much to Trevor if something (selfishness? – brotherly discomfort at their intimacy?) hadn't decided him against it.

'They're with me,' said Jay, wafting aside the doorman with a flap of his coat tails. Alastair gave the scowling steward a cocky wink. It was easy when you knew how, he thought, admiring Jay's cool confidence. He must ask him what he'd said to the carful of Rockers to put the wind up them so sharply.

Jumbo didn't see them at first. He was leaning against the wall beside a long table laid out as if for a Sunday tea with sandwiches, nibbles and cake, bottles of beer and fizzy pop, grinning his head off as he chatted animatedly away with a short, mousy girl, a half-eaten sausage roll in one hand, drumsticks twirling and tapping a rhythm against his thigh in the other.

The large windowless room had the feel of an attic about it. The low ceiling and stack of folding chairs and tables shoved in one corner, the dull bass thud of music from below, the sense that real life was going on elsewhere. Members of The Chequered Saracens and The Moondust Boys, easily distinguishable by their stage suits, stood about drinking and chatting to one another, or flitted between tight little groups of young men and women who leaned self-assuredly against the bare walls and sat cross-legged, smoking roll-ups, on the thick carpet. Fashionable lot, Alastair thought, admiring the cut of their clothes, their trendy hairstyles. Sophisticated, well off, and not at all Skegness.

'Beverage, gentlemen? On the house.'

'Thanks, Jay,' Alastair smiled, taking two bottles of beer and passing one to Trevor.

'Cheers, Jay.'

Alastair waved across to Jumbo. As he did so he felt the hopeful smile of a girl in a gold headscarf shining up at him from where she half lay among a super-cool set on the floor about ten feet away. Dark blonde hair fell over the shoulders of her white pinafore dress and the sleeves of her yellow blouse. She had a strong and very attractive face, even with the look of disappointment that came over it when Alastair smiled back at her. She'd done the same thing when they walked in, looked up expectantly only to see him and Trevor before turning away again, deflated.

The stylish young man whom she lay against leaned forward and whispered something in her ear. She looked back at Alastair and laughed a little too loudly before turning back to the boisterous male voices which echoed every now and then along the backstage corridor.

'I don't care 'ow much it bladdy well costs! Just make sure ee's there! Avver-wise I'll have him off that bleedin' tour *pronto* and he can find some avver mug to babysit him!' The smash of a telephone receiver was the cue for a grey-suited man to storm into the room. Barging Trevor aside, he made for another figure so similar in appearance they might have been brothers. In urgent Cockney accents they growled at one another about lost tickets and missed trains, furious, familiar mentions of *'Dusty'* and *'Eppy'* and *'The bladdy Motown Tour'*.

'About time an' all!' said Jumbo, slinging his sticky arms around Alastair and Trevor's shoulders. 'What kept you?'

'Steward.'

'Twat.'

Jumbo's face was dripping pink. The armpits of his shirt were black with patches of sweat which towards their outer edges had begun to dry in wavy brown islands, like the contour lines on an Ordnance Survey map.

'Urgghh, Jumbo, you're sopping!'

'Aye, and I stink an' all! So were we any good then?'

'You were bloody marvellous!' said Trevor, giving Jumbo's slippery cheek a big old squeeze.

'Fantastic!' said Alastair. *'Really* fantastic. I thought you'd be useless, you great big oaf – *Owww!*'

Jumbo let go of Alastair's testicles. 'Thing is,' he said, turning serious, 'we've got to do it all over again, later on. Probably mek a right balls-up on it this time, you watch.'

'Yer'd better bloody not, Kenny!' said a slim youth who, after clapping Jumbo matily on the shoulder, took out a steel comb and pulled it swiftly through his damp blond hair. The Chequered Saracens' singer.

'Some big noises up here this weekend – journalists, agents, record company bods. These shows could be the makin' on us, if we don't go and cock it up. So let's just make sure we don't. All right?' The singer turned to Alastair and Trevor. 'How do?' he said, 'I'm Brian. Nice to meet yer.'

Brian was a lot shorter in real life than on stage. But he was no less cocky or charismatic.

'These are my pals from home,' Jumbo said. 'Alastair, Trevor. They're staying in the caravan next to us.'

'Nice one. Well, cheers for coming, lads. I'm really glad you could make it.' Brian shook their hands, smiling as if he were genuinely pleased to meet them.

'We were just saying how marvellous we thought you were,' said Alastair. 'The group's fantastic, and you – you were brilliant! I don't know how you do it, up there. It must feel – '

Brian nodded. 'Yeah, yeah,' he interrupted. 'We're getting really good now – *bloody* good! Got to keep at it though – can't let up, you know? We need to write more of our own stuff. That's why The Beatles are head and shoulders above everyone else, they're continually writing brilliant songs. I mean, playing other folks' stuff night after night is all right, great fun, keeps you busy and all that. But it'll never buy you a Rolls Royce.' Brian glanced at his watch. 'Stick around lads. We'll have a few jars after the next show.'

'Not shy, is he?' said Alastair as Brian's tiny buttocks sprinted out into the corridor.

'Can't be can you, lead singer?' Jumbo said with a mischievous smirk. 'He's gorra big 'ead, and he can be a right cock at times. But he *is* a bloody good singer and we wouldn't be half as good without him.'

Alastair and Trevor nodded. Having seen Brian on stage they could hardly disagree.

'Here, there's somebody I want you to meet.' Jumbo beckoned the mousy girl over from where she'd been amusing herself with the buffet table. 'This,' he said, placing a gentle hand on her shoulder, 'is Amelia.'

Amelia had a sweet, angelic face, framed by a neat bob of not quite blonde hair. At close range her figure was surprisingly shapely, not half as chubby as they'd first assumed. Cardigans could be deceptive like that. In fact, she was a very attractive girl, if you liked them a bit on the comfortable side, as indeed Jumbo did.

'Amelia, I'd like you to meet my two oldest and best friends,' said Jumbo. 'Idiots, pair of them.'

Amelia smiled shyly, but then as she opened her mouth to

speak her eyes suddenly filled with painful surprise and her whole body seemed to arrest and then freeze. She coughed once, twice, and then again, turning almost as pink as Jumbo as she repeatedly patted her chest with a little fist. 'Oops!' she said after a moment, eyes streaming. 'Pickled onion! Went down the wrong hole! It's so nice to meet you both at last,' Amelia giggled.

* * *

There were about twenty of them squeezed into the box to watch Godfrey Payne and The Comforters, including some of the trendy crowd and the girl in the gold headscarf. Alastair and Trevor could hardly believe their luck when they found themselves standing right at the front, either side of Anthony Hawksmoor, lead singer and guitarist with The Berries.

'I'd kill to write a song half as good as this,' Anthony Hawksmoor shouted into Alastair's ear during the keyboard break in *Pretend She's Mine*.

'Me too!' Alastair laughed, rolling his shoulders and dipping in time with the driving groove. The upbeat, soul-tinged R&B was the perfect match for Payne's gravelly mid-register voice, which every now and then would rise to a scream as he wildly shook his hair and let his fingers run riot across the keys. The group's infectious melodies bounced along, whipping the crowd ever closer towards hysteria, one catchy hit after another. The possibility of standing still for even a second while they were on stage was zero, and by the time they closed with their two biggest hits, *Wake Up and Shake Shake* and *Locked In, Knocked Out*, the theatre was rocking on its foundations and the crowd was going completely bananas.

'How do you top that?' Trevor said, grinning from ear to ear.

'You don't!' said Anthony Hawksmoor with a reverential shake of the head. 'He's mind-blowing!'

'That was fucking blinding!' said Jumbo as they filed back along the corridor to the green room. 'I can't wait to see it all over again.'

Alastair looked around for Jay, to thank him for bringing them backstage and into Godfrey Payne and The Comforters' private box. But Jay was not there.

CHAPTER THREE

'Now we know why you've been scooting out here at every opportunity,' Alastair said, following Jumbo's eyes across the bar to where Amelia stood toying with the collar of her blouse among half a dozen sharply bobbed and beehived young girls. 'And here was me thinking you'd been rehearsing with the group!'

Amelia waved across, a giggly, beckoning smile widening her lips. Jumbo winked back and downed half a pint of bitter. 'She gives me no peace,' he said, grinning as he licked his lips.

'Loved-up, them two,' said Howie, The Chequered Saracens' guitarist, as they watched Jumbo take Amelia's face between his hands and gently kiss the tip of her nose. Something about Amelia, the way she stood with one leg tucked behind the other, hands clasped behind her back as she peered up into Jumbo's eyes, made Alastair think of *Winnie The Pooh*. She seemed so fragile next to Jumbo, the great big lummox.

Howie shook his head. 'Kenny says you play guitar.'

'Not really,' Alastair said. 'I mean, not properly, like you.'

Howie's eyebrows gave a modest lift. 'He reckons you were pretty handy. In a group, weren't you?'

'For a bit, yeah – when we were at school. Just a bedroom strummer these days.'

Howie turned away and belched ferociously into his armpit. ''Scuse me. I were ready for that. Wouldn't you fancy it again? Being in a group, I mean?'

'Watching you play tonight I wished I'd bloody kept it up, yes.'

'I could never jack it in now. If I had to go a day without picking up my guitar I reckon it'd kill me. I do. And after today – wow! They went crazy for us. That promoter bloke, Denny, is it? He said on stage we really had something.'

Alastair nodded enthusiastically. 'I thought you were even better in the second show than the first.'

'I'll say!' said Brian, returning from the bar with Trevor and more pints. 'We were bloody storming that second show. Bloody storming!'

'Kenny's a cracking drummer,' Howie said.

'I'd no idea he was *that* good,' Alastair said. 'We've been pals since we were five and I've never known him stick at anything, or get half as excited as he has about your group. Well, apart from...' Alastair nodded across the room to where Jumbo and Amelia were now lost in a kiss. Howie smiled, the lights from the fairground twinkling rainbows in his glass as he tilted it back and drank long and deep.

'It must be some life doing it all the time, like Godfrey Payne and The Comforters. Jay was telling us earlier.'

'Not half. I work as a printer on the *Argus*. Local paper. It's a good job and the pay's not bad, now I'm qualified. But sometimes, when I'm there at the machine, I drift off into my own little dream world thinking what I wouldn't give to play music and write songs for a living.'

Alastair nodded. 'Get your Rolls Royce?'

'It's norrabout money! Not that I'd say no, mind. But without going all arty-farty-pretentious-tit on you, Alastair, well... Every time I play now I get this feeling, it gets stronger and stronger, that this is what I should be doing with my life. I think music, song writing, is what I was born to do. It's all I ever *want* to do, anyroad. If I could. Jesus, I sound like a right tit, don't I? Sorry, Alastair, I'm just about pissed! Same again?'

As Howie pushed through to the bar Alastair sipped at his still three-quarters-full pint, mulling over the guitarist's earnest, heartfelt words. It was flattering Howie should think him someone worth confiding in about his dreams, someone who might understand his burning passion for making music. He didn't for a second think he sounded remotely pretentious or one bit like a tit. But he did wonder how ridiculous Howie would have thought him if he'd have said he understood exactly how he felt, because that was just the way he felt about steam engines.

The door swung open and Jay flapped into the room, raising his arms so that his greatcoat became wings. His ponytail hung forwards over his shoulder, thick as the rope on a church bell.

'Aha! Here you are! Now would any of you filthy young hipsters like to come to a proper party?'

The big party would actually be tomorrow night, Sunday. There was talk of Jeff Beck and Jack Bruce, and Dusty had promised to call in if she made it back from Liverpool in time. But Jay had done a good job of rustling up the handful of show-business faces, friends and associates, the usual assortment of pretty girls who liked a good time at others' expense, and who knew what might be expected of them in return, who packed into the upstairs function room of The Old Bell. As well as The Berries and Godfrey Payne and his boys, Alastair had already spotted a couple of radio personalities, a musical comedian, a talk-show host and a fading '50s balladeer, plus one or two stunningly good-looking girls who may or may not have been famous models. And although Dusty might not have been there in person, her voice belted out of the jukebox even louder than if she had been.

'I wouldn't know what to say to them,' Alastair said. 'They'd probably talk to you, you're a musician.'

Howie smiled. 'I can't believe we were invited to their party.'

'I know. He's all right that Jay, in't he?' said Jumbo.

Godfrey Payne and his trio of Comforters stood at the bar surrounded by girls and showbiz chums, drinking and laughing with the easy confidence of the universally adored. No doubt about it, stars really were much bigger than ordinary people, even when they were physically a lot smaller. Godfrey Payne dressed simply in beige corduroys and a black turtleneck. Yet on him they seemed to glow with some strange mysterious power, like the robes of an ancient king or a wizard's pointy hat.

'Seen Jay?' said Trevor, waving a Coke.

'Oh, he'll be around somewhere,' a well-spoken female voice purred. 'Jay's never far away from God.'

'*God*?'

'Godfrey,' said a tall, willowy girl with a wide toothy smile. Trevor took the offered slender hand, wondering what he was supposed to do with it. 'I'm Samantha,' she said.

'Trevor.' Samantha had one of those posh faces, Trevor thought as he gave the hand a limp shake, of the sort of girl who rode horses and played lacrosse. 'Pleased to meet you, Samantha. Are you here with...' Trevor broke off, noticing how Samantha wasn't listening but looking with wistful eyes over his shoulder to where Godfrey Payne and his guitarist, Eric Handley, had become hemmed into a corner by a dozen girls, all giggling and smiling as they jostled for the best positions from which to display their admiration. 'I mean,' Trevor continued, 'do you know – '

'Yes,' Samantha said, without shifting her gaze away from Payne. From behind Samantha's shoulder Alastair nibbled his nails and made a comical frightened grimace. There was an eruption of girly laughter as Payne reached the climax of another hilarious, star-studded anecdote and rose from where he'd been sitting on the edge of a table and made his way to the bar. 'What yer drinking, gels?' Payne called over his shoulder. 'My treat. Drink up, Cheryl, slowcoach!'

Samantha turned back, blinking her eyes to a moist sparkle. 'You were terrific tonight,' she said, sweeping Alastair, Trevor and all four Chequered Saracens up in her wide, elegant smile. 'You were absolutely super!' Samantha's long fingers gave Alastair a gentle prod in the chest.

'I'm, er, not in the group, myself,' Alastair said. 'We're pals of Jum – *Kenny* here. He's the drummer in – '

'Yes, I thought you were super, all of you. And I can't wait to scream for you all again tomorrow.'

'What's that all about?' said Brian, his eyes following Samantha out towards the landing.

Trevor shrugged. 'I only said "Hello" to her.'

'Think I've got a pretty good idea.' Recognising them from the box at the theatre, Anthony Hawksmoor, The Berries' singer, had fallen into conversation with Brian and Howie. 'Lavverlee gel, ain't she, Samantha?'

'Yes,' said Jumbo, with a glance to make sure Amelia was out of earshot. 'Is she, er, struck on Godfrey, like?'

'You could say that,' Anthony Hawksmoor said, puffing out his cheeks. 'Far as I know she used to be his missis – still is, supposed to be. Fing is, it's been a long tour and the Cam-fer-ters, like us, have been away a long time. And you know how it is when capples is away from each other for months.' At the bar Godfrey Payne's arm was now draped around the shoulders of a busty redhead. Alastair *didn't* know how it was, but he could very easily imagine. Godfrey looked over, raised his glass and winked at Anthony Hawksmoor.

The next few hours slipped past in a smoky blur. A bellyful of beer and a packet of unwanted fags later and Alastair was feeling hot and ill. A cigarette burned between his fingers and the warm beer he swilled around his mouth was enough to make him heave. He managed to swallow it down, only to feel it immediately wash back across his tongue. He forced it down again and tried to remain as still as possible until the twinkling rows of bottles and glasses behind the bar stopped kaleidoscoping about and floating off at nauseating angles towards the ceiling. The barman couldn't make up his mind if there was one of himself or three.

'I love this girl, Al. You know that?'

Further along the bench seat he recognised the back of Jumbo's head, the shining folds of pink skin on the back of his neck like luncheon meat as he leaned over Amelia and kissed her as though her lips were the very thing which kept him alive.

'Some good drumming today, kidder!' a passing voice called.

'Did *he* just say that?' asked Jumbo, a moment later, when the words had sunk in. 'That was Albie McPherson!'

'Huh?' Alastair's face looked blankly about.

'Albie McPherson – the Comforters' drummer!'

Alastair squinted. 'Was it?'

Amelia pushed Jumbo into an upright position, took a long sip of her drink and smiled sweetly across at Alastair before snuggling down against Jumbo's shoulder. Alastair took a drag on the stub of cigarette, gagged, then crushed it dead in the ashtray. He spotted Trevor at the bar, talking through the grey smog to Howie and Brian and a gang of others he didn't recognise. It all of a sudden seemed a much bigger party than the one he'd been at earlier in the evening. Noisier too. Faces laughed. Faces shouted. Faces drank and smoked and kissed. The room rang with booze-emboldened self-promotion, with wild tales and claims, boasts and promises no-one would remember in the morning. Somebody nudged Alastair's elbow.

'You pissed as I am?' Jumbo said, tilting at a queasy angle.

'Bet I'm twice as pissed as you are,' Alastair said slowly. 'Not used to free beer.'

Jumbo shoved his glass away into the crowd of empties on the table. 'Enough of that, I think,' he said, blowing out his cheeks, 'or I'll be chuffing useless tomorrow. Did I ever tell you, Alastair? I bloody *love* this girl!'

Alastair smiled, nodded. He was happy for his friend, but now – perhaps it was the booze – he suddenly felt very lonely and desperately envious of Jumbo having his girl to cuddle up to, his girl with whom he would later, presumably, be sharing a bed back at the caravan.

Godfrey Payne was now perched on the edge of a table, his legs spread either side those of a dark, olive-skinned girl wearing a red polo neck and a very short black skirt. Her face was obscured by Payne's as he leaned in and appeared to do something that involved his mouth and her ear, but there was no question she'd be anything other than beautiful. She was utterly entranced by the charming singer, nodding and cooing each time he drew back to look into her eyes, or stroke her hair, admiring her necklace briefly before revisiting her ear. Alastair saw with what stealth Godfrey placed a hand on the curve of her hip, how lightly he let it venture across her buttocks only for her to catch hold of it and then, shaking her head, turn it over, laughing as she read her fate in his palm.

'I feel sick,' Alastair said, dragging himself up by the table. He hadn't quite reached the landing when he felt a tremendous weight fall against his shoulder and something – *someone* – gripping tight on to his arm.

'Hey! It's my old pal! Havin' good time, are you? See y'arrr... *Upffff!*' Alastair pulled the swaying figure to its feet, averting his face from the rancid whisky spittle of its breath. 'An' when zee zye laz see you, eh? Mussuv been Gerry Bel... *Upffff!*... Ger... Gerry Bel... Bel... er, *Beldon's*.'

Neither face nor voice looked very much like the chap who hosted *Prize Box* on the telly every Tuesday evening, but it was him all right, Malcolm Tredding, purple-nosed and pissed as a fart.

'Say, aren't you...? Aren't you...? *Upfff!* You're Johnny's pal!'

'Yes, Malcolm,' Alastair nodded into Tredding's damp, twisted face. 'That's me! Johnny's been looking for you, he's over there.'

'Johnny's 'ere zee?' Not wishing to have his best jacket covered in vomit, even the vomit of a well-known TV quizmaster, Alastair spun Malcolm Tredding swiftly on his heels and with a firm shove in the middle of his back launched him towards the bar.

By now Alastair had forgotten all about being sick himself and he needed a drink. No – drink was the last thing he needed. What he needed was air. The Rolling Stones' *The Last Time* belted out of the jukebox for about the fifth time as Alastair looked about for his friends. It might have been Jay's ponytail disappearing down the stairs, though more likely chances were it was a girl. Jumbo and Amelia had gone, their places now occupied by Godfrey Payne and his olive beauty. Godfrey had made great progress from her ear, and she no longer seemed quite so interested in his palm, perhaps having decided his fate – as well as her own – for the rest of the evening. Lucky bleeder, Alastair thought as he struggled to stand still long enough to light the cigarette he found in his jacket pocket. He'd no idea how long he must have been staring, tracking Godfrey's hands as they crept about under the girl's jumper like thieves in the night.

'They're over there, chum.' Alastair realised it was Godfrey Payne's voice and that it was calling out to him.

'Eh?' he said.

'Saracen boys. That's who you're arfter, ain't it?'

Alastair nodded blankly. 'Er, yes. Yes, Godfrey. Thanks. Cheers!' Alastair smiled. An actual conversation with Godfrey Payne!

'Trev says you much prefer the Telecaster to the Strat,' said Howie, stepping forward and shoving a fresh pint into his hand. Howie seemed as sober now as he had at five o'clock that afternoon.

'I just think it's a better shape, that's all – *neater*. Never played a proper Fender though, of either. Mine's only a copy.'

Alastair sipped the froth off his beer and instantly heaved. A hand on his shoulder, Trevor's face leaned in, grinning like a mad fool. 'My dear fellow!' it said in the voice of Alec Guinness's

Professor Marcus. 'How pleased I am to see you. I feared you had been taken from us, spirited away into the night never to be seen again.'

'No, I'm still here,' Alastair said, wishing he still shared his friend's high spirits and were able to respond in the manner they deserved. A flutter of laughter rose from a large group standing nearby. He recognised Samantha, one or two of the smart set from the theatre. The rest of the room had become a noisy blur of smoking faces and merging bodies. Pianist's fingers, he thought, glancing across at Godfrey Payne and the girl. Alastair imagined himself taking her back to the caravan. He could very happily fall asleep with her later on, if only in his mind's eye.

'I'm going back to the caravan, Trev,' Alastair said. 'I don't feel too good.'

'You can't go! How often do we get invited to something like this?'

'Come over and talk to The Berries,' said Brian, wobbly on his feet. 'They're a right laugh.'

'Anthony Hawksmoor said we can sit in their box again tomorrow,' Trevor said, eyes bright with excitement. 'Come on, Al, stay!' He gave Alastair's elbow a nudge. 'There are loads of birds here. I won't say anything if you won't.'

'Sorry, matey, I'm knackered. I'll get some sleep, save myself for tomorrow.'

As he turned to leave, a slender arm curled round his neck and Samantha's face smiled dozily up from his shoulder. What was it with these people, why were they all so intent on hanging all over him this evening?

'Hello again, you,' Samantha slurred. 'You're friends with him, *Trevor*, and your name is... *Alastair*? No! Yes! Alastair. *Are* you Alastair?'

'Correct, you win tonight's first prize,' Alastair said impatiently as Samantha pulled his arm around her and intertwined her fingers with his. 'Actually, if it's a quizmaster you're after, he's over there, pissed, under that table. Right, I'm off.'

'You're not going? Please don't.'

Alastair wriggled free, giving way to a little smile as Samantha now moved across and curled herself around Trevor. 'Ah've got to get gooin' nah, duck,' Alastair said, turning up the full-on Nottinghamshire tongue. 'It's mi mam, yer see. She worries abaht me if am not 'ome for mi supper. Anyroad, it wor nice talkin' t'yer, duck. Look after yersen. Ta-ra!'

The night air was cool and refreshing, despite tasting of yesterday's fried fish. Alastair made for the coast road, his right arm windmilling wildly as he growled the opening lines of The Who's *I Can't Explain*, which chased him along the street from The Old Bell.

'I don't care a bleedin' mankees what 'is prior commitments are! Tell 'im he'll be in Saarff-end on that fakkin' stage tomorrer night or I'll have his 'air-less little bollocks for caff-links!'

There was a Bakelite-shattering crash. Alastair looked across the road to the pair of telephone boxes that stood in front of The Regency Ballrooms. One lay empty, drawing not even a moth to its bright light, but the other was swirlingly opaque with clouds of thick blue-grey smoke. Inside, a dark silhouette scuffled and then began to flail about behind the blinded windows. An angry and impatient voice cried out. 'Fakk! Where's the fakkin' Jesus cantin'... For *fakk's* sake!' Against the lower panes of the phone box the heel of a small man's shoe kicked furiously against the thick glass. 'Fakk!' The receiver took another heavy slam. 'Where's the fakkin' – *Fakk*!'

At last the door squeaked heavily open and a stocky grey-suited man, whom Alastair recognised as one of the agents he'd not so much seen as heard shouting in the green room at the theatre, stepped coughing and spluttering away from the smouldering phone box like a fighter pilot who's downed his machine behind enemy lines. The agent coughed a few more times and then stopped to scowl at the end of his cigar. 'Fakk!' He patted his pockets, looked up and down the quiet street. Spotting Alastair, he nodded. He crossed the road and started to walk quickly towards him.

'Cants,' the man said, nodding as he stopped inches in front of Alastair. Alastair nodded back, uncertain. 'Take my word for it, son. They're cants, the lot of 'em!' The man spoke quickly and decisively, and without once letting his eyes meet Alastair's. He seemed incapable of standing still for even a second and bobbed about unnervingly, shrugging his shoulders and twitching his elbows like some mad, three-piece-suited shadow boxer. You met some funny sorts in show business, Alastair had noticed.

'You mean telephone boxes?' Alastair said, smirking fearless with booze. The agent squinted, scanned the pavements and hedges as though he were expecting an assassin.

'What you say?' The agent swung back and became suddenly still. For the first time he faced Alastair directly, stared into him with the steely dead eyes of a pub nutter.

'Telephone boxes,' Alastair repeated. 'Did you mean telephone boxes are "cants"?'

'You bein' fanny?'

'No,' said Alastair, resisting the urge to add that he'd no intention of being "fanny". 'You're Denny Heyman, aren't you?' he said, remembering how Brian had pointed him out, said he was one of the top music agents in London and the organiser of the Skegness concerts. Denny nodded and rolled his shoulders. He seemed appreciative of the recognition.

'I meant people is cants, son. Lazy cants! Selfish cants! Useless cants! World's full of cants. This business 'specially. You got a light?'

Alastair held Trevor's lighter towards Denny's cigar. 'It's my mate's. I don't really smoke.'

Denny Heyman blew a cloud of smoke into the air and jerked his head across to the other side of the road. 'Them phone boxes can be cants as well, though,' he smiled. 'I was nearly incinerated in that fakker. You like rock 'n' roll, son?'

'Yes, very much.'

'Wanna cam to a party? Music, booze, plenny of nice birds.' Alastair felt a hand on his shoulder, a gentle squeeze.

'I've just left one, thanks. I'm off to get some kip for tomorrow.'

Denny looked thoughtful as he blew a thick cloud of smoke out towards the sea. 'Cheers for the light, son,' he said. And with a twitch and a wink Denny turned and marched away towards The Old Bell.

CHAPTER FOUR

Anyone visiting Skegness for its famously bracing fresh sea air would have found absolutely no evidence of it that Sunday morning. At least not in the caravan where Alastair woke, wondering if he hadn't kipped down in the camp sewerage pit by mistake, rather than in the cosy little end bedroom. The evil stink of half a dozen youths after a night on the booze had easily penetrated both bedroom door and his nostrils, and now gathered like a ball of rotting eggs and cat's fur at the back of his throat. Alastair had a clear vision of what the remains of last night's beer and chips might look like all over a candlewick bedspread, and he didn't fancy it one bit. He downed the glass of water he found at his bedside, and then, still wearing last night's clothes, dug out his wash bag, towel and paperback of *The Ipcress File* containing the envelope from his rucksack.

The bedroom door cracked dully against a snoring head. 'Stinking bunch o' bastards!' Alastair said as he scanned the blanketed heaps, burial mounds in floral and pastel shades, scattered about the floor and along the bench seats of the caravan. He swung open the door and, after adding his own noisy contribution to the sulphurous stew, stepped out into the bright morning sunshine.

* * *

'... *TWO letters from Mam last week!* (Alastair read, sitting on the toilet). *I'm not sure what's got into her, it's not like her at all. She says she's feeling a lot better and hopes to be back at work in a week or two. What do you think? I've been ever so worried about her. Her handwriting seems to be getting worse than ever — are you sure she's not drinking too much again?*'

A toilet flushed in a distant cubicle. To the sound of running water a man cleared his throat and began whistling a jaunty bring-on-the-day tune.

'... I'm sorry if I sounded rude in my last letter. Believe me, I didn't mean that YOU should mind your own business! I knew Mam had put you up to asking me to come home, because she asks me the same thing every time she writes! I expect she thinks I'll listen to you and take notice because you're so clever and sensible and handsome — that's what she calls you, you know, HANDSOME! She's always had an eye for younger men, so be very careful next time you go up or she might take you prisoner! But please tell her, Alastair, I can't come home, not just yet. And it's not that I don't care about her, you know that...'

In a distant cubicle, wind was loudly, shamelessly, broken. 'Charming!' Alastair said, not exactly to himself.

'... Isn't it funny our becoming pen pals after all this time? I'm glad. It's nice writing to you, and I look forward to reading your letters so much. It's silly, but I always feel childishly happy when I see your handwriting among the big pile of letters the postman brings every morning (our flat has its own pigeonhole in the downstairs hall — V posh!). You know, sometimes I think your letters are the only...'

This last sentence, left unfinished, had been struck out with thick black biro, but Alastair had easily been able to decipher it by studying the indentations on the reverse side of the writing paper — which of course Charlotte never used. The only *what*? he wondered.

'... Enjoy your trip to the seaside! Send my love to Jumbo and wish him lots and lots of luck. You must write and tell me all about it as soon as you get back!

Lots of love,

Charlotte x

P.S. Any more news about Trevor and Sarah? If your suspicions are correct, I think it's very sweet!'

* * *

Trevor stood at the cooker in open shirt and underpants, filling a teapot from a kettle that looked as if it had been salvaged from a house fire. 'Morning, Squire. How're you feeling?' he said, sounding a lot brighter than he looked.

'Better for some fresh air and a wash. That water's bloody freezing. Piss yourself in your sleep again, did you?'

Trevor looked down, horrified. Alastair laughed. 'Works every time!'

'Twat.'

'How about you?'

'My head's banging and my tongue tastes like a tramp's dog's arse.'

'Nice.' Alastair swung a carrier bag bursting with breakfast onto the draining board. 'This lot'll sort us out.'

'Good man! Cup o' char, love?'

'Smashing, dear, I could murder one.'

'Alastair, listen,' Trevor said, struggling to contain the excitement in his voice. 'You won't believe what's happened – you'll piss *your* pants when I tell you, I promise.'

'You didn't get your leg over that Samantha, did you?' Alastair looked interestedly between the piles of blankets that were beginning to yawn and stretch across the floor and seating.

'I wouldn't mind. She's bats, isn't she? No, Al, it's even more unbelievable than that.'

'How do, Alastair?' a familiar voice called from under its floral shroud. 'Did y'ave a good night?'

'We had a cracking day all round, Howie,' Alastair said, tossing sausages and bacon into a semi-cremated frying pan, apparently part of a matching set with the kettle. 'Did we really get pissed at Godfrey Payne and The Comforters' party, or did I just dream that?'

'Oh, it was real enough, buddy, if my head's anyfing to go by. And we'll be doing the same all over again tonight, only bigger. Tonight's gonna be wild.'

'Who's that, under there?' Alastair said, nodding towards the mysterious hairy-armed figure that lay wrapped in a delicately embroidered white tablecloth. Trevor grinned like the village idiot, a look much emphasised by his wild morning hair and his holding a pint of milk in one hand while rummaging in his underpants with the other. The heap rolled over and sat up. Alastair almost tipped the frying pan and its sizzling greasy contents all over the lino. 'Shitting hell! You're Eric Handley! What are you doing here?'

'Thanks for the welcome,' said Eric Handley, lead guitarist and co-songwriter with Godfrey Payne and The Comforters. 'Nice to meet you, too – Alastair, wasn't it?'

'Yes. Eric, you slept in our caravan!'

'I know. And I'm very glad I did, cos I hear you do a cracking breakfast.'

'Ey up, don't go givin' 'im too much!' Jumbo rose from beneath a pile of coats like some creature from the deep in purple paisley underpants. 'My stomach's rumbling like a bastard,' he said, massaging his milky-white belly. 'Christ, I'm not getting dressed just to go to the bog. Anyone mind if I have a piss in the sink?'

'Yes!!'

Learning that you'd spent the night in a comfy double bed while one of the most acclaimed musicians of his generation had slept, wrapped in a tablecloth, just feet away, in a shabby old caravan, seemed to Alastair just about the most unlikely thing (short of it being Godfrey Payne himself) that he could ever imagine. Yet incredibly, and although Eric was part of it, this was not the story Trevor and his new friends were all dying to tell him over breakfast.

Trevor chucked in two more tea bags and dragged a stool up to the table where Alastair sat, barely able to believe it, shoulder to shoulder with Eric Handley. Brian and Howie sat opposite. Jumbo propped himself against the sink, nursing a mug of tea while keeping one eye on the toast browning under the grill.

'God knows what time we left the pub,' Howie said, wiping tomato juice from his lips. 'Gone midnight. We got talking outside, us and Anthony Hawksmoor from The Berries, with Eric and Albie McPherson and decided to walk back along the prom, get a bit of fresh air and try and sober up a bit.'

'We took a crate of beer, mind,' Eric chipped in.

'So we're on the prom, pissed and talking bollocks; Eric's up front with Albie and Kenny, girls were in the middle, Amelia and a few others, that one who's got her eye on Eric.'

'Hah! I hope so!'

'Where *are* the girls?' Alastair asked.

'Listen!' Trevor said.

Howie continued. 'Brian, Trevor and me, we're at the back, sharing the last fag – '

'Where was Roger?' Alastair said. 'I hardly saw him all night.'

'In *our* caravan,' Jumbo smirked. 'Wi' some lass he picked up in the chippy. That's why we're all squashed up in here.'

'*Listen*!'

'So we're walking round the back of the fairground. It's pitch black and chuffing windy as hell – '

'Gerron wi' it, How!' Brian said. 'Be here all day.'

Trevor gulped a mouthful of tea and took up the story. 'All I heard was Albie turn and shout "Here we go lads, watch yourselves!" Next minute, this gang of Rockers jumps out of the hedge and stands blocking the path.'

'Not that lot in the Sunbeam?' Alastair asked. 'That business with Jay?'

Trevor shook his head. 'Didn't recognise them.'

'There was only three or four of them at first,' Eric Handley said, 'and I thought "No bother". Then a load more jumps out, must have been eight or nine of 'em.'

'Next thing,' Trevor went on, 'someone smashes a bottle and they rush at us – or we rush at them, I don't know – and suddenly it's all kicking off.'

'A fight?' said Alastair.

Eric laughed. 'Right old punch-up.'

'Punching and kicking – they were all over us,' Trevor said. 'It was just a blur of boots and white T-shirts. One little bastard got me right in the knackers – could hardly move.'

'One of their lot was on the ground getting a right old kicking, dunno who from, but I didn't half stick him one in the ribs.'

Howie nodded to Brian. 'He had two on him at once, big lads, until Jumbo grabs one, picks him up by his belt and collar and chucks him face first into the bloody hedge!'

'He asked for it,' Jumbo grinned.

'I think I belted a capple of others,' Eric said. 'Or it might have been the same one I belted twice. But we soon scared the fakkers off.'

'They just legged it.'

'Think they were as pissed as we were,' Jumbo said, spreading marmalade on his toast.

'But then Eric says,' said Howie, '"Where's Albie?" The last time I saw him he'd flung off his jacket and was poundin' this youth against the prom wall – geeyin' 'im a rate pastin' – but now he was nowhere to be seen. Next thing, this Rocker limps up the steps from the beach, nose pouring with blood, and scuttles off through the hedge after his mates.'

Trevor swallowed a mouthful of sausage. 'So I look over the sea wall and there he is, Albie, hopping about on the beach, he's holding his right hand and he's in agony, shouting "My fucking hand! I've fucked my fucking hand!"'

'Christ, it'd be funny if it wasn't such a fakking disaster,' Eric Handley said. 'Pissy little scuffle and now he's knackered.'

'Did they have razor blades?' asked Alastair. 'Did they slash him?'

'Albie says the lad pulled a screwdriver on him,' Howie said. 'So he jumps up on the sea wall to get out of his road. This lad follows him up, they swing a few punches, have a bit of a tussle and then they both go over the edge. It's a ten foot drop to the beach, and Albie, well he lands on his thumb – SNAP!'

'Said he heard it go like a dry twig,' Eric said.

Alastair winced. 'Ouch!'

'Up to the elbow in plaster, four to six weeks now, the dozy bastard.' Eric let out a long sigh.

Trevor, his face bursting with the excitement of a child on Christmas morning, now turned and looked at Jumbo, who seemed suddenly self-conscious in just his freckles and paisley drawers. Jumbo turned away and began frantically buttering more toast. 'What is it?' asked Alastair turning between the grinning faces squeezed around the table. 'Why are you all laughing? What's he done?'

'Thing is, Alastair,' Eric Handley said, 'we've got two more shows today...'

Brian frowned and smiled at the same time. Howie blew his fringe out of his eyes and shook his head.

'And guess who,' Trevor breathlessly continued, 'guess who Eric and Godfrey have asked to stand in for Albie?'

When Alastair turned he could see the plate of toast visibly shaking in Jumbo's hands. Alastair's eyes opened wide. He shook his head in stunned disbelief. 'No way!' he said, turning to face Eric Handley. 'Jumbo's playing drums with Godfrey Payne and The Comforters? *Today*?'

Eric nodded.

'Piss off!'

'Albie reckons he's one of the best drummers he's ever seen. So if he can play like he did yesterday, I reckon we might get away with it.'

'Bugger me, Jumbo!' Alastair said as the table erupted in a boisterous chorus of whoops and cheers. Jumbo turned to face the table, gripping the front of his underpants with both hands and suddenly looking very distraught.

'I'm ever so sorry lads,' he said, 'but I'm going to have to have a piss in this sink. I'm chuffing bursting.'

* * *

Just after four o'clock on Sunday afternoon, having already played another barnstorming set with The Chequered Saracens, Jumbo sat nervously twiddling his sticks while the crowd speculated upon the identity of the sweating stranger installed behind Albie McPherson's drum kit. Godfrey Payne looked over and gave an encouraging thumbs up before leaning forward to speak into the microphone on top of his Hammond organ. 'As you may have heard, folks, unfortunately Albie's had a little accident. He had a fight with a sandcastle last night and lost. And so, very kindly sitting in on drums for us today is a really good friend of ours – we're delighted to have him – so please give a big Skegness welcome to the fantastic Mr Kenny Moorhouse!'

CHAPTER FIVE

Norm Allinson was regarded as a champion bullshitter among the men at Langbrook. To hear him talk, the world held very little that Norm in his twenty-two years had not by now already seen, heard, read or tasted; been in, ridden on, or fornicated with until his balls were raw. No-one else at the shed could claim to have lost the father he never knew in the big push at Monte Cassino, while his audience looked on, smiling, knowing full well that a man roughly twenty years Norm's senior and with the same name and identical facial and physical features ran the busiest bookmaker's in town. Nor had any of them received a hand-written Thank You and crisp £5 note from Dirk Bogarde, for "*very kindly*" driving him to a petrol station when his car broke down late one night on the A1 just outside Grantham. So if anyone knew a ludicrous, cooked-up piece of wild fantasy when he heard one, it was Norm Allinson.

'Bollocks!' Norm said, in the enginemen's washroom, the Tuesday after the Skegness weekender. His eyes shone bright in his soot-black face as he wrung a filthy grey lather from his hands under the cold tap. 'So, you're telling me The Berries asked you into their private box, and then Godfrey Payne took you all to a party?'

'He didn't exactly *take* us,' Alastair said. 'But he did invite us, yes.'

'Piss off! If you'd have left it at that I might have half-believed you. But I'm not 'avvin it about your pal playing drums in Godfrey Payne and The Comforters. On stage? And never even met him? He-he! Giyovver, you daft sod!'

'Only on Sunday. Jumbo sat in for Albie, who'd – '

'Sat in for Albie! Hark at you! You been sniffing that paraffin again? It's a good un, Alastair, I'll give you that. But you'll 'ave to do a lot better than that to reel me in, matey. I can smell bullshit a mile off.'

Alastair realised how ludicrous and away-with-the-fairies his tale must have sounded; he could hardly believe it himself. He immediately wished he'd never mentioned it, any of it, and just told Norm he'd spent the weekend quietly with Mary.

'Godfrey Payne, eh? Your new best pal!'

'Well, it's all true Norm. And anyway, it's no dafter than you saying you picked up Dirk Bogarde one night.'

'Who's picked up Dirk Bogarde?' Stewart, a giant of a fitter, dashed into the cubicle and slammed the door behind him. 'Are thee a queer then, Norm?' Stewart called through the flaking toilet door. Stewart was in his early thirties, and while mostly all mouth, he was well aware many people found him intimidating and so took full advantage of it to torment the younger lads at every possible opportunity. 'We'll have to start calling yer Norma from now on then, wain't we? Eh? *Norma?*'

'No thanks, Stew,' Norm said, knowing it'd be a while till he heard the last of this one, till Stewart found some other tender spot to needle and poke away at.

Inside the cubicle, Stewart seemed to deflate a series of large balloons before tipping a hundredweight of gravel into a shallow pond. 'Aaah, there she is! Crikey, if am norra ston lighter when I gerrup,' Stewart said. 'So, yer like picking up chaps then do yer, Norma? Wait till the fitters hear about that, eh? Didn't have you down for a pansy, Norma. Alastair, now he looks like a poof; allus combin' his hair. Mind you, you wun't get very far wi' Dirk, either on yer. Proper ladies' man, he is. Dirk teks his pick o' t'crumpet, I bet.'

The toilet flushed. Stewart emerged from the ripe cubicle and barged his way to the sink. 'Come on, Norma, gerrout mi way!'

Terry the shed handyman's face appeared, smiling, at the washroom door. 'Hallo, lads, how's it goin', awight?'

'Ey up! Here comes David Bailey!' Stewart announced, noting the smart leather camera case that hung from Terry's neck. 'Norra peeping tom are yer, Terry?'

'No, Stew,' Terry said, quietly. 'Why?'

'Shame. You coulda joined up wi' Norma, here. *He's* a pervert, aren't you, *Norma?* Likes picking up chaps late at night – kisses their bum-holes. He wor just tellin' us all about it.'

Terry smiled and fidgeted with his camera. 'I'm jast takin' a few pictures,' he said. 'On me lanch break.' Smirking, Stewart turned away to dry his hands. Terry was the only man at Langbrook who ate "lanch". The others all called it "dinner".

'Arv been taking a lot more lately. Wanna capture this place for poss-terrat-ee. I mean, it probably ain't goin' be 'ere match longer, is it? Not like this.'

'Thank fuck!' Stewart said. Norm laughed out loud and, with a wink at Alastair, turned to follow Stewart across the workshop towards the canteen.

'I was just goin' down the turntable, Alastair,' Terry said. 'There's a Royal Scot cam on, diversion off the Midland. Like to get a few shots of her while she's here.'

'Royal Scot?' Alastair smiled. He was glad Terry had waited for Stewart to leave before he shared this information. 'Hardly any of them left now,' he said. 'Which one is it, Terry, do you know?'

'*The King's Royal Rifles* or sammink. Joe the signalman said it was due on at twenny-parst.'

'Smashing. I'll have a wander down with you. I'll just grab my snap.'

As Alastair followed Terry through the shed, between the rows of dark, simmering engines, he couldn't help thinking how far away all this was from the world he'd recently glimpsed at Skegness. True, he could hardly remember a time when he'd enjoyed himself more with his pals than during their weekend at the seaside. Yet now here, amid the hiss and woof of steam, the clanking of buffers, the rumble-crash of the coal hopper, that whole world of rock 'n' roll and show business and parties, it all seemed so silly, so utterly pointless.

CHAPTER SIX

'No, Trevor! Put it away! I've told you,' Jumbo said, getting up from his stool, 'I'm buying this round.'

'Tek it, Trev, quick, before he changes his mind,' Frank Halton said, holding out his empty glass. 'I'll have a pint of bitter, seeing as I missed all that free booze last weekend.'

It was Friday night. Jumbo had taken Amelia home to tea for the first time that afternoon, soon after which, much to his parents' disappointment, he'd whisked her away to the Fox & Hounds to meet his pals. It had been a while since they were all together like that, and following Jumbo's seaside triumph there was a definite air of celebration around their table in the corner of the taproom. Mary and Sarah immediately hit it off with Amelia and insisted on knowing all there was to know about her, where she met Jumbo, where she bought her clothes, what music she liked, as well as all the gossip from Skegness.

'Gosh, I used to love Adam Faith!' Amelia giggled as the jukebox whined into life.

'I don't need to ask who put this on,' Alastair said, shaking his fist at his sister.

News of Jumbo's brush with fame had spread quickly through Warinstowe. The *Evening Post* had even dedicated half a page to the "local lad who saved the day" when he stepped in to play drums for "chart-topping Rhythm & Blues combo" Godfrey Payne and The Comforters following an "unprovoked and violent attack by a gang of Rockers", which had left the headline act's regular drummer in hospital. Jumbo himself, meanwhile, still couldn't believe he hadn't gone to pieces and made a complete balls-up of the whole thing. Whenever he'd thought about it since it was all just one big blur of heat and lights and noise. All he knew was that he'd got his head down and played his bloody heart out, and somehow he'd managed to get away with it.

The tray shook between Jumbo's fingers as he set it down on the table. He was sick with excitement at the news he had to tell his friends. Swallowing the pickled egg he'd taken as reward for standing a hefty round, he cleared his throat and called for their attention.

'Erm, I've gorra bit of news I'd like to share with you all,' Jumbo said. The girls, excited, smiled enviously at Amelia and tried to get a clear look at her fingers which were clenched in her lap. 'Last weekend, as I think you all know, I...'

'How do? Everybody all right for a drink?' Mary grabbed Nigel Wells by the elbow and pulled him down onto the stool beside her. 'Sssh, Nigel! Jumbo's making an announcement.'

'How do, Nige?' Jumbo nodded. 'You just missed my round, I'm afraid. Erm, last weekend I was asked to play drums wi' Godfrey Payne and The Comforters...' Jumbo sank half his pint and waited for the cheers and squeals to settle. His face was the colour of tinned salmon.

'Well, Albie McPherson, The Comforters' drummer – '

'We know who Albie McPherson is, Jumbo!'

'Let him speak!'

'Turns out Albie's properly knackered his wrist up and won't be able to play for a month or two at least. Thing is, the lads are booked to play at the *NME Poll Concert* next Sunday, and, well, they've asked me to sit in for him again.'

'They haven't!' Mary said.

'At the *NME Poll Concert*?' Sarah screeched.

'With The Stones and The Kinks?'

'And The Beatles?'

Jumbo nodded. 'That's it.'

'And Dusty Springfield,' Amelia smiled. 'And Georgie Fame, and The Animals.'

'In't that in London?' asked Frank Halton.

'Yeah.'

'That's fantastic, Jumbo! Isn't it?' Mary said, turning to Alastair and taking his hand. Alastair nodded. He'd heard the news already, when Jumbo telephoned Trevor the night before. But it seemed no less astonishing hearing it again now.

'It's chuffing amazing. Brilliant! Especially considering how he played last weekend. Absolutely shocking, wasn't he Trev?'

'Bloody awful, dear,' Trevor said, camping it up. 'I was ashamed to say I even knew him afterwards.'

'Right, one of you two boggers can buy me a drink while I go for a slash,' Jumbo said. 'Pint of Best.'

Sarah had been listening excitedly at how nice Godfrey Payne and The Comforters and The Berries had been to them all in Skegness, and how Jumbo would have to go to London to rehearse every day until the concert on Sunday, when Nigel, taking advantage of Trevor going to the bar, tapped her on the shoulder.

'Hello, Sarah,' he said, smiling.

'Hello, Nigel,' Sarah said, looking him up and down. 'You've done your hair different.'

'Do you like it?'

'Yes, it looks very nice. And I like your new jacket. Trevor's got one just like it.'

Alastair held a pint out to Nigel.

'Cheers, Alastair. I was just saying to Sarah, Jumbo might be on the telly next week. It was on last year, I watched it.'

'I hadn't thought of that,' Jumbo said. 'Bloody Nora!'

'Jumbo's going to be on the telly!'

'You'll be on *Ready Steady Go!* next!'

'Giyovver! It's only for this one show,' Jumbo said, running a hand across his head. 'We're only doing three tunes.'

'I wish I were coming!'

'Well, here's to Jumbo!' said Frank Halton. 'Good for you, matey, I'm dead chuffed for you. Cheers!'

Frank had planned to share some good news of his own that evening. He'd passed his medical for Beverton Hall, the new Super Pit where Mary's father was to be Deputy, when it opened. It was a good job and he'd soon be earning a fortune compared to what he made on the bread lorries. Yet now, in the wake of Jumbo's incredible announcement, it hardly seemed worthwhile mentioning. Frank kept his news to himself and bought everyone another drink.

'You'll see if you can come, won't you?' Amelia said to Sarah in the car park. 'It'll be such fun, and the boys will look after you.'

'I promise I'll ask mi mam and dad,' Sarah said, knowing very well she wouldn't. What was the point? If she hadn't been allowed to go to Skegness for one night, there was no way in a million years they'd let her go gallivanting off for the weekend to London.

'I've already promised to help my mum,' Mary said.

'Do you want a lift home?' Trevor asked Alastair and Mary after they'd waved Jumbo and Amelia, in matching green parkas, off on his scooter.

'Don't they make a lovely couple?' Mary said.

'Yes,' said Sarah. 'She's so nice.'

Alastair looked at Mary. She was wearing his favourite navy blue mini-dress. 'I think we might take a steady walk back, thanks, Trev.'

Mary smiled. 'It's a lovely night.'

Trevor hesitated before turning to Sarah and, as casually as he was able, said, 'Would you like a lift, Sarah? I'm going past on my way home, so...'

'Well, if it's no trouble?' Sarah said, trying not to look at her brother.

'It's no trouble,' Trevor said. 'No trouble at all.'

* * *

Just as things were becoming interesting, Mary all of a sudden sat up and pushed Alastair's hand away from under her blouse. Wrapping her arms tightly around her legs, she planted her chin on her knees, a convenient plinth for her beauty, and gazed sullenly into the dark flowing river.

'Isn't it amazing, what's happened to Jumbo?'

'Yes,' Alastair said, wondering if Mary honestly thought inflating a chap's hopes and trousers like that then leaving him high and dry was in any way acceptable behaviour. 'Yes, it is. I'm over the moon for him, I really am. You should have seen him last week, he was incredible.'

'You know mum didn't believe me when I told her. She thought you and Trevor had made the whole thing up.'

'Well, it does sound like something out of a fairy tale, doesn't it? Though I can't see Jumbo making much of a Cinderella.'

Alastair put his arm around Mary's shoulder and pulled her close. You knew Mary was beautiful just from the way she smelled.

'You must be excited,' she said after a little while. 'About going to London.'

'Of course! Jumbo's playing drums for Godfrey Payne and The Comforters at the *NME Poll Concert*, with The Stones and The Beatles and The Kinks! How much more exciting than that does it get, Mary?'

Mary seemed to think carefully over her next words, so much so that Alastair could almost hear her. 'I expect you'll have a good time with Trevor – and Jumbo's pals from Lincoln.'

'Yes. They're a good bunch of lads.'

'And Amelia; she seems nice.'

'She is. Jumbo's done well for himself there.'

Mary tilted her head and rested her cheek against her knee, studying Alastair with a deep and thoughtful expression. After a moment, and in a suddenly bright voice she said, 'Can I come?'

'To London?' Alastair said, surprised. 'Why, yes, if you'd like to. Sarah won't be going though. And I didn't think you'd want to either, Mary.'

Mary enjoyed listening to pop music as much as any girl her age, but unlike Sarah, Mary was never very much one for concerts. The year before, Alastair had taken her to see The Rolling Stones and The Ronettes at the Tuxfield Granada, but all that noise and pushing, silly folks treading all over your feet all night long, it only got her back up and ruined her best shoes. Alastair didn't believe Mary wanted to go to London any more than she'd wanted to go to Skegness.

'But yes, Mary, come. Come!'

Mary held his gaze for a moment. 'I don't want to,' she said sulkily, and turned away.

'Then why did you...'

'I just wanted to see what you'd say.'

'What...? Don't play games, Mary, I'm not in the mood.'

Mary remained looking away, her eyes following the path of

the river down towards the old mill. 'I bet there'll be a lot of girls there,' she said.

'Hundreds of them, I expect – *thousands* – all screaming their silly little heads off. Of course there'll be girls there, Mary, it's a pop concert!'

'Do you think they're different?' Mary said after another thoughtful pause. 'London girls?'

Alastair, reminded of Samantha and the girl with the never-ending olive-coloured legs, was confident he had the prizewinning answer to Mary's question, but decided it was probably best to keep it to himself just for the moment.

'What happens if you meet one you like?' Mary said.

'I won't.'

'How do you know?'

'Because I don't want to, Mary. I've got you.'

Mary turned and gave him a little smile. 'Only you hear all these stories, don't you, about London?'

'What stories?'

'About nightclubs and tarts. Strippers. Good-time girls.'

'You sound like mi mam! Look, Mary, we're going to London to see Jumbo play in this concert. It'll be the biggest day of his life, and I – and Trevor – just want to be there to share it with him. Yet according to you, the whole thing's been organised just so I can run off with a bloody stripper! This is silly, Mary. Stupid. Now bloody well cut it out, or I'm off.'

'There's no need to shout, Alastair. It's...'

'What? *Common*? And you can stick all that nonsense you know where, now, before you start.'

'I wasn't going to say – '

'Really? Look, Mary, just because you enjoy making yourself miserable, it doesn't mean you have to go and ruin everything for me as well. I'm going to London to watch Jumbo, whether you like it or not.'

Alastair got up and walked down to the water's edge. Why did she always have to be so bloody infuriating? It was no wonder some of the men at work joked about one day strangling their wives. If this was the sort of thing they'd had to put up with for twenty, thirty, years, you could hardly blame them if they went through with it.

As he gazed at the moon's shimmering reflection in the water, Alastair thought how easy it would be to strangle Mary, right there on the riverbank. Belt probably, rather than bare hands. It'd be neater and seemed somehow less personal. There'd be nobody to hear her screams at this hour. A day or two before they found her, down by the mill, washed up against the sluice gate, pale and bloated, almost every trace of her teasing beauty carried away in the freezing current. A terrible shudder chased down Alastair's spine so that he had to swing round quickly and make sure Mary was still there, alive and gorgeous and sulking.

'I'm sorry,' she said, quietly. 'I'm...'

Alastair walked over and sat down beside her. He waited until she turned and looked at him, but said nothing.

'I'm sorry,' Mary said again, her lips pressing softly against his. Out of the corner of his eye he saw her legs stretch out before her, followed them all the way up to the hem of her mini-dress, where he now, cautiously, settled his hand. When Alastair pulled away and looked into her eyes, he found them wide and wet with meaning. Things she'd never be able to put into words.

'I wonder who's in the mill at this time of night?' Mary said, softly.

'It'll just be the ghost of the apprentice miller.'

'No it's not. There's no such thing.'

'You must have heard about the apprentice miller? He was killed not long before the war and has haunted the place ever since.'

'Don't be so daft, Alastair.'

Alastair made a ghostly wail.

'Stop it!' Mary made for his lips, but he drew back. He could hear it in her voice that she was frightened. He lowered his own to almost a whisper and began to speak very slowly.

'This apprentice miller, he'd been saving every penny of his wages to get married to the girl he'd loved for as long as he could remember. But it was hard, the miller paid him peanuts, and even on his wedding day he could only afford to take the afternoon off.

Of course, the night before, he goes into town with his pals and has a skin-full of ale. Five o'clock next morning, he's back at the mill, where he means to work till two minutes before he's due up at the church.'

Mary's eyes followed Alastair's to where the church stood on its little hill, in silhouette against the falling night. 'Alastair, I don't like it. Please stop.'

Alastair narrowed his eyes, rubbed his fingers over his chin. 'Well, he's so drunk, just before seven he stumbles over a bucket and falls into the workings of the waterwheel.'

'No, Alastair, stop it, that's horrible! Don't!'

But Alastair did.

'Crushed to death, he was, a horrible, splattered mess.'

'No, Alastair, stop it now, please!'

'And it wasn't as if he'd been killed instantly.'

'*Please!*'

'A slow, agonising, painful death it was. You see, he somehow fell in feet first. Took a good ten minutes for him to be ground through all those cogs and gears. His brain remained alive and felt everything right up until his head went through and – '

'No! Stop it, Alastair, now!' Mary screamed. 'Please stop it, you're frightening me.'

Alastair stopped. He'd allowed himself to get carried away and had gone too far. But for a brief moment he'd found it a pleasantly satisfying feeling to be able, for once, to torment Mary almost as much as she, in other ways, so often tormented him. He'd almost gone on to add how the miller had had a terrible job of cleaning the remains of his apprentice out of his machinery, how in the end he'd simply let the stray dogs in to gobble up what little there was left of him among the workings, but he could see from the tears that had begun to roll, one after the other, down Mary's cheeks that he'd done quite enough damage already.

When he held her close and buried his nose in her fragrant curls, Alastair could feel her trembling like a frightened animal. He hated himself for his cold cruelty. He hadn't meant to hurt her, not really, not like this. It was only because he loved her so much, he thought, as he tasted the salt on her lips.

Alastair pulled back and wiped a tear from her cheek, kissed the end of her nose once, twice. 'I'm sorry,' he said. Mary made a little smile but did not answer. After a kiss that seemed to last an age, she lay back on his jacket, giggling a little as she wriggled out of her tights on the riverbank.

CHAPTER SEVEN

'I didn't really expect you last night, Alastair, it being Sunday.'

'Sorry, Monica, I was late getting back from – '

'You needn't apologise, duck. Young lad like you's got far better things to do wi' his time than run about after an old fart like me. Still, I won't pretend it's not nice to see you now though, cos it is.'

Monica took Alastair's hands, giving them a gentle squeeze before settling back in her armchair. Her smile, he noticed, was both brighter and wider than usual. She'd put her teeth in.

'You're looking very smart, Mrs Bloomsberry,' he said, wondering what the occasion might be. 'Are you off out?'

'These, you mean?' Monica said, curling back her upper lip. 'Bloody nuisance they are, I can't gerron with 'em. But I knew you were coming, and I wanted to look mi best. And what's wi' all this "Mrs Bloomsberry"? You've not gone for a bobby, have yer?'

Alastair made a pot of tea and set it down beside the scones and jam he'd brought, on the coffee table.

'So you're ready for going back then?' Alastair said when the conversation came round to her work at the Market Tavern.

Monica blew out her cheeks and rolled her eyes. 'I'll go round the twist if I have to stay cooped up in 'ere much bloody longer. Yes, duck, I'm ready for going back and sorting the boggers out. Doctor Appleby says another month, but – eh, I never thought I'd miss that place as much as I have.'

Alastair smiled. He'd meant it when he said how well she looked. In the six months she'd been ill, Monica had seemed to be declining – in appearance at least – almost by the week (not that he'd told Charlotte). Yet now, suddenly, she seemed almost her old self again, and Alastair could quite easily see her back behind the bar, rattling away with the regulars, in no time at all.

'We could go for a little walk, if you feel up to it. Bit of fresh air might do you good. Perhaps down to Edmund's one afternoon, he's always asking about you.'

'I don't want to go mad and overdo it, Alastair. Maybe next week, eh, if you've time? Your father's allus asking me to have a turn round the allotment with him, when he comes up. He must get through some shoes, all the walking he does.'

Jock hadn't said very much, but Alastair knew he still regularly dropped in on Monica, taking her up a few groceries when she'd asked for them, a pint of milk and a loaf when she hadn't. Alastair wondered what they found to talk about, Jock hardly being the chatty type. But then, with Monica, you didn't have to be.

Monica sat forward suddenly in her chair. 'Your father tells me one of your pals is doing a concert in London now?' When she smiled, with her teeth in, the soft light of the table lamp took ten years off her.

'Yes. It's the *NME Poll Concert* – at the Empire Pool, Wembley.'

Alastair stood to remove his pullover, feeling Monica's eyes studying him quietly as he folded it neatly over the back of the chair. He smiled, remembering what Charlotte had said about her mother keeping him prisoner. You could see she'd have been a fruity sort in her time.

'Well, I never!' Monica said, shaking her head after hearing about the unlikely whirlwind of events in which Jumbo had become swept up since the weekend at Skegness. 'Good owd Jumbo! He allus were a nice lad. Is he still at the pit?'

'Yes. He's had to take a week's holiday to rehearse down in London.'

'Shame you can't join up with them as well, duck, this Godfrey what's-his-name. Mind you, they all seem to be Liverpudlians, far as I can see, The Beatles and – who did you say, *The Animals*?'

'The Animals are from Newcastle,' Alastair said. 'And The Rolling Stones and The Kinks are London groups. Gerry and The Pacemakers are Liverpool though.'

'Well, I've learnt summat then, haven't I? *The Kinks*! They do have some daft names, don't they?'

Monica left the room. When she returned a few minutes later she had a wide grin on her face and an unopened packet of Ginger biscuits in her hand.

'Got you some of your favourites,' she said. 'Well, your father fetched 'em for me. Yes, I'm glad you've come, duck, tonight, or I would've had to sit here and eat the whole packet miself.'

With a surprisingly steady hand Monica poured them fresh cups of tea and then sat back in her chair, an unusually serious look falling over her face. Alastair knew what was coming. In fact, he was surprised it had taken her so long to get around to it.

'Duck, do you remember what I asked you, a few weeks ago? I hadn't liked to bother you again about it. I mean, well, I know it's a lot to ask, but...'

Monica leaned forward and held out two Gingers. Alastair took them, balancing one on his knee while he dipped the other in his tea.

'Only, I thought that, seeing as you're going at the weekend, to London...'

Alastair nodded, sucked his biscuit dry and bit it in two. He thought Monica seemed nervous, almost as if she were frightened to ask him, though why she should be he couldn't think.

'What do you think, duck?' she said quietly. 'Do you think you'd have time, perhaps, to look in on her? Mek sure she's all right?'

'Er, yes, if I can, Monica, I'll – '

'I know I've hardly been the ideal mother. It'd serve me right if she never bothered a bugger about me no more, but I've been worrying about her ever such a lot just lately, all on her own down there.'

As Monica sipped her tea she glanced across at the handful of small silver-framed photographs arranged at one end of the sideboard. Her eyes slowly flooded with tears. 'I worry more about that girl now she's gone than I ever did when I should've done, when she was here, when she were a kiddie. We don't realise, Alastair, none of us, until it's too late.'

In the half-light, Alastair could just make out his younger self in one of the photos, taken some years ago now. He found his eyes wandering to the little corridor that led through to Monica and Charlotte's bedrooms.

'I'll try, Monica, if there's time,' he said, sounding more positive, he realised, than he should, knowing their already very tight timetable. 'I'd really like to see her myself. I'll do my best, Monica. I promise.'

Monica nodded and took a long sip of her tea. She'd seen enough life to know the value of men's promises, young and old. But she knew Alastair would not lie to her, that he would do his best for her. 'You're a good lad,' she said.

After what seemed like a long silence, one in which Alastair felt it might be inappropriate to reach for the evening paper, Monica suddenly sat up, mopped away the tears from her cheeks and let out a long self-deprecating sigh. 'Dear me, I don't know, duck. Look at me! Told you I were nowt but a silly old fart.'

Alastair smiled and held out the packet of Ginger biscuits. Monica took one, sat back and bit it noisily in two, shooing away the crumbs that tumbled down her more than ample bosom. But then, almost immediately, she sprang up again, setting her cup down heavily on the coffee table. 'Ooh, you bloody buggers!'

'What is it?'

'You'll have to excuse me, duck.' Monica held a hand up to her mouth, and with a sharp, hollow click spat her dentures into a clean white handkerchief. 'It's all right looking pretty, Alastair,' she said, her familiar gap-toothed smile restored, 'but it's no good if it only makes you bloody miserable. Me, I'd rather enjoy a nice biscuit.'

CHAPTER EIGHT

It was a glorious spring afternoon, so they'd all gone out, the four of them, for a ride to Clumber Park in the Mini. But after twenty minutes Alastair had found the tension and stilted conversation all too much, despite Trevor's attempts to distract them with his latest driving style, which now seemed to be inspired as much by James Dean as Paddy Hopkirk.

'Will you two just hold hands, for God's sake!' Alastair called over his shoulder when they'd climbed out and were strolling gently along the edge of the lake.

'Eh?' said Trevor, turning and looking at Sarah as if until then he'd been completely unaware of her presence beside him. Trevor really was the most appalling actor.

'Or kiss, or cuddle, or whatever it is you need to do so that we can all get away from this feeling like we're all about to be shot at dawn – Jeez!' Alastair stopped and turned around. 'Sarah, will you just kiss him, *please*?'

Mary laughed out loud and pressed her hands in theatrical surprise over her mouth. With encouraging eyes Sarah fiddled with the buttons on her cardigan, trying not to giggle while she waited for Trevor to stop looking gormlessly between her and Alastair and do as he was told. Alastair ran across the immaculate lawn and leapt up on to a low stone wall, all that remained of the great house after it burned down for the umpteenth time.

'Go on, kiss! Kiss or I'll jump to my death, and you'll only have yourselves to blame!'

Sarah slid her arms around Trevor, got up on tiptoes and gave him a brief but noisy peck on the lips. 'There!'

She took Trevor's hand, turned him towards Alastair and Mary and together they gave a little bow. Mary clapped, threw her arms around Alastair and gave him a little kiss of his own.

Alastair shook his head. 'About bloody time,' he said, after his sister had given Trevor's left buttock a painful squeeze and taken off, squealing across the lawn, Trevor chasing after her.

* * *

'Not real cannons?' Mary said, doubtfully.

'Yes, *scaled down.*'

Having paused a few times along the way to kiss (her idea), or skim stones (his), Alastair and Mary had fallen some way behind Trevor and Sarah, whose interlocked hands now swung with a light and joyful pride between them. Alastair showed Mary the remains of the gun emplacements from which the Duke of Newcastle (he could never remember which one) and his chums had once fired upon a specially constructed half-scale galleon anchored in the middle of the lake.

'But what if they'd sunk it? The boat?'

'*Galleon.* That was the idea, Mary. It's at the bottom of the lake.'

'Boys! Why do you always have to be so destructive?'

Mary slipped her arm through Alastair's. 'It was nice of you to do that,' she said.

'Do what?'

'What you did, back there. Let them know you don't mind them going out. I think they were worried you might not approve.'

'Water rat!'

The creature scuttled across the path a few feet in front of them, and with a gentle splash sent ripples twinkling across the skin of the lake.

'He's gone,' Alastair said, experiencing for once the sensation of Mary speeding *him* along. He slipped an arm around her waist, gave her a little squeeze. She felt warm through her clothes and his mind fizzed with filthy notions.

'I'm pleased you don't mind,' Mary said.

'Why should I? Trevor's all right. And it's hardly surprising really, when you think about it. She's always been daft about him. Just as long as they don't expect me to be their go-between, that's all.'

'I think they make a lovely couple,' Mary said. Alastair looked ahead, at his sister hand in hand with his best friend. He nodded.

'You know he got himself properly worked up a few months back. Thought Sarah was carrying on with Nigel Wells. He was driving himself crazy. And he couldn't tell me, because he didn't want me to know about him and Sarah.'

'What did you do?'

'I just let him wind himself up for a bit. Told him she'd been coming in late, all flushed and giddy. Which is true, she had, but only, it turned out, after she'd been out with him.'

'That's so cruel! How could you?'

'To be honest, I wasn't really sure myself. I still don't trust him – Nigel. You know how he always pesters her to go on that bike. I'm sure he dropped her off again, at the bottom of our street, one teatime. But she says not. I'd have brained him if he had.'

'Well, poor Nigel's out of luck,' Mary said. 'He'll see now that Sarah's with Trevor and is no longer available.'

Alastair stopped. 'And what about you, Mary Windale?' he said, slipping his hands into her coat and cupping her right breast. 'Are you available?'

He kissed her before she could answer.

'Perhaps,' Mary said, their lips barely drawing apart. 'Depends who's asking, doesn't it?'

'I wish we were here on our own, Mary.'

'Later,' Mary said. 'Later.'

CHAPTER NINE

Trevor, as usual, was almost last to emerge from the bank. Not that Alastair minded very much. It was a pleasant afternoon, and he perfectly understood that a disposition towards fannying about, checking and double-checking that ledgers and cash boxes were properly put away, doors and safes securely bolted for the night, was precisely the sort of quality they looked for in a future bank manager.

Also, he'd started to look forward, while waiting for his pal, to seeing Jean Britchardsley come skipping down the steps, to returning her flirtatious greetings before quietly savouring her glorious wiggle as she carried it homewards along Greenwood Street.

'Hello, Alastair!'

'Hello, Jean, duck,' Alastair said, paying close attention as Jean crossed the road and tinkled into the chemist. A well-remembered sighting of Jean had got him off to sleep on many a restless night before now, and he could always use another.

'She'd eat you alive, old chap,' Trevor said, making Alastair jump as he clapped him firmly on both shoulders.

'That what she did to you?'

'There wasn't much of me left when she'd finished,' Trevor laughed, pulling off his tie and slipping it into his suit pocket.

They turned into the Coal Board estate, a neat grid of terrace houses where, for the time being at least, a well-scrubbed doorstep and set of good net curtains still counted just as much as the handful of second-hand cars that gleamed from the roadside.

'What do you reckon Jean went into the chemist for?' Alastair pondered, picturing Jean buying luxurious bubble bath in which she'd soak herself intimately and at length when she got home. The reality was more likely tampons and her dad's corn plasters, but thoughts like that were no good to anybody.

'They're forever in there, far as I can make out, *women*. Chemist or the Doctor's. Always something wrong with them.'

'There didn't seem much wrong with Jean from where I was standing.'

Mrs Parkes was looking into a small rectangular mirror and patting her hair when her son and Alastair burst in, flooding her kitchen with their boisterous laughter.

'Something's tickled you pair, by the sounds of it,' Mrs Parkes said, restoring the mirror to its proper place on the windowsill and turning her friendly, mildly ironic smile on them.

'I wish it had, Mrs Parkes,' Alastair said, cheeky as he knew was expected. 'I could do with a tickle.'

Mrs Parkes shook her head. 'You are a rum un!' she said. 'Isn't he Trevor?'

Alastair had always found Mrs Parkes to be full of fun. She was pretty, too, in a sharp and shapeless sort of way, like a model you'd find in a knitting pattern, and with a youthful sparkiness you'd expect in a pal's older sister rather than his mother. Trevor pretended not to hear and asked for tea and biscuits to be brought up to his bedroom.

'I wish I were coming with you myself,' Mrs Parkes said, overhearing their arrangements for the weekend as she set a tray down on Trevor's bed. 'Do you know I've never been to a pop concert, Alastair? Or to London, even. Do you think I'd look very old and out of place if I came with you?'

'*You*, Mrs Parkes? Not at all!' Alastair said, at his most charming.

'Trevor does. Don't you, Trevor?'

'Mam, you're an ancient relic. You'd look bloody ridiculous.'

'Well, what a thing to say to your own mother,' Mrs Parkes tut-tutted. 'And how's Mary, Alastair? You've been courting her some time now, haven't you?'

'Yes. She's very well, thank you, Mrs Parkes.'

'I think she's ever such a pretty girl. Don't you, Trevor?'

'Mam!' Trevor scrunched his brow and slammed the lid of the record player.

'All right, I know when I'm not wanted.'

But Mrs Parkes got only as far as the door before she turned

131

around again. 'What do you think of him?' she said, fixing Alastair with a quizzical expression, a finger held to her lips. 'Bob Dylan, isn't it? There's one of his I like, but I can't say I'm keen on his singing very much, are you?'

'Thank you, Mother, you can go now!' Trevor shooed his mother out onto the landing. 'If *Juke Box Jury*'s short of a panellist this week, I'm sure you'll be the first person they call. Goodbye!'

When they came downstairs Mr Parkes was just finishing his tea. He seemed as excited about the boys' trip as his wife and immediately offered (as they'd hoped he might) to drive them to the station on Saturday morning, rather than leave Trevor's Mini in the car park overnight.

'Actually, Mr Parkes,' Alastair said, 'we're going from Nottingham Victoria.'

'Nottingham Vic? What on earth for?' Mr Parkes's face twisted in grotesque incomprehension. 'It'll take you a month of Sundays from there! I thought you'd know that, Alastair, you being a railwayman. No, no! You're better off going from Retford. Lot quicker than that old Midland line.'

'Great Central,' Alastair politely corrected.

'Great Central, is it? Well, whatever it is, it's on its last legs. You'll be lucky if Nottingham Vic's still there on Saturday, way they're pulling lines up round here.'

Mr Parkes hitched up his trousers and perched himself on the arm of the sofa, the height of which he seemed to misjudge so that he ended up pitched forward at an uncomfortably steep angle, his hands gripping tight on to the bony balls of his knees. But Mr Parkes was delighted with this unexpected bit of male conversation, and he was keen to make the most of it, no matter how foolish he might look.

'Dr Beeching weren't shy of swinging his axe round here,' Mr Parkes went on. 'Chesterfield Central's gone, you know. And Tuxfield. I can remember when Shireworth had *three* stations. Though I can't say I'm surprised. Half the trains running about with no bugger in them. Yes, lads,' Mr Parkes nodded decisively, 'you're better off going from Retford.'

Though he'd talk all night about trains, travel and transport, Mr

Parkes didn't really mind which station his son and his friend went from, any more than he would have minded if every railway station in the country were to be closed and the rails torn up for scrap, along with all the rusting old engines, wagons and footbridges with them. As he saw it, public transport was something people like himself had worked hard to leave behind, along with gaslights, tin baths in front of the fire, and rickets.

'Thing is, Dad,' said Trevor, an earnest little frown ruffling his brow, 'Victoria's due to close next year. So we wanted to go from there, while we still can, you see?'

'I'm hoping to take a few pictures, before the bulldozers move in and turn it into a gigantic car park,' Alastair added sombrely. 'Amazing light in that cutting.'

Mr Parkes studied the two of them with an amused expression, winking at his wife as with some relief he sat up and took the mug of tea she held towards him.

'You are a funny pair, you two,' Mr Parkes said, sucking his moustache after a big gulp. 'I thought you young uns these days were all for the latest thing – all things modern? For getting shut of the old and bringing in the new. What did Wilson call it – "*The White Flame of Technology*", was it?'

Alastair smiled, resisting the temptation to correct Mr Parkes a second time.

'Taking pictures of dilapidated old railway stations,' Mr Parkes shook his head. 'Shows what I know. Here were me thinking the pair of you were off to London for a weekend of rockin' & rollin', and having a good owd knees-up wi' some of them pretty Cockney lasses!'

PART THREE

LONDON'S A BIG PLACE

CHAPTER ONE

Another reason for travelling down from Nottingham Victoria was that Alastair and Trevor liked the idea of arriving in London for the first time at the same station as The Beatles had done in *A Hard Day's Night*. It seemed perfectly fitting, considering the purpose of their trip, and even before the train pulled away the compartment they had all to themselves echoed with smartarsed quips about clean little old men and broken hearts, delivered in those familiar, chirpy Scouse accents.

When they stepped out on to the busy platform at Marylebone, childishly excited and a little bleary-eyed after dozing for the last hour of the journey, there was no sign of The Fab Four, nor of the rabid packs of hormonal schoolgirls who'd screamed them to their waiting getaway car a year before. But there was, at the end of the telephone Trevor rang from the buffet, a snotty old actress straight out of the drawing room of an Ealing comedy.

'They've all gorn out,' the dusty voice snapped then abruptly hung up. It was the number of the hotel where Jumbo said he would be staying with Godfrey Payne and The Comforters.

'And a good day to you too, madam!' Trevor said, before turning to Alastair to relay the message. '"*They've all gorn out!*"' he mimicked. 'Stuck-up old cow.'

Trevor dialled a second number, this time for the guest house where the other three Chequered Saracens were staying in a single room, and where, successful charming – or evasion – of landlady permitting, Trevor and Alastair would also be spending the night, saving them each a couple of quid.

'I can't believe you made it!' said a very excited Howie. 'I don't think we'll have any bother with the sleeping arrangements, the old dear's lovely.'

The line crackled and popped. Trevor heard Howie's muffled voice as he called over his shoulder that they were here.

'Where are you, Marylebone?' asked Howie, returning. 'We're in Bayswater. Not very far at all. Come on over.'

'Of course, London's a big place...' Alastair boomed, pitch perfect Tom Courtenay as they strode out into a wide street lined with cars and mopeds. Smart red-brick buildings rose up on all sides. Ahead, a busy road sparkled with cars, lorries and buses. Black taxis, like giant ants, made a rattling parade, the bright sunshine bouncing off their roofs.

Trevor nodded gravely, clasped his hands behind his back. 'A very big place, Mr Shadrack...' he said, hardly believing they were really there, reciting the words they'd repeated a thousand times back home in Warinstowe. 'A man can lose himself in London.'

'*Lose* himself!'

'Loooozzz heemself!'

'A man can loo-hoo-*hoozz-ah* heemself in Lar-har-har-harndon!'

'Oi! Shadders!'

* * *

Howie lowered his mouth to his plate and shovelled in a huge forkful of spaghetti Bolognese.

'I thought *Absolute Beginners* was fantastic,' he said, licking his lips. 'Made me want to run away and see if London really was like that.'

'This place is,' Alastair said, swivelling on his bar stool, grinning as he soaked up the bustle and buzz of the little Italian café bar. 'It's just like it.'

To Alastair, the steamy clatter of the place oozed cool and sophistication. As if every yakking mouth, each wildly flapping hand, might be that of a brilliant poet or photographer; a jazz trumpeter, some mad lunatic artist and his alluringly messed-up muse.

'So why didn't you?' Brian said while seeing how fast he could spin through 360 degrees.

'What?'

'Run away to London!'

Howie laughed. 'I bought a Vox amp and took Karen Barnett to Filey instead.'

'*Karen Barnett?*' screeched Roger, The Chequered Saracens' affable bassist.

'What? She were all rate then – lovely big tits.'

'Stop that swivelling, lads,' ordered a waiter wearing what looked like a doctor's white coat with epaulettes, as he landed Trevor a heavy clap across the shoulder before diving through a badly scuffed swing door.

'Weren't *me!*' Trevor shouted after him. Brian peered round Alastair's shoulder and winked, before staring down into his dinky cup and thrusting out his tongue. 'This coffee's fucking rancid.'

'You said you wanted an espresso,' said Howie, who knew about these things.

'I didn't know it'd be like tar,' answered Brian, who didn't. 'Anybody fancy a pint?'

'I could murder one,' said Barry, the barman from the Duke of Newcastle Hotel, mopping up the last of his Bolognese. 'It's not often I get a weekend off and can have a jar or two.'

Alastair and Trevor had been pleasantly surprised to find Barry at the guest house, along with the three Chequered Saracens, not having realised that since that afternoon in February, when Jumbo had invited the barman to share his pork pie, quite a friendship had built up between the two big lads, with Jumbo occasionally dropping in to "The Duke" for a drink and a nibble on his way home from Lincoln.

'Who's buying?' asked Howie.

The light had barely begun to fail above the streets of Soho, but already the pub into which they now squeezed was carrying on as if it were ten minutes to last orders. Red-faced and rowdy punters, goaded on by a piano that had not seen a tuner in living memory, joined voices in a Cockney sing-a-long that managed to be at once both excruciating and uplifting. There were easily three times as many drinkers standing practically toe-to-toe between the tables as there were sitting at them. Men and women, young and old, all lit up and lively with booze and big talk. The heavily mirrored bar was also brightly lit – purposely, Alastair presumed – so as to guide customers through the thick smog of tobacco smoke that hung swirling in complicated clouds in the void between the heads of the crowd and the yellow-brown nicotine-tanned ceiling.

'So what're the chances of us actually meeting up with Jumbo tonight then, d'you reckon? Slim to bugger all?'

'He'll turn up, Brian,' Alastair said. 'Jumbo won't let us down.'

Trevor nodded. 'They're rehearsing till ten.'

Brian scoffed. '*Ten*?'

'If it's late,' Roger said, 'Jumbo reckons we might be able to go back to their hotel.'

'Bar stays open all night,' Howie added, impressed.

'Hmm. Bet we don't see him tonight, you watch.' Brian knocked back about half a pint, paused for a moment as if it were reluctant to stay down. 'We'll be lucky if any of us sees him ever again, except on the telly.'

Brian had fought hard during the past few weeks against the nagging feelings of jealousy and betrayal he'd occasionally suffered over Jumbo's temporary secondment to Godfrey Payne and The Comforters. But now suddenly, blown up with spaghetti and with a couple of pints inside him, plus the big sweaty bastard behind who kept on elbowing him in the back every two minutes, the whole world seemed to be rising up on all sides against him.

'Giyovver, Brian,' Howie said, frowning.

'What?'

'He's only sitting in for them,' Roger said.

'*Again*, you mean,' said Brian.

'*Bri*! It's Godfrey Payne and the bloody Comforters!' Howie said. 'You're telling me you wouldn't do the same, if you were asked? I know I would. I'd jump at the chance.'

'You would, eh? Well I wouldn't,' Brian snapped, raising his voice so that the bastard behind looked round and elbowed him again. 'I'm already in a group, Howie – *our* group – that is if we've still got one.'

'Course we have! Look. He's only helping out. And think about it; Kenny playing with Godfrey Payne – imagine how many people will see and hear about that. They'll all know his name, and they'll all know he's the drummer in The Chequered Saracens! Surely, that can only be a good thing?'

'Come on, Brian,' said Roger. 'Don't be daft about it.'

'I'm going for a piss.'

'He gets like that sometimes,' Howie said when Brian had pushed his way far enough through the crowd. 'I don't see what all the fuss's about. Tomorrow, Kenny's going to be playing in front of all those people. He'll be mentioned in the *NME* on Wednesday. And then, next Sunday, he'll be on the bloody telly! Plus, look at all the folks he's meeting – and who *we'll* be meeting – producers, agents...'

'That Denny Heyman bloke, who we met in Skeggy,' Roger joined in, 'he reckons he wants to record us, like a test disc, in a proper studio.'

'Exactly,' Howie said. 'And he hasn't heard any of the new songs yet.'

Unlike Brian, Howie was deeply optimistic about the opportunity which had presented itself through the fortuitous combination of Albie McPherson's bad luck and Jumbo's considerable (and conveniently to hand) talent. It was the chance of a lifetime, one that could very easily, if they played their cards right, lead to who knew where. Following tomorrow's concert, Jumbo would return to The Chequered Saracens with a glittering and enviable reputation, having played with one of the top R&B groups in Britain. Not to mention the countless contacts and influential new friends he'd made in all the right places. Really, anything was possible.

Brian, on the other hand, saw only that Godfrey Payne had nicked his drummer, causing his group to cancel half a dozen decent, well-paid bookings already in the two weeks' upheaval since Skegness. But what annoyed Brian most of all was that, while he did not begrudge Kenny personally his moment in the spotlight (he genuinely liked and valued Jumbo a lot), he couldn't help feeling that if any member of The Chequered Saracens should be performing at the *NME Poll Concert* tomorrow alongside The Beatles, The Kinks and The Rolling Stones, and right now be preparing himself to be lavished with an endless flow of praise and attention and more pretty girls than any decent young man could reasonably shake his cock at, then surely it should be himself, Brian, the charismatic frontman with the boyish good looks and incredible voice, not the big red-faced lump sitting behind the drums.

While all this was going on, Alastair remembered he'd promised to phone Mary. He looked at his watch. It wasn't late, but he knew he'd drunk quite enough for her to notice and to resent his having a good time. How far away it all seemed, Mary and Warinstowe, from this steaming old boozer, amid all this talk of groups and concerts and agents. It made a change from the Fox & Hounds, that was for sure.

'Well, whatever anybody says,' Howie said, after setting out his ambitions for his group, 'I'm bloody proud on him. And that's why we're all here, to support Jumbo.'

Brian now reappeared, apparently having drained off his gloom at the urinal, and with his most irresistible centre-stage smile lighting up his whole face. He rested a hand on his guitarist's shoulder. 'Sorry lads, I were being stupid. I don't know what got into me just then. Howie's right. We're here to support our mate, Kenny – *Jumbo*. He's going to be absolutely bloody brilliant tomorrow.'

They clinked and drained their glasses to Jumbo. Then, just as Brian had turned and begun to push his way to the bar for another round, a long pale hand clicked its fingers above their heads and a familiar, well-spoken voice called above the din of the Cockney knees-up. 'Allow me, Brian. Six pints of bitter, is it?'

'Jay!'

'Thanks, Jay.'

The androgynous fixer, art director, and procurer of pure new wool socks to Godfrey Payne and The Comforters made a small bow from the neck and flapped a wing of his greatcoat before cutting a path to the bar. 'I may require some assistance on the return journey,' he said, tossing his heavy ponytail over his shoulder. His friends watched impressed as Jay, after being served almost immediately, stood oblivious to the curious looks he drew, one foot on the brass rail, admiring the lethal toes of his crocodile skin winkle-pickers.

'Thanks, Jay.'

'Don't thank me, gentlemen. Thank Godfrey Payne and The Comforters, this round of rather flat ale is on them, bless their hearts. Cheers!'

'Cheers!'

'Is that all right, Jay?' asked Alastair. 'I mean, you won't get into trouble, spending their money?'

'Oh, no, no! Not at all. They're very happy to stand you fellows a jar or two. It's the least they can do, considering how you've helped them out.'

'I haven't done anything. And they've already bought me a tie,' Trevor smiled, straightening the souvenir from Skegness.

Jay tilted his head and studied Trevor's outfit, then turned to Alastair who'd decided against the shirt and tie look tonight in favour of his black corduroy sports jacket and cream polo neck.

'I thought it was you who chose the burgundy, Alastair, and Trevor the navy, no?'

'Yes,' said Alastair. 'But we often swap clobber for a night out. Can't keep wearing the same thing all the time. And I haven't got money to buy new gear every week, even if he has.'

Trevor rolled his eyes. 'Yes, I'm a millionaire, Jay. All junior bank clerks are. You know what though, Al, I think I prefer this colour to mine, now I've got it on.'

'Forget it! I want it back later. I'm wearing that to the concert tomorrow.'

'Well, it's an ingenious system,' Jay said, a mischievous smile filling out his lips as he cast his eye over their outfits. 'I must say you all look very "*with-it*", as I believe they say in these parts. Your mothers must be very proud.'

Alastair had already made a careful study of Jay's Byronesque orange shirt, with its delicate frills frothing between the buttons and wide open neck, his trousers, jet-black and which clung so tightly about his thighs and crotch they might have been regulation issue to the Bolshoi ballet.

'You're lucky actually, Jay,' Alastair said, admiring the sheer bravery of Jay's wardrobe. 'I almost wore that very same outfit myself, tonight.'

There was an uncomfortable pause as Jay frowned and for a moment Alastair feared he might have offended him. He knew how his mouth could sometimes be a liability when he was drunk.

'Now, you might not believe this,' Jay said, glancing down to appraise himself thoughtfully, 'but I meet very few people with whom I share a similar taste in clothes. Can't think why.'

Jay smiled, waited while they finished their drinks. 'Right then, gentlemen,' he said. 'Shall we wander?'

From the moment of Jay's arrival, the evening seemed suddenly to lose all sense and shape of time, to speed up and slow down, to freeze-frame and sometimes even double back on itself. The old reliable this-then-that chronology of consecutive events that usually went to make up even a lively night out with the boys no longer applied. And in the dizzying hours that followed, as Jay led them through the neon-lit streets and piss-soaked back alleys of Soho, from French pub to Spanish bar, private members' club to dodgy drinking den, it seemed to Alastair they'd sidestepped into a parallel reality, a hazy, fragmented dreamscape where a drink waited at the top of every narrow flight of stairs and at the bottom of every set of stone steps that led down to cellar after anonymous cellar into which they stumbled.

Somewhere – he'd never know where – somebody's grandmother, smoking a cigar and using a copy of *Country Life* magazine as an ashtray, had looked him up and down and stroked his cheek in a highly lecherous fashion before jabbing a button and launching the seven of them towards a painted night sky. The voice of Alma Cogan crackled, maudlin, from an invisible speaker. There was a rabbit in a woman's handbag. A young actor from a police serial. A man in a frock that, although it both fitted and suited him, failed miserably to hide his hairy chest. Every room in the city seemed to palpably drip and throb with a seedy glamour. And entry to all, along with the endless procession of drinks, whether they wanted them or not, appeared to be granted for no more than a genial nod or flick of the hand from Jay.

CHAPTER TWO

With the exception of Jay, none of them had ever seen so many black faces before, apart from on the television. Alastair had met one or two Caribbean railwaymen, of course, knew them well enough to pass ten minutes over a mug of tea while they waited for their train to be coupled at Bestwood sidings, or for an engine to be turned at Colwick shed. But here there were dozens of them, easily a third of the queue that stretched halfway down Wardour Street. Some stood alone, patiently waiting, smoking, while others larked about, singing and dancing, joking with their friends and girlfriends, both black and white.

When earlier they'd gone to a café to eat huge portions of fish and chips, Jay explained how for a long time The Blue Parrot Club had been very popular with American GIs, who, when they went home on leave to the States, would bring back all these incredible records, new and unheard sounds, jazz, blues, R&B, soul, which just blew people's socks off. Jay mentioned drugs too, pills, dope, weed, but it was the music they were most keen to hear about.

As Jay marched them to the front of the queue, drawing only a few jeers from the crowd, as well as a few respectful salutes, Alastair's stomach leapt as though he were in the back of a car as it crested a hump-backed bridge. He turned to Trevor and made an excited, bewildered face. The night air seemed to fizz with a thrilling but indefinable danger. This is *Absolute Beginners*, he thought, smiling across at Howie, it really is!

Just as they were about to go inside, a sleek grey car drew silently up to the kerb and a peak-capped chauffeur leapt out to open the rear door for a tall, pinched-faced man in a smart but old-fashioned dark suit, hair thin and grey as his smile, and his very pretty and lively looking granddaughter. Speculative mumblings rippled through the queue as the distinguished couple clipped across the pavement and slipped inside the bright doorway, where they were greeted by the joyful harmonies of The Supremes.

'Who d'you reckon they were?' said Trevor.

'Dunno, but I reckon I could do a lot more for her than that old buffer,' Brian said, smacking his lips in a sloppy cartoon kiss.

'Thinks he's John Profumo,' Howie said.

Barry craned forward, admiring as the girl practically ran up the stairs. 'Dirty old bugger!'

'Lucky old bugger!' said Brian, cracking himself up with laughter. 'Eh, Alastair?'

But Alastair hadn't been listening and he barely even noticed this glamorous arrival, which for a moment caused so much excitement among his pals. His eyes had been elsewhere, drawn to another couple, almost equally ill-matched, who'd appeared from a side street and were now walking along on the opposite pavement. She was a lot taller than him and about half his age, and from the way he gripped her elbow and hurried her along towards Shaftesbury Avenue, it looked to Alastair as if they'd just had a bit of a barney. He was a stocky bloke, fortyish, and appeared impatient and annoyed. The girl was blonde, *dark* blonde – *ash* he'd heard it called – and was clearly a little upset.

'You comin' in, man, or wha?' A huge lively faced doorman, pale mac draped cape-fashion round his shoulders and a white silk cravat plumped at the throat of his black shirt, opened his eyes wide and jerked a black thumb towards the doorway into which his friends, he saw, had already disappeared. Alastair, through some strange impulsive instinct, reached out and grabbed hold of the doorman's hand and smiled. 'Yes, please,' he said, giving the big hand an effusive shake. 'I'm a friend of Jay. Is this The Blue Parrot?'

As he stepped inside, Alastair turned and looked quickly back over his shoulder.

Upstairs a girl came towards Jay carrying a tray of black drinks in small glasses. 'Scotch and Coke,' Jay said. 'It's rather late for any more ale.'

The Blue Parrot was a dark and not especially large L-shaped room at the top of a narrow, twisting flight of stairs, with a low ceiling and a bar in one corner which, as the hours passed, twinkled more and more like a jeweller's shop window. The walls were panelled in a large red and black checkerboard design, each square about four feet across, whereas the dance floor had much smaller squares of black and white. Along three sides of the dance floor there rose a sort of terrace with an ironwork balustrade, scattered with tables as well as a number of cosy booths trimmed in red leatherette and lined up along the wall like the cars of a fairground ride. This perhaps explained the frequent shrieks and squeals that came from the mainly females who squeezed into these seats and draped themselves across the shiny black table tops. To one side, at the far end of the dance floor which was now heaving under the spell of some sax-heavy soul groove, was a small stage, empty but for the moody silhouettes of musical instruments resting between sets.

Alastair filled his mouth with sickly black sweetness, the whisky's peaty fire taking a moment or two before it scorched the back of his throat. He coughed once or twice, then took another swig before leaning forward so Howie could light the cigarette that hung from his lips. If ever there was a night for smoking, this was it.

'So this is the famous Blue Parrot,' Howie said, looking round approvingly.

'It is,' Jay nodded. 'The place for a face to be ace, so they say. The hip 'n' happ'nin' *Parrot Bleu* is the scene to be seen for all them cats who is sharp ee-nough to shine. You boys dig?' Jay raised a cynical eyebrow, smirked. 'Either that or it's a festering fleapit of gangsters, layabouts and disease-riddled old whores, it really depends on to whom one listens. Personally, I rather like it. Though of course, like any place that becomes popular, it does draw its fair share of wankers and arseholes – myself included.'

When Alastair laughed, Barry studied him with a puzzled face. As much as he liked Jay, Barry had no idea what he was on about half the time. He looked across to the bar, wondering if they had anything in the way of food.

Two smartly got-up girls, all big hair and pinched waists, excused themselves as they tottered between them and made towards the dance floor. Howie closed his eyes and inhaled a deep lungful of perfume. 'Aaah!'

'Spectacular!' Trevor shouted into Alastair's ear.

Alastair turned to Brian and winked. The singer pursed his lips. 'I could do with a bit of that. But... I reckon I'm about pissed.'

'Me too,' said Trevor.

'Excellent!' said Jay, grinning benevolently while checking the end of his ponytail for split ends. 'If we weren't all pissed by now, my friends, our whole evening would have been the most unforgivable washout. I'm only sorry I'm unable to go on boozing with you all for very much longer.' Jay glanced at his watch. 'But, unfortunately, duty calls.'

'Duty?' said Brian.

'God and the boys. They've had a long day. There's no telling what they might require, nor indeed when they might require it. As a rule, whenever I'm on duty I try to remain as lucid and sober as a High Court judge. Which, by my reckoning, leaves me room for one more drink. Same again?'

The music faded and a spotlight twitched across the stage, picking out the hats and smiles of musicians who now stepped from the shadows and settled behind their instruments. The blond young man at the organ turned and looked over his shoulder and with a casual "Okay!" launched his band into a blistering rendition of *Green Onions* that within seconds had the dance floor twisting and jiving to its outermost edges. The keyboard player, apparently the band's leader, seemed remarkably relaxed, nodding and winking at faces in the bobbing crowd, occasionally taking a puff on the cigarette that otherwise lay smouldering in the ashtray on top of his organ. His playing was incredible; skilful and filled with deep, soulful feeling, and yet it seemed so effortless, to be done with such a coolly casual air that Alastair suspected the guy must be years older than he looked. It didn't seem possible that someone so young should be able to play that well. It was only when he looked up at the end of a soaring keyboard break, his grinning face catching the spotlight, that Alastair realised who he was. He could hardly believe it. He jammed his toe into the ironwork balustrade that ran along the edge of the balcony, and, using Barry's shoulder for support, raised himself up to look out over the sea of dipping, shaking heads.

'Bloody hell!' Alastair grabbed Trevor by the shoulder and pulled him up beside him. 'Look! It's Georgie Fame!'

Trevor's mouth swung open and he almost lost his footing. 'Is it really him, Jay?' Trevor shouted, his eyes never leaving the stage. 'Is that Georgie Fame?'

''Tis indeed,' Jay said, nonchalantly waving his hand as Georgie Fame himself winked across from the stage.

'Did he just wink at *you*?' Trevor asked.

Howie slipped his arm around Jay's shoulder. 'Jay, you know everybody!' he said, impressed.

'I remembered you boys said you liked him,' Jay smiled. 'Not too bad, is he?'

'He's fantastic!' Trevor said, suddenly finding the driving tune twice as infectious now that he knew who was playing it.

'This is that place!' Alastair said, realising they were in the very nightclub where Georgie Fame had recorded one of his famous live LPs. 'I can't believe it.'

A black man with a broad chest and an air of lazy authority about him appeared at the edge of the dance floor and ordered them to get down before his hand reached up to give Jay's a comradely squeeze. A moment or two later, Jumbo appeared.

'Here you are, you pissed-up boggers!' Jumbo said, spreading out his arms and seeming to hug them all as one. 'Giz a sip on that, matey, I'm parched. Worrizit?'

'Scotch and Coke. Have it if you like. Reckon I've had enough.'

'You're not the only one, by the looks on it. You had a good night then?'

'Cracking!' said Trevor.

Alastair started to hiccup, held his breath while Jumbo quickly downed his drink. He slipped his arm around Jumbo and turned him towards the stage. 'Jumbo, look! That's Georgie Fame!'

'I know,' Jumbo smiled. 'Brilliant, in't he? We saw him this afternoon, doing his sound-check for tomorrow. He said he'd be down here.'

'Hark at him with his famous friends!' Alastair sing-songed as he took another of Howie's cigarettes. Jumbo jabbed for Alastair's ribs, deliberately missed.

'I mean he told Godfrey,' Jumbo said. 'You know what I meant, you drunken idiots. Here! We saw The Animals' rehearsal earlier. Now they *did* sound good. I'm right looking forward to seeing them tomorrow.'

'Me too,' Alastair said. 'I've never seen them before, have you?'

Howie shook his head. 'I can't wait. Didn't see The Stones, did you? Or The Beatles?'

'No, they'd already been and gone.'

'Kinks?' asked Alastair.

'They don't get back till tomorrow, from a gig somewhere abroad. They were brilliant when we saw them last year.'

Jumbo turned back to the stage, his lips pursed, his chin jutting as he started drumming along on the handrail in time to the jazzy, shuffling beat. 'Cracking though, this, in't it? Specially seeing him here.'

'Marvellous,' Alastair smiled. 'Bloody marvellous.'

A little while later, Alastair, feeling a hand on his shoulder, turned to find Godfrey Payne leaping up on to the balustrade from where he now waved across to the stage before scanning the dance floor to see who was in that was worth knowing. 'All right, cocker?' Godfrey said to Alastair, winking as he jumped down and clinked beer bottles with his guitarist, Eric Handley.

'Nice-a-see-yer again, lads!' Eric said, raising his bottle and greeting them all like old friends. 'Welcome to London! Hey, this hotel where we're staying, it's nice an' all, but the breakfasts ain't a patch on what you lads made in that caravan. You fancy camming over in the morning and rustling us up anavver?'

Alastair smiled, looked between his friends thinking how insane it was that here they all were, in a nightclub, in London, drinking free Scotch and Coke and chatting away with Godfrey Payne and The Comforters while Georgie Fame played the most fantastic run of tunes on a tiny stage only feet away. A small part of him urged the rest to stay as sober as it possibly could, so that he might remember at least some of this in the morning.

When Jay reappeared, he was accompanied by two breathtaking girls in matching black mini-skirts and sleeveless red silk blouses. The pair, one dark, one blonde, smiled delightedly as they came round with silver trays laden with tall glasses of a clear icy liquid, which Alastair desperately hoped was water while knowing very well it would not be.

'Gennulmen!' Godfrey Payne announced, swivelling on his Cuban heels at the centre of their now sizeable party. 'Just a few words. We've had a tough week getting ready for this gig, but I'm pleased to say that, thanks to Kenny here helping us out, we're in pretty good shape, considering. So please, and this goes for all of us – let's not fack it ap tomorrow, eh? Cheers!'

The rowdy moment of jubilation drew curious glances from the dance floor as well as from those who'd deliberately positioned themselves close to the scene, hoping to share in the warm fuss of celebrity, no matter how incidentally.

Godfrey Payne threw back his drink and with a friendly, self-assured smile, said, 'Right, who's for a dance, then?' But before Alastair had had time to think if he was even expected to give an answer, Georgie Fame was already halfway through the opening verse of *Baby Please Don't Go*, and Godfrey Payne was stepping onto the dance floor, a pretty waitress giggling on each of his famous arms.

After being heroically sick in the toilet, and feeling much better for it, Alastair returned to find Barry and Roger dancing close by Godfrey Payne and the waitresses with a couple of young and very stylish-looking Mod girls; while Jumbo had settled in one of the booths with Eric and Clive, the Comforters' bassist, and, with much gesticulation and face pulling, the three were running once more through some of the more ambitious drum patterns and rhythmic flourishes that would form part of the short set they'd be performing in tomorrow's concert. Howie squeezed in beside Jumbo, looking on fascinated as a toddler in a pet shop. Brian, he thought he last remembered seeing heading towards the toilet.

By now Alastair was a little unsteady on his feet. After he'd made a half-hearted, unsuccessful search for Trevor and Jay he came to rest against the balustrade at the quieter end of the balcony. The jostling ebb and flow of the dance floor did nothing for either his head or his stomach. He felt suddenly very tired and wished he were at home in his bed. A crop-headed blonde girl smiled up at him from the dance floor, whispered something in her friend's ear which made them both turn away and giggle. For some reason, which deep down he knew very well but yet which his brain was not able to fully process in its three-parts-drunken state, Alastair's thoughts kept returning to the couple he'd seen outside, earlier, walking past on the opposite pavement.

'See anything you fancy, chum?' Alastair turned to find a childish face with an unruly black cowlick springing from its high, pale forehead, smiling up at him from a little way along the balcony.

'Eh?' Alastair said.

The youth moved closer. He spoke very quickly and with a faint, kindly lilt which Alastair thought was probably Irish. 'A lady you like the look of?'

'Well, er,' Alastair hesitated.

'Take your pick. There's very little in here that can't be had, you know. That is if you're to go the right way about it.'

Alastair looked for the two gigglers but found they'd gone.

'Take her for instance...' The Irish youth nodded discreetly towards a voluptuous girl who seemed to be dancing alone near the edge of the dance floor in a shimmering black off-the-shoulder dress, and a pair of tiny diamonds which sparkled from her ears.

'What about her?' Alastair said, quietly observing not only how the girl had removed her shoes and used the slipperiness of her tights on the polished floor to great effect in her gyrations, but also the habit she had of every now and then throwing her arms up and back over her head with such wild abandon it was surely only a matter of time until her breasts leapt out of her dress.

'Avril Frederick. Looks like butter wouldn't melt in her mouth,' the youth said. 'Avril's a fondness for the beds of the rich and famous. They say they're much softer than ordinary folks' beds, but I wouldn't know about that.'

As Alastair studied the swaying figure of Avril Frederick, needing very little imagination to picture how she'd look without any clothes, he realised she was the girl who'd swished up in the big motor with the old buzzard, and that while she danced in seemingly carefree ecstasy by herself, granddad hovered at the edge of the dance floor, an empty glass twisting between his fingers as he struggled to disguise his impatience to be anywhere other than this filthy, noisy dive into which his lusts had once more dragged him.

'Eh?' said Alastair, miles away, finding the youth studying him with a cocky, wide-eyed smile.

'Said would you happen to be either of those things?'

'What things?'

'Rich. Or famous.'

'Me? God, no!' Alastair said, shaking his head decisively. He slipped his hand into his trouser pocket, covering his wallet. 'I work on the railway. You can probably guess how rich I am.'

'I didn't think so. Only I saw you was with...' The overfriendly chap turned and nodded to the booth where Godfrey Payne now cosily reclined between his two waitresses, while another girl in a bold zigzag-pattern dress leaned across the table so Godfrey could whisper in her ear.

'Godfrey? I hardly know him. But my mate Jumbo's playing drums for them tomorrow. At the *NME* concert.'

'They've a drummer called Jumbo now, have they? I never heard that. I suspect you're having me on, are you? Well, look. No matter if you're Rockefeller or poor as a church mouse, no good'll come of you standing here all miserable by yourself, looking like a leper with the halitosis. You want me to find you a nice girl?'

Alastair watched as Avril Frederick was escorted, reluctantly, towards the exit by her old man (who was almost certainly rich if not also famous), his leathery old hand creeping round her waist. Why on earth would a lovely young girl want to be with a doddery old git like him? The grim inevitability of the situation all of a sudden infuriated Alastair.

'No, I don't, thanks very much!' he snapped, causing the young Irishman to take a step back. 'I'm looking for my friend, that's all.'

The youth nodded and then, in a voice kinder than ever, asked, 'A boy about your age, is he, your friend?'

'Yes. Trevor. It's not...'

'No need to explain.' The youth took a stick of spearmint from his shirt pocket and folded it onto his tongue. 'But if he doesn't turn up – your *friend* – you'll be sure to let me know. I can always find friends for my friends.'

Alastair gave him a hard look, wondered just what exactly he meant by this.

'My name's Penny,' the lad said. 'Very pleased to meet you, er...?'

'Alastair.'

'*Alastair*,' Penny nodded as he looked Alastair carefully up and down. 'Suits you.'

'So does yours, *Penny*.'

'Short for Pennyfeather. Old family name. I prefer it to Derek. I never could see myself as a Derek.'

'No,' Alastair said, smiling with relief as he spotted Trevor and Jay weaving towards them from the dance floor.

'Jesus!' Trevor panted as he mopped his sweat-lathered face on the lining of his jacket. 'Bloody sweltering out there!'

'Penny not leading you astray, is he, Alastair?' Jay said, at last removing his greatcoat and draping it over his arm.

'No, not at all,' Alastair said, relieved his friends were back all the same.

'Penny likes to corrupt the innocent youth of England. Don't you, Penny?'

'As if I'd ever do such a thing,' Penny laughed, as with a tongue-moistened forefinger he smoothed down his cowlick.

'Is that Trevor? It *is*, isn't it? It's you!' Trevor, feeling a set of nails piercing his forearm, turned to find the narrow, humped back of a girl bent double beside him while with some difficulty she tried to get her foot back into the shoe she'd somehow cast off. With Trevor's help, Samantha rose unsteadily to her feet. 'I remember you from the seaside. You're nice. And you...' Samantha said, turning to Alastair, a sleepy smile on her lips as she repositioned the broad black band that held back her shiny blonde hair. 'You are Anthony, the... no, don't tell me! You are... the *drummer!* Aren't you? Yes, yes! And you always ring your mother if you're going to be late home for dinner! I never forget a face, Anthon-hic-Anthony.'

His face was the only thing she hadn't forgotten. Alastair smiled as Samantha was led away on the arm of an equally wobbly brunette towards one of the livelier booths nearest the stage.

'Was Samantha Godfrey's girlfriend for very long, Jay?' asked Alastair.

'Not very long, no,' Jay said, slipping back into his greatcoat. 'They were married, I believe, within a month of meeting.'

'Married? But he's with a different bird every time I look at him. There've been a dozen hanging off him since he got here only an hour ago.'

'Yes, it's a shame, really,' Penny said. 'But you see, her people are very connected. They own half of Hampshire, or Berkshire, I forget which, and Godfrey wasn't always quite so well off as he is now, if you see what I mean. She seems very fond of you, though – Trevor, is it? Have you got a girlfriend, Trevor?'

Trevor immediately looked across at Alastair. It was the first time he'd been called upon to publicly acknowledge his relationship with Sarah, and he wasn't entirely sure what to say. But as soon as Sarah's face appeared, smiling in his mind's eye, he felt suddenly very warm inside and it was easy. 'Yes, I have,' he said, rather proudly. 'Her name's Sarah and, er, she's Alastair's sister.'

'Oh, how nice!' Penny said, clapping his hands together as a mischievous grin lit up his impish face. 'And how does Alastair feel about that, you going out with his sister?'

Trevor waited anxiously, wondering now if perhaps he should have kept his mouth shut. Alastair took a long drag on his cigarette and seemed to consider the question deeply for a moment before camply tossing back his head, and in his best Kenneth Williams nasal drawl said, 'Well, dearie, if he *must* see other people, better it should be someone I can keep me eye on. Wouldn't you say?'

As the laughter subsided, Brian reappeared with a tray clinking with more Scotch and Coke.

CHAPTER THREE

They'd all left The Blue Parrot together; himself, Trevor, Howie, Brian and Barry, he was fairly certain. Roger, he was less sure about. It must have been when they'd stopped while somebody went for a slash against a parked car that they'd become separated.

In fact, it was Alastair who'd wandered off, or rather he'd just kept on walking, oblivious, while everyone else waited for Brian, so that now he found himself adrift in the gloomy streets of Soho, none of which seemed to bear any resemblance to those of earlier in the evening, or offer any clues as to where the hell he might be. The pubs and cafés were all long closed, their windows blank and shuttered against the night. As he looked about at a deserted crossroads the lights of an Italian restaurant went out and from within foreign voices rose in lively farewell. A dustbin lid slammed in a nearby yard. Two dark figures stood close together, whispering, at the top of a flight of steps leading down to a basement.

Bursting himself now, Alastair nipped into an alley, barely wide enough for his elbows, and stinking with the puddles of countless others who'd had the same idea. 'Now, boy,' he said, unzipping himself and finding Richard Burton. 'A serious night's drinking is very much like a man's life: no matter how many friendly faces there may be along the way, he will always face the end ALONE!'

Alastair had no idea where these words came from, whether he'd remembered them from a book or a play or a film, or come up with them himself, just then. Either way they were forgotten almost immediately as he tilted his head back and became lost in the minor ecstasy of a suddenly much-needed piss. Unfortunately, in his paralytic state he'd failed to fully free himself from his underpants, with the result that he'd gone off like a burst fire hydrant all down his right leg. By the time he'd realised and tugged himself clear it was hardly worthwhile for what was left. He rested his forehead against the smooth, cold bricks, watching as a steaming lake formed around his boots and the patch of warmth on his right thigh began to cool and trickle down into his sock.

When he tried to right himself again with his free hand, he overdid it and stumbled back, cracking his head hard against the wall behind. He remained there like that, a cross-beam at an unsustainable angle between the two buildings, for perhaps three or four seconds before he crumpled in a heap on the sodden ground, not entirely sure himself whether the sound that now came out of him was that of laughter or of crying.

'Christ Almighty, Alastair!' Richard Burton snarled. 'Look at you, now! Lying stinking in your own great pool of piss! Piss! Piss! Bloody Piss!'

Actually, it wasn't too bad lying on the piss-soaked flagstones, once you got used to it. It was the sight of the scabby-looking rat sniffing towards his boots that caused Alastair to leap suddenly to his feet and run screaming like a wussy old banshee towards the light of the street. After narrowly avoiding being run down by a milk float as he walked in the middle of the road, Alastair found himself in a phone box only marginally more sanitary than rat-piss alley. He fumbled in his wallet for the piece of paper on which he'd written the telephone number of the Bayswater guest house, but it was not there. Expecting to be returning with the others, he hadn't thought he'd need it; the same reason he hadn't bothered to make a note of either the guest house's name or its address. A half-smoked fag lay on the floor and he would have been tempted, had he anything to light it with.

He decided to walk to Bayswater. It couldn't be far; it had taken less than ten minutes coming in on the tube. And there were bound to be signs. If there was one thing London was not short of, it was road signs. The city seemed to sprout them like other places grew trees.

After about five minutes' brisk walking, Alastair came to a broad street which, with the exception of a theatre, two cafés and a tobacconist's, appeared to be home to nothing but bookshops. A red bus groaned past in a cloud of black smoke, gears crunching, its windows illuminated with misty shadows. A taxi, then another, rattled up towards what looked like a big junction. Here, though, the traffic lights and Belisha beacons put on their pretty little show for no-one, as if they were quietly rehearsing for the forthcoming rush hour.

Alastair started towards the junction. He rather liked the idea of a good walk, alone. His head had begun to clear slightly, and his mood now brightened with every step. Rather than a disaster, the thought of being thoroughly lost in the middle of London suddenly opened out before him like an unexpected and thrilling adventure.

In the window of one of the larger bookshops an elaborate display of Ian Fleming's *James Bond* novels had been arranged, featuring life-size cardboard figures of the late author and Sean Connery. Alastair stopped for a moment to study it, his eyes almost immediately drawn to the jacket of a *Dr No* paperback. He'd read the book a couple of years before, in an earlier edition, but decided it was probably worth buying again just for the picture of Ursula Andress in that white bikini.

The couple paid him no attention as they walked silently past, and Alastair, miles away on a desert island with Honey Ryder, would probably not have noticed them either if the man hadn't dropped his car keys thirty yards further along the pavement. As soon as he saw her – only a brief glimpse from the side, but it had been enough – Alastair felt sick, though not with booze this time. Sick with fear, and something else he couldn't quite put a name to, but whatever it was it set his heart banging and left him gasping for breath as if James Bond himself had stepped out of the window and socked him in the windpipe.

Of course, he'd known it was Charlotte the moment he saw her from the doorway of The Blue Parrot, being hurried along on the opposite side of Wardour Street by this same cannonball-headed goon she was arm in arm with now. Alastair had taken a dislike to the bloke on sight, the way he walked with his confident, heavy, short-legged strut, the way his well-cut and expensive-looking suit showed off his broad, solid figure, but now he simply hated him. Who was he? Where had they been? What had they been doing till this time?

There was nothing to stop him calling after her, saying hello and finding all this out – she was his friend after all. Yet something did. The rush of delight he'd felt on seeing that it really was Charlotte was immediately crushed by the conflicting feeling that he so desperately wished it weren't. Alastair was still drunk. Far more than he realised.

He kept his distance, moving stealthily from one shop doorway to the next, but neither Charlotte nor the man once looked back. Nor did they exchange a single word, as far as he could tell. When a bus trundled past, the word "Bayswater" seemed to stand out especially bright among all the other exotic-sounding destinations on its indicator board. But Bayswater could wait.

The couple turned down a side street and for a few moments Alastair lost sight of them. Having run to catch up, it was a miracle he wasn't spotted. About fifty feet around the corner Charlotte and her companion (whom Alastair was further annoyed to see was quite handsome in an ageing, thuggish sort of way) had come to a halt in the middle of the pavement, and the man, having turned back the way they'd come, was now facing Charlotte. The doorway of the hectic-looking bookshop, pictures cut from magazines of Bob Dylan, Marianne Faithfull and the Rev. Martin Luther King messily taped to the glass, was positioned on the corner of the building at such an angle Alastair was able to look through the door and out again through the huge window that ran along the side street without being seen. Huddled in the shadows, his heart thumping, he watched as the man took out his car keys, unlocked the passenger door of a dark blue Rover and, smiling creepily, urged Charlotte to get in. Alastair could see only the back of her head, but her dark blonde hair shook determinedly enough for him to be certain she'd said 'No'. The man looked down at the pavement and blew out his cheeks. He tried again, this time his face not so much inviting Charlotte to get in as ordering her to do so.

'Come on, gel,' the man said, impatiently. Charlotte shook her head. 'Good girl', Alastair thought, wincing as he felt his teeth grind together.

Charlotte physically jumped as the man slammed his palm against the car roof and nodded to the open door. 'Charlotte, get in the bloody car. I ain't got all night, even if you have.'

'No,' he heard her say, quietly. There was fear in her voice, or something very much like it. And when she turned round, looked back over her shoulder and almost straight at Alastair, he saw there were tears in her eyes. She hadn't changed a bit in nearly three years. She was just as lovely as he always remembered her. Only he didn't remember ever seeing her look quite so vulnerable as this, so helpless, so frightened. He swallowed his heart back down from where it had leapt up and become stuck in his throat. His fist clenched tight against the glass of the bookshop door. Whatever situation Charlotte had got herself into with this nasty piece of work, he had to get her out of it. Yet as bad as it already seemed, Alastair hadn't for a moment expected it to take the turn it did now.

'No,' Charlotte said again, lowering her head and nervously tucking her hair behind her ear.

'Fine. Have it your way.'

The man slammed the door and moved rapidly towards Charlotte. Alastair could see he was the sort of bloke who wouldn't think twice about giving a girl a good hiding if she refused him. Perhaps he'd bundle her into the car and... It didn't bear thinking about. He could feel the anger rising inside him, his fist starting to shake. He held it still, squeezing his knuckles. 'Lay one finger on her, and I'll break every fucking bone in your body, you mean little bastard,' he threatened under his breath.

But the man did neither. Instead, he did something that just at that moment seemed far, far worse. He slid his hand inside his jacket, pulled out his wallet and began tearing out £5 and £10 notes. There must have been seventy, eighty quid – a hundred even. He handed the money to Charlotte, practically threw it at her, and she stood there looking at it for a moment or two before stuffing it into the pocket of her suede coat. When she turned and looked back over her shoulder, Alastair could barely see her face through the haze of tears that now filled his eyes. He shook his head, burning from head to toe with rage. 'No!' he said, refusing to believe this terrible thing he was witnessing. 'Not Charlotte.'

The overpowering stink of aftershave didn't go particularly well with the metallic tang of blood that coated his lips and tongue, but after the third or fourth time the man's head smashed against his mouth, Alastair hardly noticed it as he struggled hard to cling on to the broad shoulders and land as many punches as he could in the bastard's eyes, ears and throat.

He rode him like a rampaging bull, the man spinning in wild, frantic circles and smashing against the Rover as he fought to throw off his attacker, wondering where on earth he'd sprung from, and what the hell this was all about. When he'd pounded one side of the bloke's face until his knuckles ached, Alastair switched hands and started on the other, raining down blow after blow upon the furious, greying head. It was like punching a brick wall that wouldn't stay still.

As he'd launched himself from the kerb, up onto the chap's back, he'd heard Charlotte's surprised voice call out his name. He heard it again now, as briefly at the edge of his vision he saw her, beneath the street lamp, as she spun dizzyingly past.

'It's Alastair!' she said. It was hard to say whether or not she sounded pleased to see him. With all the force he could muster, Alastair smacked his fist hard into the bucking man's windpipe. Then everything went black.

CHAPTER FOUR

'*Three chips-un-egg, one scrambled wi' beans on toast?*'

Sarah sighed. 'They treat me like a five-year-old, sometimes,' she said, a resigned smile widening the muted pink lips she was permitted to wear at work. She blew her tea and took a small sip. 'Mind you, I didn't even bother asking this time. They'd never have let me go.'

Mary nodded understandingly as she splashed a sugar lump into her cup from an unnecessarily great height. 'I know I've never cared very much for going to concerts, but I really would have liked to see Jumbo play with Godfrey Payne and The Comforters.'

'It would have been marvellous. And to see The Rolling Stones. I missed them last year when they came to the Granada. I had a bad stomach, remember?'

A cocky youth, not bad-looking, but with skin a little froggy from teenage acne winked across from where he sat with five or six mates at a table by the door. Sarah smiled politely and looked away.

'Still,' Mary said. 'At least we'll be able to watch it on the telly next Sunday.'

'Can you believe it? Jumbo on the television! Why don't we all watch it together, you and me and the boys, at our house?'

'That'd be nice. Perhaps Jumbo will bring Amelia?'

'*Three chips-un-egg, one scrambled wi' beans on toast? Come on, where a-yer?*'

The dumpy, yellow-haired waitress scanned the Café Milano for her elusive diners.

'*Ere y'are, duck!*'

'*Wor yer 'iding from me, Johnny? Eh? I'll 'ave to gee it a-summon else, if yer 'iding from me.*'

'*Yer know I'd never 'ide from you, Joyce, duck.*'

Mary found it impossible not to smile whenever she looked at Joyce, proprietor of Café Milano. On one of their very first dates to the pictures, she had asked Alastair how difficult he thought it must have been for Joyce to apparently tattoo her own forearms. To which he'd answered, '*Very*', though not half as difficult as it had been for her to do the bulldog she had tattooed on her arse.

'Sarah,' Mary said, dropping another lump in her cup. 'Do you think they'll be all right in London?'

'What do you mean?'

'Alastair and Trevor.'

'Yes, of course. I know they can be daft as a brush together, sometimes, especially when Jumbo's with them. But Jumbo'll be too busy with the group. And they'll be at the concert most of the day tomorrow.'

Mary took a dainty bite out of her slice of fruitcake and, nibbling, sat there looking very thoughtful for a moment. Sarah could see something was worrying her. She appeared quite miserable behind the beauty that for a long time Sarah had envied and always known she'd never have herself. She was fine about it now. She was quite happy with the way she'd turned out, more or less; although she wouldn't have minded being just a couple of inches taller.

'What made you ask that?' said Sarah. 'What is it?'

'Oh it's... I'm just being silly, I suppose.'

'What?'

Mary made a pretty frown. 'It's just that... I keep thinking Alastair might be getting fed up with me.'

'Don't be daft! Mary, he thinks the world of you. You've only to see the two of you together. Course he's not fed up with you!'

'But I'm always nagging on at him, about work and settling down and things like that. And we had a terrible row the other night about him going to London. We made up, but...'

'What about? Didn't you want him to go without you? I didn't really want Trevor to go either, but I knew they would. They wouldn't have missed seeing Jumbo.'

'I know,' Mary nodded. 'I was just a bit worried he might, I don't know, go off with some other girl, meet somebody he likes at the concert, or in a pub. You know they're all going out tonight, don't you, in London?'

'I know they are, but it doesn't mean they'll be looking for girls. You know what they're like. They'll be too busy drinking and messing about, talking about records and cars – or trains.'

'That's another thing I've been getting on at him about,' Mary said glumly, 'his beloved railway.'

'Well, you're wasting your time there, Mary. You know how long my dad went on at him about it and got nowhere.'

'*Black coffee, slice o' fruitcake. One knickerbocker glory, one banana milkshake.*'

'Ooh, I just fancy a milkshake! Would you like one, Mary?'

As Sarah clip-clopped back to her seat, careful as she sucked a frothy mouthful of strawberry milkshake through her straw, the eyes of the froggy youth and his mates followed her closely.

'Yer wun't get many o' them t'pound!' one of them leered, much to the amusement of the others.

'Cheeky boggers,' Sarah said, giggling as she fastened a button on her cardigan. 'I brought an extra straw for you, Mary.'

'The thing is,' Mary said when they were halfway down the glass. 'I don't mean to get on at him. I hate it when I nag, but it feels like that's all I do sometimes. I only want him to do well, Sarah. To make the most of himself. I mean, look at Trevor. He's always liked trains as much as Alastair, but he doesn't want to clean them, or drive the filthy things for the rest of his life. It just seems a waste for someone as clever as Alastair. He could do anything.'

'*One black coffee, slice o' fruitcake. Last time 'for I tek it back?*'

'*Ovver 'ere, Joyce!*'

'*Serve you rate if it's cold.*'

'*I'd nipped for a tiddle, duck.*'

'*Enough o' that, folks's eating.*'

'It's like he doesn't care about his future at all. Sometimes I think he lives in a dream world.'

'It's not about how clever he is, Mary, or whether the job's good enough for him. Alastair had his heart set on working on the railway ever since he was little – he's always been train mad, you know that. It wouldn't have made any difference what school he went to, or what any of his friends did, Alastair was going on the railway and that was that.'

'I know,' Mary said, almost smiling.

'Anyway,' Sarah continued, 'I think it's nice he has a job he loves so much. Don't you think it better he does something that makes him happy, rather than makes him rich, or appears more... *respectable*? I do.'

Mary nodded. 'Yes. Yes, I do, Sarah. All I want is for him to be happy.'

Sarah touched up her lipstick in a daisy-shaped plastic hand mirror. 'Come on,' she said, pouting into the glass. 'If we're quick we might just catch the ten past.'

As Mary reached for the door, Froggy leaned across the table of dirty plates and puckered his lips. 'Ey up, duck. Give us a kiss before you go.'

Mary tilted her head to one side, gave him a withering once-over and then, curling her lip, said, 'I don't think so.'

One of the others, quite handsome, winked at Sarah. As Mary pulled the door open Froggy nudged his pal and sprang up. 'Well, how's about a squeeze on yer tits, then?'

Mary turned and looked back over her shoulder. 'How's about you go and squeeze your face, instead?'

'I don't know how you dare say such things!' Sarah said, giggling as they ran up the hill towards the bus stop. 'He didn't know what to do with himself, poor sod.'

'Sarah, can I ask you something,' Mary said when they were seated upstairs at the back of the bus. 'You know how Alastair's been looking in on Monica Bloomsberry?'

'Yes,'

'Well, I know Alastair's been writing to Charlotte. You don't think...'

Sarah turned to Mary in disbelief. Taking her hands, she looked into her eyes. 'Don't be so silly, Mary! They've gone to a concert, to see Jumbo! And Alastair loves *you*!'

For the past hour Nigel Wells had waited patiently, sitting astride his motorbike, across the street from Café Milano. He hadn't bargained on Mary Windale turning up and getting in the sodding way.

CHAPTER FIVE

Apart from the large damp patch that had formed against his cheek where he'd drooled into the pillow, it was a lovely, comfy bed, whoever's it was. Alastair wished he could stay there forever, and the way his head felt, heavy as lead, fragile as blown glass whenever he so much as tried to lift it even an inch off the pillow, he thought he might very well have to. Sunlight poured in through a pair of flimsy orange curtains. To fully open or even attempt to move his eyes with much haste was a masochistic act, like inviting a wrestler to take his fat thumbs and force them back, deep into his skull.

His first thought on finally peeping out from under the bedspread was that he was in the Bayswater guest house, though how he might have ended up there he had absolutely no recollection whatsoever. A bus flickered hazily past in some distant recess of his memory, but vanished before he could find out whether he'd climbed aboard. But the furniture was all wrong for the guest house. When they'd dropped off their bags yesterday afternoon (had it really been only the day before?) he hadn't remembered noticing the little electric fire that sat in the old hearth, nor the heavy looming wardrobe with its suitcases piled on top, hangers of clothes and underclothes dangling from its handles. Neither were any of the lads there, you could tell that simply by the fragrance of the room. It smelled fresh and sweet, a little sickly perhaps (though that might have been his stomach), somewhere between a florist's and a sweetshop. But there was also, coming from beyond the bedroom door where a drawing-pinned Mick Jagger pouted from a fur-lined hood, another smell, one which was not at all sickly, was delicious in fact. Frying bacon. Alastair's mouth watered, reminding him of the countless ashtrays and cattle farmer's wellingtons that, according to his tongue, he must have spent the whole of the previous night licking. But if he weren't at the guest house, where on earth was he?

The sound of a teaspoon ringing against the rim of a blue and white striped mug. He must have nodded off.

'Tea, one sugar. Bacon and egg on thick white bread, with far too much butter and a big blob of brown sauce. I'm sorry it's not caked in coal dust like you normally have it, but I couldn't get hold of a fireman's shovel at such short notice. I hope it'll do?'

'Charlotte!' Alastair drew himself up against the headboard and waited while the strange room and the vision at the end of the bed gradually came into focus. He remained there a moment, blinking and wincing a little, thinking he must be dreaming, though he knew he couldn't be. In a dream he'd have made himself a damn sight more presentable than the triptych of grey-faced, cockerel-quiffed ghouls he saw reflected back at him from the mirrors of the dressing-table that stood in the corner with its clutter of little bottles, pots and jars of perfumes and potions, its hairbrushes, bows and powder compacts. It was not the look he ideally would have chosen to present himself to Charlotte again after nearly three years.

'How're you feeling?' Charlotte said, after he'd swallowed most of his tea in one gulp.

'Like death,' Alastair said, smiling as he self-consciously ran his fingers through his hair. 'And a little bit confused, if I'm honest.'

Folded neatly over the back of a wicker armchair, Alastair recognised his jacket, cream polo neck and black cords. He wiggled his toes. Socks, too. He glanced down, grateful for his vest and, hopefully, underpants, but still feeling a bit of a fool sitting there in what he assumed was Charlotte's bed, eating the bacon sandwich and drinking the tea she had made for him. He'd no recollection of getting undressed.

Charlotte, though, didn't seem in the least bit surprised or put out. And as she sat there, in the middle of the big bed, legs curled beneath her, wearing nothing but a quietly amused smile and a very plain and not at all fetching white nightshirt, it was as if this was the sort of thing they did all the time together, as if he was her roommate or an old friend invited down for the weekend.

'That was delicious, Charlotte,' Alastair said, swallowing the last of his tea and setting his mug down on the tray between them. 'I feel a hundred per cent better already. Thank you.'

'You're very welcome,' Charlotte said, raising her own mug between two hands and slowly sipping her tea. As she peered over the rim he was reminded what dark eyebrows she had, black almost. She wore no make-up, so far as he could tell, and her skin was just as peachy and unblemished, her blue-grey eyes as deep and calm, as he remembered them. His mind rewound through the night before, to when he'd spotted her outside The Blue Parrot, before then tumbling through various jumbled and fragmentary scenes of pubs ablaze with light and bawled conversation; scenes of Jumbo and Godfrey Payne, of girls, dancing and rock 'n' roll; on a tiny stage Georgie Fame plays James Brown. There was booze, fags, booze and *more* booze; a rat scuttles through a puddle of piss, and fists, fists, pounding fists; the bristled solidity of a big grey head smashing repeatedly against his lips and teeth.

Alastair became suddenly aware of a pain at the back of his head, noticed how the knuckles of his hands were tender, the right ones scrubbed raw. When he looked up he found Charlotte studying him with, not a pitying look exactly, but certainly one of friendly concern. He felt he owed her an apology, though for what he wasn't quite sure.

'Thank you,' he said again, hoping that might cover it for now.

'I'll go and make us a fresh pot of tea,' Charlotte said brightly, rising with the tea tray. Before she reached the door Charlotte halted, her back to the tall sash window. 'Bathroom's one floor up,' she smiled. 'When you're ready, I mean. There's no rush, it's Sunday.'

Alastair felt his cheeks begin to burn, convinced Charlotte must surely notice how he struggled to remain looking at her face while the orange sunlight poured through her nightshirt, making it virtually transparent. She seemed to remain there an age, though it could only have been a second or two, and he was in no doubt now that he still had his underpants on. The second the door had fully closed, he reached down and freed himself from where he'd grown trapped in the fly.

Just before eleven, Alastair dialled the number of the Claremont Guest House, Bayswater. The name had come to him as he freshened himself up in Charlotte's bathroom, and sure enough there it was in the phonebook.

'*Charley Bloomsberry*?' Trevor gasped. 'You're joking! Bloody hell, where'd you find her? We all thought you'd turned and gone off with that fruity little Irish fella who took such a shine to you at The Blue Parrot.'

Alastair frowned, dredged the broken frames of the night before. 'Bloody hell – Penny! I'd completely forgotten about him.'

'Bet he's not forgotten about you, dearie. Ooh, I say! So, how's Charley then, you dirty old man?' Trevor said, slipping into Harold Steptoe.

'Nothing like that,' Alastair said, smiling as he waved through the glass of the telephone box to Charlotte, who sat smoking on a bench at the entrance to what looked like some sort of public garden. 'I must have been so pissed. I can hardly remember a bloody thing. And my head's *banging*.'

'Mine too. We didn't half sup some ale. Mind you, I threw most of mine up in a bin on the way back.'

'Trev, I haven't got much change. Look, later on – '

'I've got your ticket here. Shall we say a quarter to two at the box office?'

'Righto. I'm sure I'll find it.'

'Where are you, anyway?'

'Place called Camberwell.'

'Never heard of it. Well, say hello to Charley for me. Hey! Why don't you bring her along? We should be able to get her in, there was a spare ticket for Frank.'

Charlotte prised open the door of the telephone box and whispered that the bus was coming.

'Trev, I've got to go. I'll see you later, quarter to two.'

They strolled along the south bank of the Thames, a light but determined breeze blowing into their faces, bright sunlight glinting off the crests of the waves churned up by riverboats. For some of the time they chatted away excitedly and non-stop, about London and work and old friends, Alastair amused at the casual pride Charlotte took in pointing out some of the better-known landmarks of her adopted city – St Paul's, The Tower of London, The Houses of Parliament off in the distance. But there were also periods when neither of them felt the need to say anything, were equally happy and content in the easy silence that settled between them as they wandered arm in arm among the smiling tourists.

Neither of them had made any reference to Alastair's unexpected presence in Charlotte's bed that morning, nor the circumstances that had led to his being there. Perhaps it was his stinking hung-over state, or simply the thrilling strangeness of walking beside the famous river on a glorious spring Sunday morning with Charlotte, like a scene from some daft romantic film. Either way, Alastair felt himself wishing with all his heart that neither he nor Charlotte would do or say anything that might jeopardize this oddly familiar feeling of comforting closeness; that this moment of unanticipated bliss might never end.

At Tower Bridge they waited while a merchant ship laden with tarpaulin-covered humps of some heavy dark mineral – coal perhaps – passed between the elevated sections, its deep, throaty horn sounding gratefully as it made towards the sea.

As they walked on, Charlotte pulled him closer. 'I never imagined I'd find *you* in my bed this morning, Alastair Braymoor!' she said.

Alastair looked into her eyes. 'No,' he said, smiling thoughtfully. 'Awfully rude of me not to have telephoned ahead, given you notice.'

Charlotte smiled. 'Lucky I had room. You kept me nice and warm though, so I'll let you off.'

'It's funny. I sort of promised your mam I'd try to drop in and see you, though I didn't really expect there'd be time, with the concert. And as I hadn't heard back from you in the week... Anyway, turns out I'm a man of my word, after all.'

'Mi mam? Sending you to spy on me now is she, nebby cow?'

'She worries about you, Charlotte, that's all. Down here all on your own. I do too, sometimes.'

The pleasure cruiser frothed its way up to the pier where a sizeable gaggle of tourists, some with very exotic-sounding voices, waited eagerly to board. As Charlotte skipped across the gangplank and led the way to the front of the boat, Alastair thought she seemed smaller than he remembered her, but then probably everybody did in a place like London.

'There's no need to worry about me, Alastair. You or mi mam,' Charlotte said in a kind voice when they were out on the river. 'I'm quite all right, you know. I can look after myself.'

Alastair nodded, a pained expression coming over his face, not so much in response to Charlotte's confident assertion as to the wind he suddenly felt cutting through his jacket and polo neck. He cursed, wishing he had the clean granddad shirt that was folded neatly, uselessly, in his rucksack in Bayswater. For what little use it was he turned up his jacket collar and stuffed his hands deep into his pockets.

He looked at Charlotte, where she nestled in the crook of his arm, her brown suede jacket pulled tight around her. 'You warm enough?'

'Yes,' she said. 'Lovely, thanks. Are you?'

'Yes,' he said. 'I'm all right.'

By the time they reached Greenwich, most of the other passengers had long since retreated into the warmth of the cabin, leaving the for'ard deck clear for Charlotte to run, at times very animatedly, through the events of the night before. Alastair had no clear recollection of how he'd come upon Charlotte and this 'Eddie' (that was apparently the chap's name, though Charlotte remained vague regarding her relationship to him) as he stumbled through the Soho streets, though he continued to get odd flashes of vision, glimpses of scenes in which he was clinging to some hefty bloke's neck, punching away for all he was worth. A glance at his knuckles, swollen and scuffed, was enough to set them throbbing again.

'It's a wonder you haven't got a great big lump on the back of your head,' Charlotte said as they climbed towards the Observatory. 'Let me see.' Their cheeks almost touching, Charlotte reached around and ran her fingers gently through his hair. It was all he could do not to take her in his arms and kiss her, but he knew that that would be a mistake, that such a move would surely break whatever spell it was they had both fallen so deliriously under.

'Oww!'

'Oops, sorry! Still, it's a lot smaller than the dent you made in Eddie's car.'

From the highest point of the park you could see almost the

whole city, stretching away in all its grey vastness to the hazy beyond. The river, which had seemed fairly straight on the boat, with just the odd gentle turn here and there, was in fact a giant snake, alternately pinched and bloated along its twisting length, uncoiling slowly, darkly towards the horizon. If Alastair had had his camera, he'd have taken a few pictures, but that was also in his rucksack, in sodding Bayswater.

After they had lunch in a pub on the edge of Blackheath, they sat for a while with a drink beside a pond where geese and ducks and model boats glided happily together between the reflections of trees and the kites that danced high above the heath.

Charlotte lit a cigarette and held the open packet towards him. Alastair shook his head. As they talked though, he watched her smoke, the way she tilted her head back and blew her thoughtful clouds high up into the air, how she'd then lick her lips before taking another drag. Her hair was long now, shoulder length, and her figure very much that of a beautiful young woman (he hadn't missed how her breasts pushed perkily forwards under her shirt), but there still remained something of the tomboy about her – the casually assured air, perhaps, a certain toughness of attitude, rather than in her looks.

They talked a bit about Alastair's work, about Monica, and Jumbo, Amelia and the groups. Charlotte was delighted to hear Trevor was now officially going out with Sarah, though she told him he'd been cruel to torment Trevor so relentlessly about it. They laughed about scrapes they'd got into as kids, the things they used to do, the people they once knew. It was all so easy, so comfortable. To be with Charlotte was no effort whatsoever. And he was only mildly annoyed when, perhaps inevitably, she started asking about Mary, if they were all right, was she still very pretty, and did he love her (he laughed), though even then his annoyance felt directed more at Mary, as if she'd physically appeared from nowhere and deliberately sat herself between him and Charlotte, ruining their intimacy. Charlotte said she wondered why he rarely mentioned Mary in his letters. Alastair said he didn't know, changed the subject and did his best to push Mary totally and completely out of his mind. You couldn't feel guilty about somebody you didn't think about.

The clock of All Saints' church struck the half-hour.

'You'd better get going,' Charlotte said, 'or you'll be late for your concert. Come on, the station's just down the hill.'

They'd only a few minutes to wait. The station was quiet, the platform empty but for a couple of cyclists in full road-racing gear and a group of white-haired old dears in their Sunday Best, sounding very excited about a visit to some art gallery. As the rails began to tingle, Charlotte laid her head against Alastair's shoulder, her hand squeezing his where they lay together inside his jacket pocket. The thought that they'd soon have to say goodbye made him feel suddenly very depressed.

'Bloody horrible trains you've got,' he grumbled as the electric unit squealed up to the platform.

Inside the train, Charlotte slammed shut the compartment door and sat down close beside him. 'Alastair, the concert...'

'Will you come?' he said, his face lighting up. 'I'm sure we'll be able to get you in.'

Charlotte shook her head. After studying his face for a moment she suddenly leaned forward and softly pressed her lips to his. When she pulled away, her eyes were sparkling under their dark brows as she shyly nibbled the corner of her lip. 'Will you come home with me, Alastair?' she said. 'Please. Come home with me.'

CHAPTER SIX

'You can get up and change it yourself, next time. If you're going to criticise,' Charlotte said, pressing her nose gently against his.

'It wasn't a criticism. I just said it was a bit soppy, that's all. As it happens, I like it very much.'

'I thought you usually preferred something a bit more *noisy*.'

'I do. Doesn't mean I can't do soppy every now and again.'

Alastair saw how Charlotte's eyes smiled, felt her hand give his side a gentle tickle through his jumper. Her breath was warm against his face and smelled of toothpaste. 'I can see that,' she teased.

As the record turned and Donovan accepted the bittersweet impossibility of capturing either the wind or the girl, Alastair's palm grew hot in the hollow of Charlotte's waist, against the small patch of bare skin where her gingham shirt had broken free of her tweed trousers. Her hand lay between them, its fingers doodling shapes upon his chest. They had lain like this, close and yet at a distance, either side some invisible barrier, for however many 7-inch singles could be stacked on a Dansette, making intimate small talk while gazing nervously, expectantly, into one another's eyes. The last time he'd held her like this – the only time – had been almost three years ago, that sweltering July afternoon, on her mother's bed. A week later she was gone, without a word to anybody.

'I'm sorry you're missing the concert,' Charlotte said as the record player clicked off. The sound of children playing now echoed up from the street. A bus shuddered past. At the partially opened window the orange curtains flapped in and out on the gentle breeze. Alastair recalled how she'd stood there that morning, in her see-through nightshirt.

'*I'm* not,' he said.

'Really?'

'Really.'

Charlotte put her fingers to his mouth, slowly tracing his lips.

172

She stroked his nose, the bristles on his chin for which he'd already apologised, his shaving tackle being, along with everything else, in his rucksack at the guest house. Alastair shifted his hand along her side, where it had become sweaty, slid it further under her shirt. The top three or four buttons were unfastened. By dipping his eyes he'd a very clear view of what lay inside. To be locked in such blissful tenderness was agonising. He wondered how long they were supposed to keep it up.

'Shall I put another record on?' Alastair asked, spying an opportunity to adjust his trousers, which had grown increasingly tight at the front. But Charlotte shook her head. Instead, she raised herself on one elbow and, after looking into his eyes rather seriously for a second or two, lowered herself and began to kiss him, softly and slowly. Although you wouldn't have said so to look at them, Charlotte's lips felt larger, *plumper*, than Mary's when kissed. There was also a much greater sense of urgency about them, even at this gentle pace, in the way they circled, pecked and nibbled, leading rather than being led, which Alastair found infectious as well as most arousing.

After a little while Charlotte rolled over onto her back so that his fingers found themselves caressing the gentle curve of her stomach, the shallow well of her navel, the small, dark mole immediately below. He had an urge to kiss her there, but decided this might be too ambitious a move, so early on. Instead he traced the lacy edge of her bra, felt the silky heat of her breasts where they pushed together and overflowed their tight cups. The throbbing discomfort where he'd risen awkwardly (but majestically! he was sure) inside the flytrap of his underpants was becoming unbearable. But before he'd time to discreetly unsnag himself, Charlotte had pushed him over onto his back and was tugging very determinedly at his belt. With a sigh of relief, he felt himself sprung free, flushing only a little self-consciously as their eyes met and he lay there, looking up in to her eyes as she sat astride him, nibbling her lip with a dreamy, almost drunken, smile on her face. She appeared suddenly like another girl. Another Charlotte at any rate. And for a moment, when she lowered her head, opened his trousers and began nuzzling among the dark tangle of hairs that covered his belly, Alastair thought he might be about to disgrace himself by – as he'd heard Shep once sportingly put it – "blowing his whistle before they'd even kicked a ball".

Yet somehow Alastair managed to hold back, to cool his ardour and play on, at least for now. It helped a little that he'd momentarily become distracted, wondering if Charlotte might ask why his underpants reeked of ladies' perfume – hers, which he'd used to douse his pants and cords that morning to try to disguise the smell of last night's dried piss – but she seemed either not to notice or to care. On the contrary, she now moved her lips up to meet his, and within seconds he felt her fingers tickling against his sides as she pulled him out of his vest and polo neck and fell hungrily upon him. He slid his hand inside her bra, prised it up and over her breasts. The softness of her body, so smooth, so delicate against his rough worker's hands made him feel clumsy, even though he knew his way around a girl plenty well enough by now. He took a sharp breath, scrunched his eyes tight as she pulled back the waistband of his underpants and took him tightly in her hand and...

'Who was that bloke?' he said, suddenly pulling his lips away from hers. It was as if someone else had stepped into the room and asked the question. For although the voice sounded like his, and Charlotte was now looking at him with an expression of stunned disbelief on her flushed face that seemed to point to him definitely having asked it, Alastair had absolutely no idea why he'd chosen to ask such a stupid bloody question – or *any* bloody question – at a time like this. He wasn't entirely sure that he really *had* asked it, or at least that he'd had any say *in* asking it. For some while up until that point he'd been miles away, lost in Charlotte, lost in burning sensuous bliss, his mind as empty as his underpants were full. The words had come from nowhere and burst out of him, seemingly of their own accord.

'*What?*' said Charlotte.

'That bloke, last night. Eddie. Who is he?'

'Doesn't matter now,' Charlotte said, and, smiling indulgently in a way that made him feel like a mardy little boy, she leaned forward and kissed him hotly on the lips. 'Ssshhh!'

His hand was making good progress inside her shirt again,

when suddenly she sprang up, and with an impressively deft action pulled both it and her bra over her head and flung them to the floor. She sat there a while, long enough for him to savour her delightfully perky display, before she fell forward and kissed his mind blank all over again. What did it matter who this Eddie was? She wasn't with Eddie now.

Alastair turned Charlotte gently onto her side so that he could undo the zip on her trousers. She made a little sound as his fingers brushed across the front of her knickers. With his mouth he moved gently down her neck, kissing a gentle path towards her breasts, cupping them in his hands, stroking, circling. He looked up as he felt her shake off her trousers, their eyes meeting as she now moved her fingers up between his legs. Alastair thought that if he became any more aroused something must surely either snap or burst.

There isn't much in the way of material to girls' knickers, and Alastair's hand slid easily inside Charlotte's. A gentleman, he made round the back at first, lingering a while over the firm, shapely curves of her small buttocks, before moving to the front where, with his first two fingers he began very gently to...

'Alastair, what is it?' Charlotte said as he pulled away again. She leaned over him, bare-breasted and confused, irritably tucking a length of dark blonde hair behind her ear.

Alastair frowned. 'I saw him give you money,' he said.

'*What?*'

'In the street. That bloke gave you money, a great big bundle of notes, fivers and tenners.'

Charlotte's mouth fell open a little and she shook her head. 'Alastair, we were – '

'Why? Who is he?' His voice sounded shaky and his jaw felt suddenly very stiff. 'Why did Eddie give you money?'

He knew he was behaving like a bloody idiot, making a terrible, terrible mistake, but he couldn't help himself. By now he and Charlotte should have been lovingly entwined, discovering each other all over again, making up for the years they'd lost, but suddenly there was Eddie leaping before his eyes, Eddie arm in arm with Charlotte, Eddie handing Charlotte a great big bundle of notes in a dark Soho street. Of course, it was no business of his what Charlotte did, nor with whom, but it made no difference. The thought of her being with anybody else was unbearable. He wished Eddie would walk into the room just at that moment, so that he could smash him in the face again.

Charlotte looked at him searchingly for some time. 'You see a man give me money,' she said, 'and the first thing you think of...' There was a look of bewildered desolation in her welling eyes that seemed somehow made worse by the fact she was wearing only a pair of little white knickers.

'Alastair, do you really think that I'd... That I could ever... Oh, Alastair!'

'No,' he started to say, pathetically, as she swung herself off the bed and snatched up her trousers. 'I didn't... I just... Charlotte I'm sorry!'

Why couldn't he have kept his big jealous mouth shut? Why had he had to go and ruin it all and hurt Charlotte so horribly, so unforgivably? The girl who he'd struggle to deny he was still madly, head over heels in love with after all this time, and who, just a few moments ago, had been the only thing that mattered to him in the whole world. As she zipped up her trousers and stood there with one hand inadequately covering her breasts, tearfully fixing him with a look of wounded disappointment, Alastair couldn't imagine that she, or anyone else, had ever looked quite so beautiful. Without taking her eyes off his, Charlotte made a tight little smile, shook her head slowly once or twice, then turned and walked out of the room.

For a good few minutes Alastair remained where he was, shaking with dumb rage in the middle of Charlotte's big old bed. Whatever the beautiful thing they had found together, so briefly, here in this room among the feminine piles of unironed clothes and ramshackle mix of cast-off furniture, whatever it was, or might have been, he knew it was something they could now never get back, that it was gone for ever. He felt angry at Charlotte, at Eddie, and most of all at himself. But of course he'd gone berserk! A man twice her age, who looked like a proper thug and a gangster, giving a young girl money in the street, trying to get her into his car – what else could it have been? He began to wonder if there'd been others, and if so, how many, but something stopped him. Did he seriously believe that Charlotte could ever do that? Not Charlotte.

As he pulled on his polo neck, Alastair caught his reflection looking back, puffy-eyed and sorry for itself, from three dressing-table mirrors. 'You stupid bastard,' he said to himself. 'You stupid, stupid bastard.' He looked across to the bedroom door, pictured her coming through it and throwing her arms around him, the pair of them falling onto the bed. But all that came was the sound of a kettle whistling in some far-off part of the house.

Alastair had pulled on his cords and was just tidying his hair when there came a knock at the door and a polite-looking young man, aged about twenty-five, and with a head full of springy dark curls and a trendy leather jacket which he appeared to wear against his own will, stepped cautiously into the room.

'Oh!' the young man said, his face flushing with a mixture of embarrassment and annoyance at finding Alastair (who was even more disappointed) looking suspiciously back at him. 'Er, do forgive me. I'll pop back some other – '

'Oh, go on in, Gordon!' Charlotte shooed Gordon into the room, set down the tray of tea things she was carrying on the dresser – two mugs, Alastair noted, regretfully – before shifting a pile of clothes from the armchair onto the floor so Gordon could sit down. But for her white bra, which she'd put back on, Charlotte was naked above the waist.

'Don't be silly, it's only Alastair. Alastair's an old friend from home. Known each other since we were babies, haven't we, Alastair?'

'Yes,' Alastair nodded cheerfully, forcing a smile. Charlotte smiled back, her head tilting slightly as she gave a little shrug of her shoulders and which he took to be her way of privately letting him know that she was sorry for Gordon's poorly timed intrusion. She showed not even the slightest sign of the pain and upset he'd caused her just a little while ago. Promising to not be a minute, Charlotte snatched a handful of flimsy items from the clothes pile and padded lightly out of the room, leaving the image of her breasts trembling like two perfectly set jellies hanging in the uncomfortable silence.

Gordon sat forward in his chair, smoothing his trousers over his knees. 'I do hope I'm not intruding,' he said, attempting what he thought was an ingratiating smile. He glanced down at his watch and began to wind it. 'Alastair, wasn't it? Yes. Only, I thought she was expecting me, you see, but... I mean, if you and Charlotte have made...'

'Don't mind me, pal,' Alastair said. 'It's my fault. I'm the one she wasn't expecting. But I'll be off shortly.' Gordon nodded. Alastair studied him for a moment, wondering what business he had calling on Charlotte. Perhaps that was exactly what it was – *business*. He certainly looked the type. And he hadn't seemed the least bit surprised to find her wandering about half-naked, no more than Charlotte had minded parading herself in front of him. Alastair went over and knelt by the record player, hoping The Kinks might take his mind off wanting to smash Gordon in the face and throw him down the stairs. It was either that or burst into tears. Right now he felt he could very easily go either way.

Gordon gave a nod of approval to Dave Davies's opening riff, and turning to Alastair said: 'You say you've known Charlotte for a – '

The door swung open and Charlotte skipped over and sat at her dressing-table. She'd put on a navy blue and white striped sleeveless dress, which went very well with the sharply pointed white stiletto-heeled shoes she now slipped into. 'I'm sorry, Alastair,' she said, rapidly brushing her hair before drawing it back from her face with a broad white band. 'I completely forgot I promised Gordon I'd go along with him to this party – for some friends of his.'

Alastair nodded, he and Gordon looking silently on as Charlotte now popped a large pair of white plastic rings through her ears and skimmed her lips with a pale pink sparkle, pouting in each of the three mirrors in turn. She looked like a film star and Alastair could not have felt more miserable.

Charlotte swivelled round on her stool. 'Why don't you come too? It'll be a lot of fun, and I think there'll be one or two people you might know there.'

'Really?' Alastair looked across at Gordon.

'You'd be very welcome,' Gordon said, not entirely convincingly.

Charlotte flashed an encouraging pink smile. 'You know where the bathroom is. Go and get ready.'

CHAPTER SEVEN

The clock on the dashboard said almost seven. The concert would be finished by now, and Trevor and the boys would already be celebrating with Jumbo after his big performance with Godfrey Payne and The Comforters. He hoped it had all gone well, that the sight of the television cameras and the thousands packed screaming into the Empire Pool hadn't got the better of his pal's nerves so that he'd gone and made a complete balls-up of it. But knowing how Jumbo had played at Skegness, Alastair didn't think that was really very likely. He wished he'd been there to see it. He should have been there, yet he'd chosen not to be, and for what? A bit of tit and a stupid, jealous tantrum. A disastrous and humiliating afternoon, which had surely put paid to the precious bond that had for so long existed, however loosely, between himself and Charlotte.

Alastair wished he was with his friends. Or better still, at home, in bed. Anywhere rather than in the awkward silence that filled the back of the chauffeur-driven Daimler which Gordon, on seeing Alastair's look of surprise as they climbed in, had shrugged off as being simply "*The firm's*".

But Alastair had agreed to go to the party, if only for an hour, so that he might get Charlotte alone and properly apologise. He owed her that much at least. As soon as he'd done that he'd make his way to Marylebone and the first train back to Nottingham. Through the window, he recognised the gates of Greenwich Park. When he turned and looked at Charlotte she gave a little smile then turned away.

Alastair had been told the party was to be held at somebody or other's house, and that's what he'd expected, a house; not what in fact appeared to be some sort of modest stately home, at the end of a crunchy half-mile drive of tree-lined gravel. Beneath the tall gables and darkly gothic windows, bell tower with castellated weathervane, a sweeping crescent forecourt was jammed with cars and the odd small van. Gordon led them round the side of the house, past a converted carriage-house into which the chauffeur now slowly reversed the Daimler, and through a large and apparently uninhabited stable yard, which in turn, via a small gate set into the wall, led to the sprawling grounds at the back of the house. There was a kitchen garden to one side with a long greenhouse and various small outbuildings, while on the other, screened off by tall, manicured hedgerows, was a sweeping terraced garden, dotted about with all kinds of flowerbeds, fountains and statuary – chipped and mossy, and apparently a great deal older than the house itself. Alastair couldn't imagine what sort of people must live in such a place, short of being royalty. But royalty were hardly the sort to pitch a giant marquee in the middle of their lawn, were they? Let alone fill it with a hundred or more young men and women, all drinking, shouting and dancing along to Godfrey Payne and The Comforters' *Wake Up and Shake Shake*, which only a moment before had been exuberantly introduced by the voice of a very well-known disc jockey, from his makeshift station at the side of the small stage.

'Some party,' Alastair said, his mood lifting a little as he noted the musical instruments and amplifier cabinets set on the stage, presumably for use later on. Gordon smiled as he passed back their drinks, a pint for Alastair, white wine for Charlotte, and then saluted them with his rather suspect choice of a bottle of ginger ale. Declining a cigarette, Alastair watched as Gordon then lit two at once, leaving one dangling from his lips while he placed the other between Charlotte's waiting pout.

'Gordy!' A rosy-cheeked fellow in a creased middle-aged suit waved above the jostling heads as he pushed towards them, taking Gordon's hand and shaking it with great, grinning enthusiasm. Steering Gordon aside, Alastair heard the man say '*Thank you*' half a dozen times before making a string of effusive noises about '*the lovely house*', of somebody being '*immensely grateful*', how Denny Heyman was an '*utter darling*', and somebody else having '*always done SO much to help them.*'

'Let's go outside, while it's still nice,' Charlotte said, taking

Alastair's hand and leading him quickly through the dancing crowd. There were more people outside now, standing about the lawn in countless little groups, glasses, bottles and cigarettes moving frequently to and from their mouths. A few lay about on the grass, or sat cross-legged like naughty, overgrown Scouts.

'This is amazing,' Alastair said, when they were alone, walking along the terraced garden.

'Yes, it is,' said Charlotte, sliding her arm through his.

Alastair brought them to a halt by a dribbling fountain. 'Charlotte,' he said, turning to face her. 'Look; about this afternoon.'

'It doesn't matter.'

'It matters to me. Charlotte, what I said, what it sounded like I was...'

'Charlotte!' a sharp female voice called. 'Charlotte! *Hi*!'

'Samantha!' As the girls exchanged kisses on both cheeks, Samantha, although she appeared to look directly at Alastair, neither greeted nor showed any sign of having previously met him twice before, the most recent time being less than eighteen hours ago. He smiled at her anyway, thinking how odd it was that she kept turning up all over the place, first at Skegness, then last night, and now here. But then suddenly it all made sense.

'Yes, Godfrey's here,' Samantha said, waving limply in the direction of the marquee. 'He's over there with the boys, or rather he was, anyway.'

Alastair looked at Charlotte. 'Told you you'd know people,' she said, giving his elbow a gentle squeeze.

'Oh, Charl! They were so marvellous this afternoon,' Samantha said. 'Fabulous! You should have been there. I mean, everyone really *dug* them, you know? Isn't Gordon such a darling to do this?'

While Samantha babbled on, Alastair scanned the vast lawn for Jumbo and the boys, wondering why Charlotte hadn't bothered to mention that the party was for Godfrey Payne and The Comforters, knowing very well that Jumbo had been due to play with them that afternoon and that Alastair had missed the concert to spend the afternoon (disastrously) with her. He didn't understand. But then there were a lot of things he didn't understand about Charlotte and her strange London friends.

'We missed you too, Charlotte,' Samantha said, still babbling. 'Gosh! It was such a super show. They were better than The Beatles-uh-huh, *easily*! And The Rolling Stones too... Well, maybe not *The Stones*! I mean, Mick's like just so *crazy* and er, Wow! You know? Huh? Yes. We're all going down to Dorset on Friday, to Collie Bentham's house. He's in New York for Karl and Raphaella's *opening*.'

Alastair was itching to go and find his friends, yet he couldn't bring himself to leave Charlotte, feeling that he hadn't been able to apologise to her as fulsomely as he'd have liked, as he felt she deserved.

'*Sir*?' Alastair turned to find a waiter smiling as he leaned towards him with a tray full of brimming pints of beer.

'Me? Thanks very much!'

'Thank *you*, sir,' bowed the waiter, swivelling on his heel and marching stiffly back towards the marquee. Alastair had barely sipped the froth off when the waiter's twin appeared with a tray laden with fizzing champagne. Charlotte and Samantha thanked him, giggling as they clinked and sipped.

'Hey, I know *you*!' Samantha said through her posh, toothy smile, sounding as surprised as if he'd materialised suddenly out of thin air. The fading daylight was less kind to Samantha than the nightclub or smoky pub, where they'd previously met, had been. She looked tired, yet still very attractive, and Alastair found her haughty fruitiness strangely appealing. 'You're *Arthur*, aren't you?'

'That's me!' Alastair said with a cheeky grin. 'And you, if I remember rightly, madam,' he teased, going all music hall, 'are *Susan* – am I right or am I right?'

Samantha threw her head back and laughed like she'd never heard anything so hilarious. 'You're so funny!' she said. 'Such a tease! You're not Arthur at all, you fibber! Let me see, you're... *Adam*!'

'Nope.'

'*Alan*!'

'Nope.'

'*Andrew*!'

'Nay, nay, lass!'

On the previous occasions he'd met her, Alastair had put Samantha's forgetfulness down to her always being blind drunk, but he saw now that that was not entirely fair, and that this whole dizzy act was part of some flirtatious little game she liked to play, presumably under the impression that men found dippy rich girls utterly irresistible. Alastair could easily believe there might be some truth in that theory, though personally he was more impressed by her bra-less nipples which poked like two grapes through the thin material of her neat yellow mini-dress. She was drunk again, but no more than half-blindly so.

'*Aloysius*?'

'Aloysius is Sebastian's teddy bear, in *Brideshead Revisited*,' Alastair drawled.

'Really? Then who are you? Are you a teddy bear?'

'No, although I am rather cuddly. Hello, I'm Alastair. Nice to meet you, er, *Sandra*, wasn't it?'

'Oh, you do make me laugh so, Alastair! I'm so pleased you could come tonight. Hey, do you know Hugo Merchant-Hill?'

'Not sure – is that a person or a local landmark?'

Alastair noticed how, as he flirted with Samantha, Charlotte looked on almost proudly at the way he made her laugh. He was thinking how he'd much rather it was Charlotte he was entertaining so effortlessly when suddenly he felt a crippling blow against the back of his thigh and crumpled to his knees in agony.

'Dead leg for being a lousy let-down bastard!'

'Jumbo, you dozy bleeder! You've broken my pissing leg! *And* you've spilled my pint!'

Jumbo kept at a safe distance, shaking with laughter until Alastair had regained enough feeling in his throbbing leg to get up and chase after him, the drummer squealing like a girl as, cheered on by amused onlookers, they zigzagged across the lawn, leaping over flowerbeds and dodging in and out of thick shrubberies. They came to rest after a minute or two, grinning and breathless, against the weathered base of a large stone urn. 'I've heard you were the highlight of the show,' Alastair said, flexing some blood into his numb leg.

Hunched over, hands on his knees, Jumbo nodded slowly, panting like an old dog. 'Was the best... the best day of mi life... Pffff! Tell you, if I die tonight, Alastair... I'll die happy.'

Alastair smirked. 'By the look of you, I'd say there's a very good chance of that happening, you big fat bogger. Do you need an ambulance?'

'You'll need an ambulance when I catch you, you cheeky little bastard.'

But this time Alastair did not run away. He remained where he was and held out his hand to his friend. 'Well done, matey,' he said. 'For today, I mean. I'm so proud of you. And jealous.'

Jumbo looked down at the hand, wafted it away as he threw his big arms around Alastair and almost crushed the life out of him. 'Thanks, pal,' Jumbo said. 'Means a lot. Even though you couldn't be bothered to come and see us this afternoon.'

'I'm sorry, Kenny. I meant to, you know I did. I'd been really looking forward to it, but...' Alastair sighed, wondering where to begin, or if he should even bother. This was hardly the time.

'I heard all about it. Trev filled me in before he went to catch his train. Barry's gone wi' 'im,' Jumbo said. 'I've just seen her, actually – Charlotte. She's changed a bit.'

'Yes,' Alastair said, as he turned and looked across to where he'd been talking with Charlotte and Samantha. But Charlotte was no longer there, and Samantha and another girl were now noisily flirting and laughing between Howie, Brian and Roger, and some other lads he didn't recognise.

Alastair wrinkled his nose. 'What's that stink? Is that you, you sweaty bleeder?'

'So would you be sweating, if you'd... Oh, piss off!' Alastair dodged Jumbo's boot. 'Hey, look Alastair, I've got summat to tell you, but I can't just yet. I'm under strict instructions to keep mi gob shut for the time being.'

'Make sure you do, Kenny! Stick this in it, I find it usually helps.' Alastair nodded in awe as Godfrey Payne gave him a friendly wink and handed Jumbo a bottle of stout. Behind Godfrey, two waiters followed with trays of beer, along with members and friends of The Comforters and The Chequered Saracens. 'Get stuck in,' Godfrey said, as he began passing out the bottles. 'Plenty more where this came from.'

Alastair took a bottle, clinked its neck against half a dozen others, as well as the rim of Amelia's champagne flute as she appeared at Jumbo's side. 'Cheers, Kenny!'

Jumbo downed his stout and called the waiter for another.

'I'll have a pink gin, Sonny, if you can find me one. Yes, a *pink* gin.' Recognising the voice, Alastair turned to see that Denny Heyman, the agent, was standing not very far away with the disc jockey, who, with his bleached scarecrow hair and sequin-trimmed gold kaftan, looked even creepier in the flesh than he did on television. 'I know it's an old poof's drink,' Denny said, waving his cigar about, as if to show how much bigger it was than the DJ's, 'but I don't care, I like it. Now where's that cant Gordon? I need to make a very important phone call and the fakkin' house's all locked up.' The DJ laughed, and Alastair thought he heard him say something about "eager young lovelies", but by then he'd become distracted by the sound of a leather greatcoat flapping across the lawn towards him.

'Jay!'

'Cheers to you, Mr Alastair!' said Jay, bowing a little as he raised his bottle. Alastair smiled, noting with impressed amusement the blue silk scarf Jay wore like a cravat, tucked into the neck of his blue and white striped Breton sailor's shirt, the white jeans that tapered into dodgem-sized brogues. 'Having a fun time?'

'Yes,' Alastair said, smiling as he realised he was rather enjoying himself, in spite of everything. 'I didn't know you'd all be here. I was just saying to Jumbo, I keep expecting a bill for all the beer I've been supping.'

'The waiters come round at the end with a tab. Just be sure to run like the proverbial wind.'

Alastair laughed. 'Hey, I think I just saw Oliver Reed. Going into the tent,' he said, as to the sound of a boogie-woogie piano a dark figure stumbled through the flaps of the marquee.

'Very likely,' Jay said, frowning a little as his eyes made a thoughtful study of Alastair. 'I see you're wearing the same clothes you had on last night. *Intriguing.*'

Alastair shook his head. 'I could have done without intrigue, Jay. I wish I'd just gone back with the lads, and been at the concert today, like I was supposed to be.'

'Like that, eh? Sorry to hear it, my friend. I'm afraid you missed a terrific show. The audience were wild. A little too wild at times. But the sound in there was incredible, considering.'

'I feel awful about missing it, letting Jumbo down. Some pal.'

'I heard you were waylaid,' Jay said, as he snapped the elastic band from his ponytail and shook out his lustrous hair like some beauty in a shampoo advert. 'Young lady from The Blue Parrot?'

'No. Sounds ridiculous, but I got lost and ended up bumping into an old friend from home. She invited me here. Her name's Charlotte. Charlotte Bloomsberry.' Alastair turned again and looked across to where lights now flickered within the marquee as the group on stage belted out an impressively rousing version of *Good Golly, Miss Molly.*

'Oh, I know Charlotte,' Jay said, nodding and smiling vaguely through his full lips. 'Lovely girl.' Jay made another little frown. 'Shame Trevor was unable to stay for the party. Nice fellow, very funny.'

'Yes, he is. I wish he were here too. He's got work in the morning.'

'He's taken your bag, by the way. Said to tell you.' Jay raised his finger, relieved a passing waiter of four bottles. 'Fancy a look about the grounds?'

As Jay led him along the gravel path through a fragrant arch of hedgerow into the kitchen garden, drawing his attention to the various sprouting and budding crops, the immaculate frameworks of climbing vines, as if they were the work of his own hands, Alastair was reminded of Ridgetop Allotments (not that they were comparable to this miniature Eden). He took comfort that if nothing else this weekend he had at least kept his promise to Monica, to drop in on Charlotte and see she was all right, no matter how unintentionally, and in circumstances neither of them would ideally ever have chosen. It would mean the world to Monica that he should return with good news.

'I *say* it's Gordon Bryce-Hart's place, I mean his father's, Lord Manningtrove,' Jay explained as they turned back towards the house. 'They rarely come up here now; it's mostly just Gordon and his friends. He's an odd fish, Gordon, but very decent and proper. He's been very generous to the group. Think he finds it all rather rebellious, this playing at rock 'n' roll. A lot of these public school types seem to. He's an old school chum of Godfrey's — I know, you wouldn't think it to look at him, would you?'

'God's posh?'

'Oh, yes. *Very*. Unfortunately, not in the way that matters these days. His family are very much of the historically titled but presently penniless variety. Hence what you heard last night.'

'Samantha?'

Jay nodded. They came to a stone seat at the far side of the house, overlooking suburban southeast London. Alastair hadn't realised how high up they were, and down below, in the gathering darkness, beyond the dockyard and the river, the lights of the city twinkled liked a grounded constellation.

'And is that how you know them?' Alastair asked. 'From school?'

'Me?' Jay laughed, sweeping back his hair from where the wind had blown it like a scarf across his face. 'I rarely went to any school long enough to make friends.' Jay took out a cigarette and bent to light it within the shelter of his coat. 'My mother was — *is* — a painter. A sort of "free spirit" you might say. We moved about a lot — here and abroad. It was exciting for a kid. My mother used to joke that I had a passport before I even had a name.'

'So that's where you get it from?'

Jay blew out a long plume of smoke and turned to Alastair with question-mark eyebrows.

'Your artistic talents. That brilliant poster you showed us, outside the theatre at Skegness.'

Jay nodded. 'Oh, yes. Yes, I suppose I must. Although my father painted a bit too. He was a writer really, apparently one of great promise according to some critics. He never came back from the war, so we'll never know. Mother would sometimes read me little bits he'd published, poems, short stories. I never knew him.'

They sat a while in silence, drinking slowly as they looked out across the fields and rooftops towards the city. A ship's horn sounded melancholy from the dockyard. The smell of hot food came wafting across the lawn.

'Is this what you always wanted to do then, become an artist and work with groups, theatres, that sort of thing?'

'Heavens, no! I never really thought about doing anything for a job. Still don't,' Jay laughed. 'I've always been able to draw and paint a bit; there wasn't much else to do. I just sort of fell in with Godfrey and the lads because, well, I suppose I knew a lot of the same people from just always being around, a face on the scene, you know?'

Alastair nodded, coolly. He felt rather proud now at having first-hand knowledge of "The Scene", by which he presumed Jay meant the non-stop concerts, parties, nightclubs and girls they all seemed to live for. No doubt it was a very exciting life for a young man – or woman – to lead. Yet it wasn't one he could imagine himself fitting into very easily on a regular basis, or that it would ever really suit him, like it suited Jay. Perhaps it just took practice.

'One day I knocked up a poster for a gig they played in a pub, at Richmond, I think. Then shortly after I took some pictures for a Sunday magazine. It's always been very cool and casual, you see.' Jay stubbed out his fag. 'But it looks like that may all be about to change. PhonoDex Records have asked me to do the sleeves for the group's new LP and next three singles.'

'Wow! That's fantastic, Jay.'

'Suddenly it's all contracts, deadlines and copyright clauses. Hellish stuff. Where's the fun in that? It's nice to be paid for one's work, of course it is, and paid very well, too, I must say, but it all makes me very anxious. The idea of *having* to work, being tied down. I like to feel that if I ever wanted to just throw everything up and push off, then I could, whenever I like, you know?'

Alastair smiled, took a sip of his beer. 'And do you? Feel like pushing off?'

'Not right now. But who knows, in the morning...' Jay tossed the glowing end of his cigarette down into the dark grass. 'And how about you? The trains still keeping you busy?'

The Hollies came jangling across the lawn on the breeze. Alastair, licking his lips, nodded. 'Mm.'

'If you don't mind my saying so,' Jay said, 'you don't seem like a typical engine driver.'

'I'm not. I'm only a Passed Cleaner. But I'm on the footplate a fair bit these days.'

Jay nodded, then, reaching deep into his pockets, pulled out two bottles of Guinness and cracked the tops off, one then the other, against the edge of the stone seat.

'Cheers,' said Alastair, brushing a wispy beard of moss from the glass neck.

'Trevor said you were a scholarship boy, earmarked for university, cap and gown and all that.'

'My dad was always set on the idea, after I got into grammar school. He's a very proud Scot, "all for books and self-improvement, the value of a good education, yi know?"' These last words were uncannily delivered in Jock's careful Lanarkshire drawl.

Jay laughed. 'Sounds like a good chap, your father. And what does he do himself?'

'He's at the pit. Lamp Cabin, these days. He came up with bad skin, from the dust.'

Jay stood and lit another cigarette. 'My mother's a Scot. Argyllshire. She's in Australia at the moment. Hitched up with some fellow daubster and gone to capture the uncapturable Outback, or some other god-forsaken desert.'

As Jay looked out across the city, cigarette smouldering between his fingers, tails of his greatcoat flapping round his knees, Alastair thought he seemed like some ghostly romantic figure from a highland epic. But perhaps that was them talking about his father.

'And was he very disappointed, your father?' Jay asked. 'When you chose not to go to university?'

'Yes, he was. We made this sort of deal where, after a year on the railway, I'd agree to review the situation and then, depending on how I got on, I'd maybe think again about applying to Nottingham. I've been at the shed eighteen months now, and I'm sure he knows what it means to me, but I don't think he's really given up.'

'To study...?'

'English. *Literature*. We never actually got that far, to properly discussing a course, but I think we both just assumed. As I said last night, I've always loved reading, love books – I get that from him, but...'

Jay tilted his head back and blew smoke high into the air. 'It's your life, Alastair. You jolly well drive steam engines, if that's what you want to do. You can't live the life your dad thinks you ought to live – the life he perhaps would have liked to have had himself. If life, such as it is, is to mean anything, you must do what *you* want to do, no-one else. To kill the dream is to kill the spirit.'

'Who said that?'

Jay lowered his drink and looked up to the stars. 'Me,' he smiled. Alastair laughed and took a long thoughtful swallow of Guinness. Jay hadn't said anything Alastair had not already told himself countless times before, though perhaps not quite so artfully, but it meant a great deal coming from him nevertheless.

'The railway's the only thing I ever wanted to do, and since I started I've loved every single minute of it. It's bloody hard work, sure. And I know it must seem ridiculous to you, anyone wanting to be up to their eyes in muck and filth all day, but even now, talking to you, I'm already looking forward to tomorrow night, wondering what sort of a run I might be sent out on. There's nothing like it, Jay, honestly, when you're on the footplate, hammering along; the smells, the heat, the noise – it's glorious.'

'I thought it was only vicars and poets who came over all rhapsodic about steam engines. The sort who never has to get his hands dirty, but you prove me wrong.'

'I've always quite liked getting my hands dirty.'

'Me too,' Jay said, frowning at his closely gnawed, ink-stained fingernails.

'You must do those record sleeves for Godfrey and the boys, you know, Jay. It'll be an amazing thing to have done. Even if afterwards you push off and never do another day's work ever again.'

Jay nodded. 'It wouldn't be very difficult. I've already got an idea – a *concept*, as they call it.'

After a little silence, and when they'd almost drained their bottles, Alastair caved in and took a cigarette. 'Jay,' he said, the smoke catching in his throat and making him feel light-headed. 'How did you say you knew Charlotte?'

'Charlotte? Oh, she's a – ' Jay turned suddenly to where the sound of female giggling seemed to come from beyond the tall hedge. 'Someone's having fun.'

As footsteps scurried away along the gravel path, Jay tossed his half-smoked cigarette into the grass and lifted his eyebrows. 'Time I went and off-loaded some of this ale. I'd go in the bushes, but one never knows who might be prowling about among them.'

CHAPTER EIGHT

The sandwiches – dainty triangular things, lightly filled with cucumber, egg and cress – seemed more suited to a village hall tea party or cricket pavilion than a sweaty tent full of boozy rock 'n' roll types and their various hangers-on. But they tasted delicious, and Alastair, who by now was feeling very hungry as well as being fairly drunk once again, wolfed down as many as he could before the tray was swept away, empty, by a pretty waitress.

On the little stage, a quartet led by a stocky black man on piano raced through a dance floor-pleasing set of soul, blues and R&B standards, his voice sounding equally convincing as Elvis and Mick Jagger as it did for James Brown or Little Richard. And if it hadn't been for the group of people who danced close by him and his friends, Alastair could quite happily have stood there, entranced by their performance, all night. There were perhaps ten or twelve of them, men and women, including, Alastair noticed with surprise, a stunning and well-known film actress and two middling male actors with whom she'd recently appeared in an acclaimed film adaptation of Thomas Hardy; one of the less amusing TV satirists; a suave and perma-tanned male crooner and a top Scottish racing driver. But it was the figure at the centre of this circle, leading a proud and merry jig, who drew Alastair's attention. Skinny, bearded and impeccably attired in tweed jacket and collar and tie above the waist, this odd little chap was, below it – apart from a stout pair of brogues – completely naked. At first, Alastair, noticing the bushy fringe that flowed from the hem of his jacket, thought the man was wearing a lavish but unkempt sporran, on the front of which bobbed some sort of pink acorn insignia. But no...

'Jay,' Alastair said, indicating with a corner of his last egg and cress triangle. 'Why's that chap got his cock hanging out?'

'Cock? Ah, that'll be Willard,' Jay said, through one of his customary frowns. 'He does that sometimes, especially at bashes such as this, where he knows it'll be seen.'

Alastair looked at Jay a moment before turning back to Willard. 'I think I'd avoid drawing attention to myself if that were mine.' Jay laughed, and for a moment the two of them, along with Jumbo, Brian and Howie, who'd come over to see what they were finding so amusing, looked on at this bizarre scene, as the bare-arsed Willard, gleefully clapped and cheered on, leapt and bobbed about among the famous faces and beautiful girls. It was the sort of the thing you sometimes read about in the Sunday papers, the sort of thing you thought never really happened, not in real life.

Brian blew his fringe up out of his eyes. 'And I thought *I* was pissed!'

'What're you all looking at?' Amelia asked, slipping her arm through Jumbo's. 'Urgh, yuk!' she giggled. 'That's horrible.'

'Won't be two ticks,' said Alastair, after Jay had told him, in confidence, of a quiet toilet where there'd be no need to queue. It took him a while to push his way out of the marquee, and once or twice he hovered momentarily, intrigued by the conversations he overheard.

'... well, if he doesn't pull his finger out soon he'll be for the push, I'm afraid...'

'... oh, yes. Exquisite! But unfortunately she also has the sort of thighs which can so often leave a girl lonely...'

'... I say, have you ever been inside an *actual* television studio?'

'... said to Larry, a four hundred seater's about all they can fill these days. And they should think themselves lucky if they even manage that, lazy little turds...'

'... yes, but Vanessa says he's terribly generous in the ways in which he *uses* it. Though I can't for the life of me imagine what she means by that...'

'... no, just ham and a couple of gherkins...'

'... bet you'd look smashing on camera. You know, there may be a position for a pretty, intelligent girl on this new project I'm developing for Rediffusion, but I doubt you'd be interested...'

'... three hundred and sammink thou's all they recovered, so's I 'eard. What, me? Not bleedin' likely, Simon. Mice-well blow me *own* bleedin' 'ead orf!'

'... well, *pigs*, I should imagine – somewhere near Devizes...'

'... you're as pretty as any of our regular girls. Oh, yes... prettier, I'd say, in many ways. But then, it's not just about looks, of course, there's...'

'... tried to get them on this tour with Billy – Eh? – *Fury!* 'Course, he's got The John Barry Seven, ain't he? Well, you can't do better than John...'

'... could be anywhere by now – Spain, Australia, South America. They'll never get it back, though, *never...*'

'... so very few girls have that "special something" that's required for television. I've got the Bristol parked round the front – it's really not very far...'

* * *

Jay's secret toilet was situated in one of the outbuildings at the far side of the kitchen garden, in some sort of gardener's workshop-cum-potting shed. It must have been a treacherous enough place in daylight, but in the pitch dark, after four or five pints, Alastair was lucky not to have broken his neck while negotiating a path between the carelessly parked lawnmowers and rollers, the upturned rakes, lethally dumped forks and pairs of sharp, open shears. The air inside was a rich organic mustiness, thick and heavy as a greenhouse. A little light followed him in through the open door, and around the walls the shelves bowed with the weight of stacked boxes and trays, glass bottles, jars, cans of two-stroke motor oil and numerous unravelling balls of string and twine. Bags of compost and seed packets lay open on the benches, beside a selection of hand tools and a leaning tower of variously sized plant pots.

Alastair had not, in the strict biological sense, *needed* to sit down. He'd simply felt like taking the weight off his feet for a minute or two, and at parties previously he'd always found the toilet as good a seat as any for enjoying a little breather. But he'd never actually fallen asleep on the bog before.

He'd no idea how long he'd been out; seconds, minutes, an hour or more, only that when the noise – a sharp, piercing scrape, like the sound of a heavy wooden table being dragged across a flagstone floor – woke him with a disorientating start, he'd lost all feeling in his legs, so that for a moment or two, until his eyes adjusted, he feared that while he dozed they'd been amputated by some lunatic gardener, using the pair of shears he'd tripped over on the way in.

The noise came again – the scrape. And again. It was coming from the other side of the toilet door, from the potting shed, the table (or whatever it was) shifting repeatedly, although not very far, an inch or so at most each time. As Alastair rose, carefully hoisted his trousers over his numb buttocks, while simultaneously trying to silently stamp the pins and needles out of his legs, he thought he heard another, different, sound. A human sound. It was a sort of long, drawn-out sigh, punctuated occasionally by soft little gasps, rather mournful in their way, though not entirely. The scrape of the table again. Little gasp. Sigh. A girl.

When it fell silent for a moment or two, Alastair pressed his ear hard against the door. Suddenly the girl moaned, briefly, but very loudly. Alastair almost leaped out of his skin. There was something else now, too... Yes... A man's voice. Or rather a deep, poorly suppressed grunt which every now and then would accompany the girl's gentle rhythm of gasps and squeaks.

'Bloody hell,' Alastair said to himself, hopelessly hoping that what was going on out there was not what he suspected. At first he'd thought the noise might simply be somebody who'd had a skin-full escaping to the potting shed for a little privacy in which to throw up their gallon of bitter or Babycham. But the increasingly urgent puffing and panting that now came from beyond the door told him otherwise. The table scraped and the girl whispered '*Ooh-hh!*' and then, a moment later sighed '*Hmm-mmm.*' The man now made a sudden gasp, as if he'd stepped on a carpet tack or put his hand on a scalding iron, and was biting his lip in a desperate effort to not swear.

As Alastair wondered how he was to get himself out of this ridiculous situation, unseen, he noticed at roughly waist height an open knothole in one of the planks of the toilet door. The hole was small and whorled inwards at an unhelpful angle, so that he had to crouch and twist his neck in a most unnatural position in order to see through and into the potting shed, but it was enough to make out the upper portion of a man's back and one broad, steadily rocking shoulder. Of the girl he could see nothing, apart from the fingers of one hand that occasionally gripped the man's arm, or clung tight around his neck as she pulled him towards her, and yet, as her cries and whispers became increasingly more fraught, she seemed as close as if her back were pressed against the other side of the door. It was a curious sensation, being so near to such private intimacy, yet Alastair did not find it the least bit arousing. He was more annoyed at being held captive against his will in a cold and windowless outside toilet.

The table scraped further than previously and something metallic, a trowel maybe, rang out against the flagstone floor. The girl's breathing had become so rapid and so short she sounded like a carpenter's saw hacking through a length of particularly stubborn timber. Alastair thought she might be asthmatic. He knew he had to get out of there fast. If he were discovered hiding in the cubicle after it was all over they'd think he was some sort of peeping tom, which he most certainly was not. At least not intentionally. His experience of such moments told him that if he moved now, immediately, he should be able to slip out and away before this randy young pair finally reached their inevitable end among the bags of seeds and fertiliser.

Very carefully, Alastair slid back the bolt and drew the toilet door slowly inwards, praying that it would neither squeak nor scrape and give him away (he'd taken no notice on the way in, it had hardly seemed important at the time). The girl sighed. The man grunted and made a sudden sharp hiss. The table scraped against the floor. The door opened without a sound and Alastair, relieved, peered out. Less than fifteen feet stood between him and the open door, the moonlit path beyond, and for a moment as he stepped out of the cubicle and stood in the middle of the potting shed, careful not to trip over the snake of hosepipe that lay coiled on its nest of dusty sacks, he thought he could probably have swung his jacket round his head and sung *I'm in the Mood for Love*, for all these two would have cared just then.

Treading as carefully as if he were skirting the edge of an enemy trench on the Somme, he made swiftly across the debris-strewn floor. A quick glance over his left shoulder revealed a pair of slender

196

male buttocks, pale as young mushrooms and going at it like the beam-end of a Victorian pumping engine. The girl sounded as if the carpenter's saw was just about through. Alastair was more than halfway to freedom when suddenly the man made what sounded like a startled growl and started pumping away faster than ever, faster and faster and faster, until suddenly, when Alastair was only two steps from the threshold, there came a horrible wounded cry and the beam-end shuddered and shook to a gasping, knee-trembling halt. Outside, beyond the greenhouse and kitchen garden, Alastair could hear the marquee thumping away on the lawn. Behind him, in the musty shadows, the girl giggled before whispering something soothingly intimate, the sound of lips kissing, of lips being kissed. And then CRACK! Alastair stepped on a rogue plant pot. A landmine. Frozen to the spot, eyes fixed on the moonlit path, he waited for the explosion.

'Who the fakkin' hell's that?' demanded a furious male voice.

'Alastair!' said the girl. 'It's Alastair!'

Alastair slammed the potting shed door hard behind him and ran as fast as he could. There'd been no need to turn round and make sure. He knew it was Charlotte.

* * *

As he skirted the lawn past the marquee, a female singer stretched to reach the high notes of the chorus of *(There's) Always Something There to Remind Me*. Jumbo and Eric Handley both had their backs towards him and he would easily have slipped past unseen had Amelia not just at that moment stepped through the flaps and called him over.

'You found it all right?' said Jay, before turning to the others. 'See, I told you he hadn't left.'

'Have you heard?' Howie asked, his face a picture of childlike wonderment.

'What?' Alastair said, noticing how they were all staring between himself and Jumbo and grinning excitedly. Jumbo opened his mouth as if to speak, but then, seeming to come over all self-conscious, started to read the label on his beer bottle instead.

Eric smacked Jumbo playfully across the shoulder and shook

his head. 'We was just sayin', we're doing a show in Nottinum in a capple of months – June, I think – and you lot should all cam along and see us. Bring your missus.'

'Trevor's going to take Sarah,' Amelia smiled.

'Thanks, Eric,' Alastair said, still barely able to believe the famous guitarist was talking to him at all, let alone as if he were a friend. 'That'd be brilliant.'

Alastair turned and looked back over his shoulder, across the lawn towards the kitchen garden.

'We thought it'd be a larf,' Eric continued. 'Bit of a do, you know – a sort of homecoming for Kenny.'

As Alastair nodded he saw how everyone else was now grinning again. It took a moment for Eric's words to sink in. He wondered where Godfrey Payne was. The last time he'd seen him he was lying on the lawn between three beauties and a bottle of champagne.

'*Homecoming*? How'd you... Are you gonna let him play with you till June?' Alastair looked at Jumbo. 'That's fantastic, Jumbo!'

Jumbo ran his hand over his prickly head and took a long gulp of beer. Eric nodded, a knowing smirk on his face as he said, 'He'll be with us a lot longer than June, my friend.'

'Eh?'

'As of this afternoon, Kenny-boy is now officially full-time drummer with Godfrey Payne and The Camferters.'

'What? No! He's in the group? *Properly*?'

'Yep.'

'*Jumbo*?'

'Yep.'

Amelia squealed as she threw her arms around Jumbo and kissed his grinning lips.

'That's...' Alastair looked around the table at his smiling friends, old and new. 'That's bloody unbelievable! Shit! Congratulations, Ken, that's... Wow! You're in Godfrey Payne and The Comforters!'

'I know! Stop staring at me like that, Al, and have a drink!' Jumbo held out a bottle. Alastair smiled, but shook his head.

'I'm afraid I've got to get going,' he said, glancing at his watch.

'What? We're havin' a party!' said Eric.

Howie tapped his elbow. 'Thought you were staying with us

tonight?'

'I can't. They've switched my shift at work tomorrow. Forgot to say. Look, have a good night, and, er... I'll see you all soon. Well done again, Kenny, and er, thanks, Eric. Brilliant.'

As he ran along the terrace, past a dark porch on the side of the big house, the scene in the potting shed returning vividly to the front of his mind, a voice called after him from the shadows. 'Did you manage to find your friend tonight, Alastair?'

'Yes, thanks, Penny,' he said bitterly, without looking back. To avoid a couple who were getting very cosy against a sundial, he leapt a low hedge and cut across the grass towards the courtyard. More cars had arrived by now and it was a job to weave between them at any great speed, so that in his angry impatience he smashed carelessly against protruding bumpers and wing mirrors with his shins and elbows. When he was in sight of the long drive he stopped to have a piss against a Dormobile. The music from the marquee seemed louder than ever.

'Boo!' It took a moment to locate the voice. But then Alastair saw Samantha grinning devilishly from the half-lowered window of an old grey Wolseley shaped like a jelly mould. 'I do hope you're not running away from me,' Samantha said, in a sultry, whimpering voice. If she hadn't been blind drunk when he'd spoken to her on the lawn earlier, then she certainly was now. Alastair was perhaps twenty feet away from the car, but it was close enough to see that Samantha's dress was unzipped and that she was struggling to hold it over her front while at the same time lean through the window with a glass of champagne. As Alastair looked at the dishevelled girl, the fogged rear window squeaked slowly down and another girl he recognised from earlier appeared in a halo of cigarette smoke.

'Pam, this is Aristotle,' Samantha slurred. 'Aristotle, this is Pam. Pam thinks you're sexy, Aristotle. Don't you, Pam?' Pam giggled but did not speak. On her top half Pam wore only a cream bra and a small silver crucifix.

'Aristotle's from the north,' Samantha said. 'Where was it you said again?'

'Nottinghamshire.'

'Notting-*ham*-shire.'

199

'Ooh, I know Nottingham,' said Pam, her breasts pushing against the glass of the lowered window. 'Do you work down t'pit, lad?' she sniggered, setting Samantha off.

'No, I don't.' Alastair said. He was in no mood for this pair now and he turned to walk away.

'Yer don't work down t'pit, lad? Wi' t'coal 'n' t'donkeys?'

'T'pit!' Samantha repeated, giggling. 'T'pit! Oh, go on, Alastair. Be a darling and say something *northern* – like you did before. Oh, *go on*. He's *so* funny, you know, Pam.'

As she tilted her head and fixed him with her empty-eyed smile, Samantha's dress slipped off her shoulder. She looked down at herself, smiling as very casually she re-covered an exposed breast. Pam, who'd started hiccupping, dipped inside the car and returned a few seconds later, a cigarette glowing between her fingers. Alastair stood there, digging with his toe in the gravel. The sight of these two silly, pissed-up girls filled him with pity as much as anger. The tightness he'd felt in his chest since the scene in the potting shed was now almost suffocating. Now, the more he looked at them and the longer he remained there, the more he wanted to shout, to lash out, at them, at anybody. He took a few steps closer. 'What are you doing in that car?' he asked.

'Drinking!' Pam said. 'Would you like some champagne? You'll have to go and fetch some more, though, ours has all gone.'

Samantha reached out as if to touch him, but couldn't quite reach. 'Got a light?'

'Afraid not.'

As Pam flicked her lighter towards Samantha she smiled, noticing him eyeing her body. 'You can come in here with us, if you fetch some champagne,' she teased. 'Or you and I could perhaps go somewhere a little quieter...'

'Told you she liked you,' Samantha said.

Alastair knew exactly the sort of somewhere a little quieter Pam had in mind. The thought of it again now almost choked him. It was not Pam's fault, he knew, but just then he could have smacked her clean across her stupid face, the silly little slut. Samantha too, while he was at it. He stepped away from the car, shaking with rage, his fists clenched tight as rocks. He was about to tear off down the drive when a voice called jovially from behind him. 'Shampers!'

As the two girls clapped excitedly, Alastair turned to see Willard crunching across the gravel towards them, his bushy acorn jiggling at the hem of his jacket as he waved a bottle of champagne high in the air. Willard came to a halt beside Alastair, tilting his head and smiling ingratiatingly as he presented the red label and said, 'Who would like to share my lovely bubbly shampers?'

It was terribly poor timing on Willard's part. He couldn't have known Alastair didn't like champagne, nor that he was no longer in any sort of mood for partying, especially with upper-class arseholes who went about with their pitiful cocks hanging out. Alastair smashed his fist about as hard as he could into Willard's hairy little face, spinning him through 180 degrees before he bounced off the wing of a Zodiac and fell in a pathetic heap among the gravel, where he lay bleeding and bewildered between shards of fizzing glass. 'Now put some fucking trousers on!' Alastair growled.

Fists still clenched, he shook with the temptation of giving Willard some more, but he knew, the way he was feeling just then, that if he started he might never stop. When he looked up, Samantha and Pam were watching him, horrified. 'I'm sorry,' he said. Then he turned and ran as fast as he could towards the gates at the end of the long gravel drive.

CHAPTER NINE

The main road was quiet and mostly downhill, and in no time at all he'd covered easily three miles before it levelled off across the dark, open heath. By now the last train north was long gone, but Alastair did not run faster than he'd ever run before just to get to a railway station, or to anywhere else. He ran only to get away. His fists bunched, teeth clenched, he pounded the uneven pavement, throwing every last bit of energy he had into each long, seething stride, hoping that if not this one then perhaps the next might be the one that finally made his heart burst. When the taxi clattered up alongside him and Charlotte opened the door and pleaded with him to get in, his cheeks were wet with tears, so he was grateful for the light rain that had begun to fall a short while before.

He returned from the bathroom to find her pouring tea into a pair of Coronation mugs on the tray she'd set out on the ottoman at the foot of the bed. She'd changed out of the blue and white striped dress and was once again wearing her drab old nightshirt. Her hair, now she'd discarded the white band, fell forward over her face as she carefully poured the milk. There was no sunlight behind her now, only the light of a pair of table lamps and the sleepy glow of the night through the orange curtains.

After hovering awkwardly for a moment on the threadbare rug, Alastair turned his back on her and leaned against the mantelpiece, waiting, though for what exactly he hardly knew.

'Your tea's there,' Charlotte said, sounding as sweet as she had when she brought his breakfast that morning. 'Won't you come and sit down and drink it?'

If he'd have kept his mouth shut, if he'd kept his suspicions to himself and they'd slept together – *properly* – that afternoon, would she still have gone to the party? he wondered. Would they both still have ended up here, now, like this?

'I'm sorry,' Charlotte said, for perhaps the fifth or sixth time since they'd arrived back at the house. 'And anyway, what does it matter?' Her voice remained calm, but Alastair knew from her expression that her patience was wearing thin. Before he'd gone to the bathroom they'd already spent twenty minutes going round and round in bickering circles, he demanding an answer, she refusing to give one, over and over, neither of them willing to give in until eventually, exasperated, Charlotte had got up and stormed out.

'What difference does it make *who* it was?'

'I'd just like to know, that's all,' Alastair said, tap-tapping his bruised knuckles against the edge of the mantelpiece. 'Why can't you just tell me?' He turned round. '*Who* was it?'

Charlotte lifted her mug slowly to her lips, sipped her tea as if she'd not heard him. Alastair went to the dressing-table, picked up a heavy crystal bottle containing perfume, glanced at the label and put it back down again. He watched in the angled side mirror as she resettled herself in the middle of the bed. When she curled her legs under her, her knees poked out of the hem of her nightshirt. She seemed suddenly very vulnerable and childlike. And yet the last time he'd seen her knees, in the potting shed, they were...

'You surely can't have forgotten already?' he sneered. 'Let's see, was it... *Gordon*? With his chauffeur-driven car and daddy's fairy-tale castle?'

Charlotte looked down into her mug.

'Well?'

'Please don't shout, Alastair.'

'Tell me then. *Gordon*?'

'No,' she said, very quietly.

'What?'

'I said, *no*, it wasn't Gordon.'

Charlotte swept one side of her hair away, tucked it behind her ear. In all the years they'd been friends she'd never known Alastair behave like this, had never seen him particularly upset, as far as she could recall. So to see him now, and know that all the pain, all the hurt and confusion she could see in his eyes and hear in his voice was all because of her, was unbearable. She hadn't meant for this to happen, not any of it.

Alastair shoved his hands deep into his pockets. 'So who, then?' he said after a short silence. 'The one with the poncey fag-holder – actor, was he? The Welsh bloke you seemed to be on such friendly terms with? Perhaps it was our friend *Willard*, Willard-the-fucking-wisp, the stupid... Christ knows what the hell he thinks he's supposed to be. But why not Willard? He's already dressed for the part! Well if it *was* him, I'm glad I gave him a damn good pasting.'

'*You* hit Willard?'

'And he'll get another if I ever see him again. *Who* was it, Charlotte?'

Alastair felt his temper rising, starting to get the better of him again, and in a way it was a relief to them both when they were interrupted by a gentle knock at the door.

'Charlotte, is everything all right?'

'Yes, Deanna, it's okay. We were only messing about. *Night*, love.'

Charlotte remained still for a moment, her eyes fixed on those of Mick Jagger peering out from his hood on the back of the bedroom door, while Deanna's footsteps receded across the landing. When Charlotte turned to Alastair she did so with a sigh that seemed to say, enough, let's stop this now, *please*. They were both very tired as well as having had far too much to drink. All this upset was just so *unnecessary*. It could never serve any purpose other than to make them both feel even more bloody miserable than they already did. But Alastair could not stop.

'Perhaps it was that other chap, big moustache and leather waistcoat. No? Or Mr Toad, who came sucking up to Gordon – *him*?' While Alastair glared at Charlotte a thought struck him. 'Not Godfrey? Yes, I should've thought of him before. Was it Godfrey Payne? The greedy bastard, he can't walk past a skirt without having a look underneath to see if his name's written on their knickers. Was it him, Charlotte? Was it Godfrey? *Tell me* if it was Godfrey!'

Charlotte buried her face in her hands, her head shaking slowly from side to side as she began to sob. 'No,' she sniffed.

'Wasn't Godfrey.'

'*Not* Godfrey?'

Charlotte, openly crying now, but trying to keep it down so Deanna wouldn't hear, shook her head again and repeated 'No.' Alastair stood shaking in helpless rage, trying to hold back the tears he felt welling at the corners of his eyes. She would never tell him, he realised, no matter how much he screamed and shouted, and in a way, though he perhaps didn't know it himself just then, Alastair didn't really want to know who Charlotte had been with in the potting shed. There are times, where the heart is concerned, when the truth is the very last thing you need.

'What about the letters?' Alastair said, quickly wiping his face.

Charlotte shook her head, confused at this sudden swerve. 'What letters?'

'The letters you wrote to me. That I've been writing to you, all this time.'

'What about them?'

'Why did you write them?'

Charlotte frowned, shook her head, baffled. 'I like writing to you, Alastair. And I thought you liked writing to me. We're friends, aren't we?' Alastair let the question hang in the air. Charlotte took a sip of tea. 'And I told you, that for a long time after I left home I... I missed you.'

'Missed me! You missed me so much that the first time you see me after three years you're off, within half an hour, banging Christ-knows-who in a fucking greenhouse! *When* did you miss me? When there was nobody else to take you out in their fancy cars, get you pissed-up on pink champagne and do what they bloody well please with you? Is *that* when you missed me? Well thank you very much! S'pose I should be grateful. It must've been hard to find five minutes to write a few lines to muggins Alastair, up north with nothing better to do than sit about waiting for the soddin' postman! I'm not blind, you know, Charlotte. Jesus, how many fucking boyfriends *have* you got?'

Charlotte uncurled her legs, her nightshirt riding up as she slid off the bed and padded barefoot over to him. When she put her hands on his shoulders all he wanted to do was to gather her up in his arms and kiss her all the way back to yesterday afternoon. But how could he, after all he'd seen?

'It was nobody, Alastair. Please try to forget about it,' she said, slipping her arms through his and resting her head against his chest. She held him tight. 'I don't have any boyfriends. I don't have anybody. Never have done, not really – not in the way you think. And I write to you because no matter what you believe, I *do* miss you, Alastair.' Charlotte took a step back and, taking his hands, looked up into his eyes. 'You're my oldest friend, Alastair. Or at least you were. You've never been anything but lovely to me, you've always found time for me – which is more than I can say even for my own mother, who never has, always too busy having a good time herself to take any notice of me, her selfish, inconvenient daughter. Ha!'

Charlotte lowered her eyes and fell silent. Alastair watched her a moment, confused by her beauty but also by the sadness that filled her faraway expression. He saw how her throat rose and fell when she swallowed, her chest as she breathed. The first few buttons of her nightshirt were unfastened, as they had been that morning, and a deep shadow fell between her breasts. He pushed a horrible scene out of his mind and took her in his arms, Charlotte, just as she was, here and now.

'I'm surprised she even noticed I'd gone,' she said, pulling him close once more. 'Oh yes, mam was always quick to notice if the gin was low, or when her fags went missing. But not me. I don't know why I'm surprised. She never wanted me in the first place.'

'Don't be daft,' Alastair said, his chin brushing against her hair. 'I know you've had your ups and downs, but your mam thinks the world of you. She asked me to come down and spy on you, remember? Monica loves you. You're everything she has.'

A few minutes earlier, he'd have been sharp to point out how it was a bit rich – considering the company she kept and the way she carried on – for Charlotte to be criticising her mother for her loose and slatternly ways. But for the moment he was trying to remember exactly how Monica had suddenly crept in and derailed their argument.

'Maybe. But it's true,' Charlotte said, very shakily. 'She didn't want me. That's why she's always hated me. I'm a constant reminder of how she tried to get rid of me, and herself while she was at it. It's only thanks to your dad she didn't manage it.'

Alastair took her shoulders. 'Monica has never hated you, Charlotte. Don't be so silly. What are you talking about? Where's this all come from?'

'From Eddie.'

'*Eddie*!' The bitterness and hatred which had begun to ebb away these past ten, fifteen minutes came suddenly flaring back up again and Alastair stepped back, throwing Charlotte's hands away, her touch, which only a moment ago he'd found so comforting, now filled him with utter disgust.

'Yes, *Eddie*,' Charlotte said, a note of defiance in her voice as Alastair turned his back.

'I'd forgotten about bloody *Eddie*!' he snapped. 'I thought you had too, the way you dropped your knickers for your new mystery man in the potting shed. Who was it, Charlotte? Tell me! I'm surprised you didn't have them form a queue across the lawn, let them all have a go – Come on! Charlotte's open for business!' And in a sudden vicious swipe, Alastair sent the contents of Charlotte's dressing-table flying through the air, bottles, jars, boxes, creams, powders, perfumes – the lot – smashing against the wall and clattering across the floor. Boiling with rage, he was hardly aware of what he was doing as he grabbed Charlotte by the arms and flung her backwards on to the bed, knocking over the teapot as he leapt after her and sat across her chest, twisting his fingers into the fabric of her nightshirt as he pulled her face up close to his. His hands shook like he was holding a road drill as he glared into her frightened eyes. He felt utterly confused, didn't know whether to push her away as far and as violently as possible, or take her in his arms and hold her so tight and never let her go ever again.

'Charlotte? Are you sure you're – '

'Go away, Deanna!' Charlotte said, her eyes not leaving Alastair's. 'It's all right, love. I'll see you in the morning.'

'If you're sure?'

Alastair released his grip on Charlotte's nightshirt. Deanna's door banged shut.

'It's not what you think, Alastair,' Charlotte said calmly, as one plump tear after another raced glistening trails down her cheeks, turning the blonde hair dark just above her ears. 'Not with Eddie.'

'Isn't it?' He felt her whole body begin to shake under him, and then Charlotte covered her face with her hands and began to cry as if she'd been saving up a whole life's worth of heartache just for this moment. He could have cried himself as he looked down at her.

'No, Alastair. Eddie... Eddie's my dad.'

Outside it was Monday morning. The heavens had opened and Alastair could hear the rain pouring down on the Camberwell pavement.

CHAPTER TEN

For nearly half an hour they lay in one another's arms while Charlotte sobbed herself calm enough to tell him all about her life in London and her search for her father, Eddie Gardner. Perhaps not all; there were one or two incidents – one in particular – that she chose deliberately not to mention, as much to avoid reminding herself of their unpleasantness as to protect Alastair from any more hurt and upset, which she knew they were only bound to cause.

At first she'd worked in a biscuit factory, on the south side of the river, not far from Tower Bridge. It had been a dull, monotonous job, but the other girls had been nice, and it paid enough that she could afford to spend two or three evenings a week trawling the clubs and bars of Soho, nursing halves of lager and lime while she looked out for an Eddie who resembled the grinning young soldier in the twenty-year-old black and white photograph she kept in her purse. Monica had said he'd gone back to run some such dive straight after the war, and was still there as far as she knew, or cared. It hadn't been much to go on. The best part of a year passed and Charlotte had all but given up when a friend whom she'd arranged to meet in Leicester Square, to go to the pictures, failed to turn up, and so, in no hurry to return to the dismal bedsit where she then lived, she decided to have a quick drink by herself. The sign promised "Live Jazz Till Late" but it was still very early, so she presumed that was why the dingy basement was almost empty and the jazz piped-in through speakers. Charlotte got talking with the barmaid, a friendly girl named Deanna (who soon became her housemate) and, for the sake of conversation more than anything else, found herself asking if there might be a job going.

'You might be in luck,' Deanna had said, but she'd need to check with Eddie to make sure he hadn't already got some other girl in mind. He usually had. Charlotte's heart skipped at the name, and when, a little while later, Eddie appeared, leaning casually against the bar beside her, she knew him immediately. He was handsome and very charming, in a rough sort of way, though fatter and shorter than she'd imagined, and after quickly looking her up and down he'd nodded and said she'd "Do just fine", sealing the deal by giving her a sharp slap on the bottom as she climbed the narrow steps back up to Frith Street.

As hostess, Charlotte said, snuggling tight against Alastair's chest, she'd been able to observe Eddie very closely as he went about his business at The Hot Foot Club – and a pretty shady business it was too, at times. At first she'd tried hard to get to know him, to see the sort of man Eddie was, and had waited patiently for the right moment to reveal herself as the daughter he'd never seen, the child he'd fathered while stationed at Nettleton Camp, a few miles north of Warinstowe, in the summer of 1942. But it was difficult to talk to Eddie. The club was mostly busy whenever he was around, it being popular with tourists as well as the freewheeling coterie of regulars – boozers, artists, writers, the highly acclaimed musicians it was renowned for drawing most nights of the week – so he was rarely ever alone. But in the end Charlotte was glad she hadn't just rushed in.

As for women, well... There was no question that Eddie liked female company, but of what kind! They came and went frequently enough, but none ever stayed for very long, sometimes only minutes. More than once Charlotte had absent-mindedly wandered into Eddie's office, to lock away the night's takings, and found him with a woman – two, on one occasion – half-undressed and drunk, or worse. Dolly birds. Tarts. Rough sorts. Once she'd found him face down on the old moth-eaten sofa wearing only his underpants, an empty whisky bottle at his feet and his turned-out wallet lying on the grubby lino. Late one night a thin woman had slashed her wrist in his office with a broken bottle, though neither she nor the incident were ever mentioned again.

Soon afterwards, Charlotte made up her mind to quit The Hot Foot Club. Eddie Gardner was a vile, sleazy man, a drunk and a racketeer who used prostitutes and took drugs, the sort of man she couldn't bear to work for a single shift longer, let alone acknowledge as the father she'd waited her whole life to meet. She decided to leave as soon as she next got paid, without telling Eddie who she was. But then Eddie did something which left her no choice.

'Oh, Alastair!' Charlotte began to shake and sob uncontrollably in his arms all over again. He held her tight, told her it was okay. 'I'm here,' he said, smoothing back her hair where it had fallen over her hot, tear-stained face.

'He asked me to go to his office one night,' she said, when she'd settled down once more. 'He asked how I liked working there, said how pleased he was, how I'd soon be running the place all on my own. He was *very nice*, Alastair.'

Alastair nodded. His left arm was numb where she'd been lying on it. As he tried to wriggle it free, Charlotte pushed him onto his back and laid her head upon his chest. He put his arms around her and kissed her hair so gently she'd never feel it.

She went on. 'Then he poured us a drink. I said I didn't like whisky, not even the smell of it. So he drank mine as well as his. Then he started laughing and saying all these horrible, vulgar things, like how he knew what I *did* like, what girls like me liked. He kept on saying it, over and over, "I bet I know what you *do* like." I stood up and said I was leaving and... He just came at me like an animal.'

Alastair swallowed hard, the anger steadily building again as Charlotte told how Eddie had then gripped her arms so tight she couldn't move, how he'd hurt her as he kissed her "horribly". She had tried to turn away, to push him off, but he had easily overpowered her and she felt herself being shoved down onto the sofa where, after slapping her hard once across the face he'd stuck his hand up her skirt and actually torn off her knickers. His belt buckle fell with a heavy thump against the lino and Charlotte screamed out as she felt her skirt being pushed roughly up her thighs. She smelled the whisky on his breath. Cigars. This could not be happening. With all her strength she hammered her fists against his arms, his face, his shoulders, shouting 'Get off! Get off me! No, Eddie! *No*!' When Eddie paused for a second, grinning viciously as he leaned back to wrench off his tie, Charlotte took her chance and kicked out as hard as she could, smashing the heel of her shoe right between his legs and then, just to make sure, as he fell back wincing in agony, she punched him full in the face with her trembling fist. 'Stop it, Eddie! You must stop it, now, *please*!' she said, leaping up and straightening her skirt. 'I'm Charlotte, Eddie. Monica Bloomsberry's baby – remember? I'm your daughter!'

'I thought he was going to kill me,' Charlotte said, shaking, 'but he just turned away and told me to get out.'

Alastair drew her close. 'I knew I was right about him. I should have killed the bastard last night. How could he? His own daughter.'

'He hadn't known that when...'

'I don't care! If I ever see him again...'

They lay in silence a while, Alastair feeling his fingers wet where they stroked her cheek.

'When did all this happen? I mean, when he – '

'November before last. A few days after, he told Deanna to ask me to go in to see him. I never went back. But then, last week, out of the blue, he turns up here and invites me to dinner. That's where we'd been last night, when you saw us near The Blue Parrot. He said he didn't want us to remain on bad terms. After a year and a half! He asked about mam, how she'd been, if she had married. And he told me a bit about his life, though not much I hadn't already worked out for myself. He'd known about me, though, right from the beginning. That was a surprise. I sometimes used to wonder if mam had ever even told him.'

Charlotte stopped to find a tissue and blow her nose. 'He said that they'd had a lot of fun together, at the time, him and Monica. But he hadn't thought it had been anything more, to either of them, than just a brief romance, a fling, like everybody had in the war. He said it was "complicated" when he found out about me. His regiment was sent abroad. And then, when it was all over, he came back home, to London, and forgot all about us. He said people did a lot of forgetting after the war. I told him I hadn't. It was hardly the reunion I'd imagined all those years, how what a

212

lovely surprise it would be when we first met, all the fun we'd have getting to know – ' Charlotte began to sob again, softly this time.

'And did he apologise? For what he did to you?'

'He was very sorry about that.'

'But now that he's met you, finally, isn't he at all pleased?'

Charlotte shook her head. 'The money you saw him give to me, that you thought was for...'

'I'm sorry,' Alastair said. 'I was very drunk, and him giving you all that money in the street, I didn't know what to think.'

'A hundred pounds.'

'That's very generous.'

'It was a gift, on the understanding that I never try to contact him ever again. That's how pleased Eddie Gardner was to finally meet his daughter.'

'But...'

'He said he was glad we'd met, but it was probably best for all of us if we left it at that.'

When Charlotte gazed up at him with a resigned smile, her tears were drying on her cheeks. But the sadness remained in her eyes and Alastair felt utterly useless for wishing he could drive it away, knowing he never could. She lay on his chest and began to speak now in an almost cheery voice.

'After he carried you up here last night, Eddie said you were a hot-headed young pup who couldn't hold his drink, but that if you were anything like your father you'd be the sort of bloke I should be very lucky to have as a friend. It was a funny feeling, hearing him drive away while I struggled to get you undressed.'

They lay for what seemed a long time breathing into the silence, against the ticks and creaks of the old house. A car sloshed past in the rainy street below. But the mention of his father had reminded Alastair of something Charlotte had said in the heat of their argument.

'What did you mean earlier, when you said that if it weren't for my dad you wouldn't be here?'

There was a short pause while Charlotte pulled a blanket over them and repositioned herself on his shoulder. She cleared her throat. 'She tried to do herself in – Monica. In that little flat over

213

the paper shop. She nearly succeeded as well. Ginned-up to the eyeballs and a bellyful of pills. Eight months gone with me, she was. It was only luck that Jock happened to be passing. He was home on leave and, well, I suppose Eddie must have told him Monica was up the spout, but anyway he went to look in on her and... He found her on the floor. Jock saved her. And me.'

'*Mi dad*?'

'Mam told me once that it was your dad who she'd really fancied. They all met in the Fox & Hounds. She thought he was lovely. But Jock only ever had eyes for Gladys, so she had to settle for his pal Eddie instead. And look where that got her, eight months later – Tuxfield General, with a thick head and me bawling in her arms. Served her right, selfish cow.'

'It can't have been easy for her,' Alastair said, wondering as the details of this many-layered drama slowly sank in, why his father had never bothered to say anything to him about all this. But then he wouldn't, would he, not Jock. Same as he probably would never have mentioned it either to Gladys or to anyone else, had it not been for the gawping circus which had gathered that afternoon to see Monica's anticipated corpse being carried out and driven away in the ambulance, a salacious cloud of tittle-tattle ringing in its wake. It sounded more like the plot of a black and white film than anything real, especially with his father, the unlikeliest of heroes, at the centre of it all. But it explained a lot, about Monica, about Eddie, about Charlotte. It still left several dark corners unexplained, of course. But, as it had now begun to dawn on Alastair, it was perhaps better to leave them that way.

It was not how he'd pictured his weekend in London drawing to a close. And yet as he lay there, wincing at how foolishly he'd behaved, and how only forty-eight hours earlier, if asked, he'd have said he was going steady – and quite nicely too, more or less – with Mary Windale, there seemed somehow a sort of inevitability about now finding himself in Charlotte's bed. He realised how all this time he'd been clinging on to some hopeless adolescent fantasy; that for three years some precious part of his heart had been kept warm, *alive*, by the remote possibility of Charlotte. Pointless, he knew. Yet even now didn't a part of him *still* hold on to some slight sliver of hope?

Charlotte might have been eavesdropping on his thoughts, for suddenly she put her lips against his ear and whispered, 'I love you.'

'Do you?'

'Yes.'

Charlotte raised herself on one elbow and, smiling, studied his face as if she had for a moment completely forgotten what he looked like. 'I love you like I've never loved anyone else. And like I know I will never love anyone else. Ever.'

Alastair felt tears pushing at the corners of his eyes, but managed to prevent them from getting any further. '*But?*'

'But not in the way Mary loves you, Alastair. Not in the way you love Mary. And I know you *do* love her, and you should.'

It was a curious sensation to be thinking of Mary while Charlotte leaned over him, the neck of her nightshirt gaping open so that he could see inside, all the way down to the patch of dark shadow between her legs.

'I love you, too,' he said. 'I have done since *forever*. I always thought – hoped – we'd be together, even when you went away, the week after we... I thought that one day you'd come back and... I suppose I just wish...'

Charlotte shook her head. 'You don't.'

'You could've come back; you still could. Why not? We could forget about all the stuff that's happened, this weekend, the party, everything. We could...' Alastair heard his voice crack and it was all he could do to keep his quivering chin under control.

'We couldn't, Alastair,' Charlotte said. 'It wouldn't...'

'But I still love you.'

Charlotte tilted her head. A tear ran down her cheek; Alastair caught it, very gently wiped it away with his thumb.

'Alastair, you know you don't like what you've seen. The sort of people I go about with, how I live. The Charlotte you love, she's not me. The girl I was when I was sixteen, seventeen, she's the Charlotte you love. But I'm not her. She's gone. She changed, she – she grew up, I suppose.'

'I still think about that afternoon, you know. On your mam's

215

bed. You were nineteen then.'

He felt a heavy tear crawl down his cheek now. Charlotte nodded. 'I know,' she said. 'I think about it too.' And she leaned forward and kissed him softly on the mouth. Her lips were hot and salty with tears. His hand found its way to her hip, felt the warmth of her curves through the thin nightshirt.

'I want you,' he said, as Charlotte pulled the blankets over them and snuggled under his chin.

'It's not me you want, Alastair. You only think you do. What you really want is a version of me that doesn't exist. A Charlotte that lives and behaves like Mary. But I can't be like Mary, Alastair. I never was and I never could be.'

Alastair wrapped his arms tight around Charlotte, kissed the top of her head and closed his eyes.

CHAPTER ELEVEN

'I hope you appreciate me trailing all the way across London, this time of the morning,' Charlotte said, glancing up at the huge clock. It was a little after half past nine, and beneath the twin-arched roof of King's Cross Station diesels throbbed, restless for the north.

Alastair nodded. 'But you really didn't have to, you know,' he said, thinking how much easier it would have been if she had let him come alone.

'Yes I did,' she said. Gently nibbling the corner of her lip, Charlotte peered into a half-empty ten-pack of John Player's before, perhaps thinking she might have greater need of them later on, slipping them back into her coat pocket. She followed Alastair's eyes along the platform, towards the front of the train. 'Looks like *The Flying Scotsman*'s on time.'

'Aye. Thi can set tha watch by it.' Charlotte smiled. It had been one of the things he'd used to say, in that daft Yorkshireman's voice, whenever the famous train hurtled past at Gamston Crossing, when they were kids. He fidgeted with his hands in his pockets, made sure his ticket was still in his wallet where he'd seen it was, not five minutes before.

'Thank you for letting me stay with you,' he said. 'I'm sorry about... all the bother.'

Charlotte shook her head. 'You've nothing to be sorry for. It was nice to wake up with you in my bed two mornings in a row.' Alastair nodded again. He could find no words to give any better answer.

Considering the night they'd had, he was amazed how she still managed to look so lovely, barely a scrap of make-up and fresh as a daisy. After her bath that morning, he'd struggled to focus on his toast and the week-old evening paper he'd pretended to read while she towelled herself dry at the foot of the bed and then dressed as casually and unselfconsciously as if there'd been nobody else in the

217

room. He wondered if she hadn't done it on purpose.

'I'm the one who should be sorry,' Charlotte said, as three rising notes rang out.

'*Passengers for the ten o'clock Flying Scotsman service to Edinburgh Waverley...*'

'I'd better get going.'

The prospect of having to return to Camberwell alone, without Alastair, sent a sudden cold shiver through Charlotte's whole body, and for a moment she wanted more than anything to beg him to go back with her, like she had done the previous afternoon. She knew there was a good chance he might still come, even after everything. 'I suppose so,' she said, capturing him forever in her blue-grey eyes. Alastair saw she was trying not to cry, and that it was a battle she was not going to win. He gazed up into the echoing roof for guidance.

'I don't want to leave you, Charlotte, all on your own,' he said. 'Won't you come back with me?' Charlotte seemed as if she were about to speak, but then instead threw herself into his arms and buried her face in his shoulder. The ticklish smell of her freshly washed hair rushed in like a dose of sadness. 'You don't have to stay here. I can come back at the weekend and fetch your stuff. I get cheap travel, being staff.'

He could feel her body trembling in his arms where he held her inside her coat.

'No, Alastair. I'm all right here. And you know me, I can look after myself.'

'But I don't want you to look after yourself,' he said pathetically, softly kissing her ear. '*I* want to look after you. I love you.'

'I know. And I love you. But you must go home now, to your friends, to your work. To Mary. You know I'm right,' Charlotte sniffed. 'Don't you? And what about mi mam? You promised her you'd go back and let her know I'm all right. Will you do that – *for me*?'

'*Platform Two for the ten...*'

Charlotte drew back and, taking him by the shoulders, gave Alastair a playful shake. It took all her strength not to let him see how her heart too lay torn to shreds in the pit of her stomach.

'Come on, don't let us get all silly again. You'd better hurry, or you'll miss your train.'

'Yes.'

'Thank you, Alastair,' Charlotte said, taking his hands and giving them a gentle squeeze.

'For what?'

'Just for being nice.' Her eyes suddenly flooded with tears which, a second later, came tumbling over her pale round cheeks. 'I'm sorry I've made you so unhappy. If, when you get back, you think it best if you no longer write to me... I'll understand.'

The throbbing drone of a diesel engine grew suddenly much louder as a guard blew his whistle and sent carriage doors slamming like dominoes from one end of the platform to the other. Alastair took Charlotte's face in his hands and drew her gently towards him. By the time they stopped kissing the last coach of *The Flying Scotsman* was already clear of Copenhagen Tunnel and the train thundering towards Peterborough. No matter. There'd be another in twenty minutes. And besides, *The Flying Scotsman* didn't call at Retford, anyway.

When finally his train was announced, they held each other tightly until the very last minute, leaving just enough time, after she'd kissed him once more, gently and on the mouth, to look back over his shoulder and see her disappearing down the steps to the Underground.

* * *

An inch or two closer and he would have been mown down, crippled in the station car park under a Mini driven by a lunatic. Trevor grinned through the open window. 'Now then, yer dirty little stop-out! Ah thought thee were never comin' 'ome.'

'How did you know I was on that one?'

'Little bird told me. Telephoned to say you were rather tired, so to look out for you in case you'd nodded off. Late night again?'

'Hmm. I slept like a baby. Ticket Inspector gave me a nudge at Newark.'

'Get in, then. I want to hear all about it.'

Alastair ran round the front of the car and dropped himself

into the bucket seat.

'Cheese and onion sandwich and some crisps there, if you want them,' Trevor said, flooring the accelerator and roaring out into the traffic. 'And your clobber's in the back. It's all there, except your copy of *Goldfinger*. I started reading it on the train last night and couldn't stop. You can have it back when I've finished it.'

'You do spoil me,' Alastair smiled, shoving a sandwich into his mouth. 'This is delicious.' When a moment or two later Trevor threw the car through ninety degrees into a narrow lane, Alastair's sandwich ended up on the floor, but he was far too hungry to mind a few bits of carpet fluff and the odd piece of gravel from the station car park.

Trevor looked at him with a wrinkled nose. 'You do know you stink like a perfume factory?'

'Eh? Oh, yes. I pissed my trousers on Saturday night. Twice, I think. After I lost you lot.'

'Sounds like I'm in for quite a story.'

'You are,' Alastair sighed. 'But I think we should save it for later. There's rather a lot to tell, and I don't want to distract you from the road any more than is absolutely necessary.'

In no time at all they were turning into Welgrove Terrace. Sarah was standing in the porch and a police car occupied the space outside number 7 where Trevor would normally have screeched to a halt. Sarah rushed towards them and crouched beside the open driver's window. 'It's Monica Bloomsberry,' she said. 'Dad found her this morning.'

CHAPTER TWELVE

'By! I wish my missus could bake half as a good as you, Mrs Braymoor,' the sergeant said politely. 'Oh, go on then, if you insist. It's delicious.'

Gladys smiled modestly, blushing till her cheeks turned almost as red as the curls that tumbled over the shoulders of her best floral-patterned dress.

'Mi gran does a good sponge, but it's norra patch on this,' smiled the young constable.

'There's plenty more, if you'd like some. Let me fill you up, Sergeant.'

'Thank you very much, Mrs Braymoor, you're very kind.'

The two policemen would happily have sat there all afternoon, eating home-made ginger cake and drinking gallons of tea out of Gladys's best china while Jock calmly told them of the grim discovery he'd made that morning at number 1, Ridgetop Allotments.

He'd taken Monica a few groceries, a pint of milk, bread, potatoes – the usual – as he and his son had done, once or twice a week, since she'd been poorly. It was no bother, top of the street. No, he mostly went up late afternoon, teatime, he said, rubbing his hands drily together, but he'd had a doctor's appointment that morning, so had arranged to work a later shift. It must have been just after eight o'clock, after he'd fetched his paper and picked up a few bits for Gladys, as well as for Monica, from Edmund's, the shop down the way.

Jock hadn't thought it at all unusual when Monica hadn't immediately answered the door when he knocked; she rarely did. And so, finding it unlocked, he'd stepped into the kitchen and, as he always did so as not to startle her, given her a wee call. 'Are yi there, lassie? It's only me – Jock.' While he unloaded her groceries onto the sideboard he'd whistled to himself, quite loudly, to be certain of making her aware of his presence, in case she was in the bathroom, or had the radio on in her bedroom and hadn't heard him. All the while, Jock said, opening his eyes wide, he'd expected at any moment to hear her come up behind him with one of her typical greetings. 'And about time an' all, Jock! A woman could be dead o' thirst before you bothered to come and put the bloody kettle on!' Jock looked between the policemen and smiled. Aye, he did sometimes stay for a cup of tea and a chat, he explained, feeling a strange and unnecessary twinge of guilt as he acknowledged his wife's supportive smile. She got very lonely, did Monica, having been more or less housebound since before Christmas. And she'd always been a night owl, worked in pubs and clubs all her life, aye. She would often stay up into the small hours, listening to the radio or reading a book, along with a small glass of something or other – 'a wee nightcap, yi know?' Yet no matter how late she sat up (Jock didn't bother adding 'or how much she put away'), Monica would always round her night off with a strong cup of tea, before washing up and setting out her breakfast things for the morning. It was a habit from the pubs – 'Nivver start the morrow wi' a mess yi made today.' That's how he knew something was amiss, Jock said. There'd been no breakfast things set out. And when he'd gone to light the kettle he'd found it empty and the teapot, still under its cosy, half-full with a stewed and filmy brew that must have been cold for hours.

The thought had briefly crossed Jock's mind that Monica might have gone back to work last night, something she'd talked a lot about lately. And where, enjoying being back among her old pals, she'd perhaps decided to stay over with the landlord and his wife. But having seen her coat and shoes by the back door, he'd soon dismissed this idea. He'd put the kettle on and washed up two cups and saucers ready, before wandering into the living room and giving her another shout. 'Are you there, Monica? It's only me, lassie, Jock. Ah've put the kettle on...'

That's when he found her. She was sitting bolt upright in her armchair. Her eyes were open, and on her face she wore an expression of deep concentration, as if she were listening, very interestedly, to what someone sitting in the chair opposite was telling her. Peaceful, aye. As he stood there before her, blank and shaken with surprise more than horror, it struck Jock he'd never seen Monica either so still or so quiet. Only her mouth had anything really deathly about it, the plump barmaid's pout, the mischievous 'Tek me as yer find me' smile gone, and in their place the pale lips of an old woman which hung slack and half-open to reveal the gaps where she hadn't bothered to put her teeth in. Jock wondered where all that energy and vivaciousness had gone, just like that, where it had all ended up. He thought how amused she'd have been to know that even in death she couldn't keep her big gob shut.

As he'd knelt to pick up the glass which lay on its side by Monica's feet – he'd done it without thinking, but trusted it wouldn't hinder the sergeant's investigation (it wouldn't) – Jock hoped his dear friend hadn't suffered too much at the end, and that perhaps the photograph album which lay open in her lap, turned to a picture of Charlotte and Alastair, aged about sixteen and fourteen, sitting with their guitars on the roof of a shed on the allotment, had been some small comfort to her in her final moments.

Jock had almost had a heart attack himself when the kettle suddenly began to shriek, but he was grateful of the opportunity to turn away from the dead woman and make himself useful. As he flicked off the gas it was perhaps only natural his thoughts should return to that afternoon, twenty-two years before, when he had called on Monica at her little flat above the paper shop. A packet of Monica's cigarettes lay on the sideboard. Jock took one, lit it, and, leaning against the draining board, inhaled deeply. 'I'm sorry, lassie,' he said, as the dirty dishes began to blur and shimmer before his eyes. 'I was nae soon enough to help yi. Not this time.'

Of course, Jock, hardly being the sort to come over all wet and sentimental, especially in front of policemen and his own family, left out the more personal elements – his feelings, the superfluous historical details about his relationship with Monica Bloomsberry – from his statement. He stuck to just the bare and necessary facts, which he knew was all that was expected.

* * *

'I'd no idea about all that stuff during the war,' Alastair said, as he strolled back with his father from the funeral directors. 'I mean, about Monica and Eddie.'

'Aye, well. It was nae such a joyous affair, yi know? He was a decent chap, Eddie, good company, good soldier. But he was always abysmal wi' the women.'

'So I gather. She told me about what you did, about the time you found Monica.'

'She knows about that, Charlotte, does she? I would nae think Monica would...'

Alastair shook his head. 'She found out at school, from a friend whose mam remembered it. She said they never really got on after that, Charlotte and her mam.'

'And yi say he wants nothin' ti do wi' her, now – Eddie? And wi' her mother gone as well, poor lassie.'

Jock stepped off the road, rested his foot on the bottom rung of the fence overlooking the allotments. The bright spring afternoon had lured out a few plot-holders, one or two who now waved from their little patches between makeshift sheds and greenhouses thrown up from old windows, doors and blacked-up corrugated sheeting.

'It was good of you to sort everything out,' Alastair said. 'The funeral and things.'

'She's no-one else, son. And it's nae bother. Few phone calls. Still no word?'

Alastair sighed. He'd written to Charlotte as soon as the policemen left on Monday afternoon. It was Thursday now and he'd heard nothing back. When he wrote again that morning, with details of the funeral on Monday, he'd enclosed the money for a return ticket, along with Trevor's parents' telephone number for her to get in touch. He half-remembered seeing a payphone in the downstairs hall of the Camberwell house, but it had never occurred to him to take down the number.

'There'll be a little money for her, when her mother's affairs are settled,' Jock said. 'Nae much, mind.'

'Eddie gave her a hundred quid.'

'It was a father she was after wi' him, no' money.' Jock turned to his son. 'Yi say yi had a wee falling oot, no?'

Alastair shrugged his shoulders. A train whistle screeched in the distance. 'The Fish,' he said, pulling back his sleeve to check his watch. 'I had a bit too much to drink – not *that* much. But I said a lot of not very nice things, about Charlotte and the sort of folks she goes about with.' He shook his head and puffed out his cheeks. 'I saw her with Eddie, on Saturday night, and... I thought he was her boyfriend, so, well there was a bit of bother and that's how all that came out, about Eddie and Monica and you, and a lot of other things besides. I didn't behave very well about it, really, Dad. But it was only because I...' Alastair looked away, across the allotments.

'Yi care aboot the lassie. I know.' Jock nodded and together they watched as the fish train belched its rattling silhouette across the horizon. Jock turned to Alastair with a careful expression and said, 'I'd say it must've been some showdown yi had, the two of yiz?'

'You could say that.'

'Yi think yi wiz mebbe still carrying a wee flame for the lassie?'

Alastair shrugged. 'I don't know. She'd changed such a lot – in some ways.'

'Aye, that can sometimes happen, son, with women. And yi'd been friends a long time, two of yiz. It can be hard when people – ' Jock gave Alastair's elbow a gentle nudge, his eyebrows shooting up into a bushy steeple as he nodded across the street. 'Look sharp, I think you're wanted here, the noo.'

'She's early,' Alastair said, as Mary came clip-clopping towards them, smiling in her bright red dress, the one with the white collar and matching band around the hem that ended nearer her knickers than her knees.

He felt his father's hand on his shoulder. 'You'll be all right, son, aye?' Jock said out of the corner of his mouth.

Alastair nodded. 'Yeah, I'll be all right, Dad. Thanks.'

'Hello, Mr Braymoor.'

'Hullo, Mary, love,' Jock said, straightening his tie. 'Go on then, away with yiz. Enjoy yersels. And dinnae forget, Alastair, you're at work the neet.'

CHAPTER THIRTEEN

After dropping a long rake of empties at Warinstowe sidings, they'd taken a heavy trainload of coal over the Trent towards Lincoln and on to Snipe Junction, from where it would probably make its way, later on, with another train crew, to High Marnham Power Station.

It was Friday, and the third night that week Alastair had fired the 22.25 for Walt Goodman. It was a good run, especially in the dark where, once you were clear of the yards, the pits, the lights and suffocation of the towns, and beating along through open country, the world beyond the cab windows would suddenly just fall away and become as black and endless as the night sky. You might have been whizzing across the universe in a space rocket, were it not for the infernal heat and noise, the constant back-breaking effort of feeding the fire and watering the boiler to remind you there was no machine quite so elementally earthbound as a steam locomotive.

Snipe Junction was never at its busiest at that hour and there was only one other crew in the enginemen's canteen, a bleakly strip-lit prefab lined with lockers and noticeboards, and with a long, battered table and bench-seating running down its centre. As they walked from the washroom, between the tracks, Alastair, at Walt's request, had hummed a couple of chart-topping tunes, but as the driver tore the lid off his snap tin and folded himself onto the bench, he stuck out his bottom lip and shook his head. 'Ah've heard on 'em, a course,' Walt said, reaching for a well-fingered copy of *Boxing News* that lay top of a pile of reading matter on the table and giving it a quick glance. 'But ah wun't know Godfrey Payne and his Comforters, or their music, if they were to come and play it in mi front room. I'll 'ave a look at it on telly, Sunday, though, if thee pal's on it. Drummer, you say?'

'Yes,' Alastair nodded, dropping a couple of tea bags into two mugs he'd quickly scrubbed out. 'You might like 'em, Walt.'

'I'm a bit too old for rock 'n' roll, duck. But don't think I don't see what you young uns get out on it, all yer Beatles and yer Crickets and whatnot. When I were your age, we 'ad it wit jazz bands, concerts and dancin', just same. It's all about gettin' wit lasses, in't it?'

Alastair smiled. He would miss working with Walt when he retired, determined as he was not to retrain for the diesels. 'There's no point me learning owt newfangled now, Alastair,' Walt had said on more than one occasion these past few months. 'I'll hang on while ever Langbrook does, then that'll be me done. No, duck; I started wi' t'steam, so I may as well end wi' 'em.'

Walt held his snap tin under Alastair's nose. 'Want an onion?'

'Bloody size of them! You pickle them yourself?'

'Ah did, arr. They're good uns. *Strong.*'

'Thanks.'

'Ah shall miss thee though, young un,' Walt said with a fond grin as he lifted his cap and gave his thinning grey-black hair a good old scratch.

Alastair winced. 'That vinegar, Jesus! You'll miss *me*, Walt?'

'Aye, ah will. If only to remind me how much better-lookin' I am than thee. Now if tha's done crunching, that kettle's boiled. It'll be cold again if tha's not sharp.'

Alastair pushed a mug of tea across to Walt and opened a packet of crisps. 'When do you think it will close, Walt, the shed? Shep keeps saying not to worry, but...'

'New diesel depot's about finished now. I shouldn't be surprised if we're not starting to wind up by end o' the year. They're taking most of this power station traffic from us now. We'll keep gooin' a bit yet, I should think. But I reckon by this time next year we'll about be shutting up and done.'

Walt, after examining some bright pink spread on his sandwiches, made an ungrateful face and pushed them aside.

'Cheese and pickle, if you want one?' Alastair said, tearing the lid off his grubby sandwich box. Walt took one, nodded appreciatively.

'You'll be all right, you young lads. Tek to these diesels in no time. Why, I bet tha can already drive a diesel wi' thee eyes closed.'

'In mi sleep, Walt. But only when Shep's not looking. It's like operating a train set; forward, reverse, brake. Rubbish.'

'Tha wants to join t'navy, Alastair,' Walt said, lighting an untipped cigarette as they stepped out into the clanking yard. 'Goo and see the world while tha's young and daft enough. Tha'd meet some lasses then, by God yer would! Eh? Every size, colour and shape tha can think on. Bloody 'ell, if I 'ad my time again!'

Alastair laughed. And then, tapping Walt on the shoulder, he nodded to where a huge Britannia class locomotive was being reversed off the turntable, gleaming under the floodlights as it barked huge and billowing clouds of smoke into the night air, so that for a moment the whole yard – sidings, wagons, signal box, coaling plant – was lost in a swirling fog of grubby cotton wool. They waited while the engine hissed and ground past them, the sleepers beneath their feet trembling under a small earthquake. 'It wouldn't be like this though, Walt, would it?' Alastair said, making a mental note of the name – *John Milton* – so that he could check it off against his *Ian Allan ABC*.

Walt's eyes visibly twinkled as he watched the engine being coupled up to their return working, a dark, glistening snake of petrol tankers for Tuxfield Concentration sidings.

'No, lad,' Walt smiled, shaking his head. 'It wouldn't be like this. Now, has tha remembered to fill them two mashing cans wi' fresh tea?'

'They're in my bag, Walt.'

'Good lad. Come on then, let's get this 'ere engine checked over. If tha's quick about it, I might even let thee have a turn at driving on t'way back.'

CHAPTER FOURTEEN

Gladys Braymoor very carefully folded her handkerchief in four and snapped it away inside her glossy black handbag. 'See you later, Mary, duck,' she said, in almost a whisper as she gave the girl's hand a gentle squeeze. She turned and blinked up at her son. 'It was nice for her, wasn't it, the service, and all them lovely flowers?'

'Yes, Mam, it was,' said Alastair. 'She'd have liked them a lot.'

'Will we see yi at the Fox & Hounds?' Jock asked, stepping forward, a vague, reassuring sort of smile on his lips. 'Some of her pals from The Market are having a wee drink, afore they go back.'

'She did have a lot of friends, didn't she? We'll only be stopping for one, mind,' Gladys reminded her husband. 'We won't be boozing it up all afternoon, even if others might.'

'Aye, he knows that, lass. He knows. I'm hoping Jumbo might let me have his autograph, now that he's a what-yi-call-it, a pop star, on the television.' Jock winked. 'Well, bye for now, Mary.' As he turned away, Jock caught his son's eye, pursed his lips and gave a little nod. Tiny gestures, but which seemed to say infinitely more than any words might have done just at that moment.

'We'll catch you up, Dad,' Alastair said. 'Tell the others we'll see them there, will you?'

Jock waved over his shoulder before offering Gladys his arm and leading her down the steep path through the churchyard towards where the group of young friends, Trevor and Sarah, Jumbo and Amelia, Frank and his new girl, Lindsay, dawdled in their mourning clothes among a handful of older neighbours at the edge of the car park. Just before the gate, Nigel Wells smiled proudly as Jean Britchardsley, using his shoulder for support, emptied a stone from her shoe and then quickly slid her hand back into his.

As Alastair peered one final time into the dry, crumbling earth, at the dead box with its shiny brass plate, the name and two

229

dates barely fifty-six years apart, a gravedigger cut across the grass to join his mate who'd been lurking behind the delicate screen of a willow. 'I've put kettle on,' he said, none too quietly. A wide smile spread across Alastair's face and for a moment he waited, half-expecting to hear Monica's voice bawl up from her dark hole 'And about bloody time an' all!'

He'd done well to hold it together this far. But when Monica did not call out, and he pictured her leaning towards him as she delved into her biscuit tin and said, through her gap-toothed grin, 'Mi last two Gingers, duck. You 'ave 'em. I know they're your favourites,' it all just came out. He burst like a silent dam.

'You really thought a lot of her, didn't you?' Mary said, taking his hand and resting her head lightly against his shoulder.

'Yes, I did. She was... She was just a very nice woman.' Alastair bit his lip and took a long, deep breath. 'And I didn't mind, you know,' he said, sniffling, 'I didn't mind running about after an old fart like her.'

Mary smiled, knowing it had been one of Monica's sayings. She turned Alastair towards her and slid her arms through his. 'I know you didn't. And she knew that too, Alastair. Monica knew that. You were a very good friend to her. You *and* your dad. I think she'd have liked to have adopted the pair of you, if she could have done.'

When Alastair had whispered a final farewell to Monica Bloomsberry, and nodded to the gravediggers that it was okay for them to commence shovelling back the earth they'd spent all morning digging out, he and Mary wound their way slowly down the path, hand in hand, towards where a wedding party had already begun to gather by the gates.

'So, you knew about Nigel and Jean?'

Mary looked mischievous. 'Maybe. I think it's lovely. Don't you?'

Alastair lifted his eyebrows. 'Well, yes, I suppose, but how – '

'It was Sarah's idea.'

'Our Sarah?'

'You know how Nigel's always had a thing for her.'

'Obsession, you mean.'

'Well, Sarah's always liked him, too – as a friend. And of course, she knows all about Trevor and Jean, what went on.'

Alastair doubted Sarah knew *all* that went on. How could she? She was Trevor's girlfriend, not his best pal.

'So she decided the best way to stop Nigel mooning about after her, and to keep Jean away from Trevor, was to get them together. It was simple really. When Nigel gave her a lift home that time, on his motorbike, Sarah told him Jean quite fancied him. Then we told Jean, in the Fox & Hounds, that Nigel was desperate to ask her out but was too scared in case she said "No". He took her to Matlock last Sunday, when you were in London at Jumbo's concert.'

'You scheming pair of witches! Well, good for Nigel. *And* Jean.' Alastair laughed. 'Crikey, *she'll* keep him on his toes.'

As the church bells began to ring, a ripple of joyful anticipation lit up the small crowd of friends and well-wishers who, armed with confetti and best-clothes smiles, awaited the bride's arrival. Beside a Morris Traveller, a photographer and his assistant bent over their variously sized cases, hurriedly assembling their equipment.

'She'll be here any minute,' said an old man on a three-wheeled pushbike. Women held their hats as they squinted along the main road.

'Awight, Alastair?'

'Terry! What are you... ?' Terry, smart in his dark grey suit, came over, very coolly winding on the film in a fancy-looking lightweight camera. 'Are you doing the wedding?' Alastair said, impressed. 'Blimey, you never dress like this to take pictures of steam engines. Mary, this is Terry from work.'

'Hallo, Mary,' Terry said shyly. 'Yes, I find steam engines is a lot more interesting to photograph than 'appy capples. But there's decent money to be had in this game, if you're any good at it. I'm only helpin' Ray out, here, but one day I'm finking I moight give it a go on me own. Shall see. You been at your friend's funeral, have you? Go off awight?'

Alastair nodded. 'It did, thanks, Terry. It was nice.'

'I can see the car!' a little girl squealed, excitedly.

'Here she comes!' said the tricycle man.

'Better get moiself ready,' Terry said, giving Ray a thumbs up.

231

'You on days this week, Alastair? See you in the morning, then. Nice-a-meet-you, Mary.'

They waited on the bridge, opposite the old mill, to see the big white car float past, silent but for the bonnet ribbons which fluttered in the breeze like a pigeon's wings. Mary waved good luck, squeezed Alastair's hand as the bride's father helped her out of the car and she became lost among the fuss of friends, ushers and bridesmaids.

Alastair and Mary turned onto the path to walk along the riverside. The water was low, the lazy current busy with ducks and swans.

'Alastair,' Mary said, after a thoughtful while. 'Did you think she'd come today? Charlotte?'

Alastair studied the path for a moment or two, chipped a small stone with his toe into the water.

'No,' he said. 'I don't think I did, not really.'

'I saw she sent some lovely flowers. They must have been very expensive.'

Alastair stopped, slid his arms around Mary and very gently kissed her lips. She did make such a lovely mourner. But he could imagine her reaction if he suggested getting down on the riverbank for a quick cuddle straight after a funeral.

'I feel like I haven't seen you for ages,' Mary said, pouting up at him. 'What with London, and then you being on nights all last week.'

'Yes, it does feel a bit like that, doesn't it?' The breeze off the river blew a mass of thick dark curls across Mary's face. Alastair swept them carefully aside to kiss first her nose, and then her lips.

'Alastair, were you serious, earlier, when you said to Frank that you might leave the railway?'

Alastair nodded slowly. 'Yes. But it won't be for a while yet. I'll stay on as long as Langbrook keeps going – another year maybe.'

'But what are you going to do then? Afterwards?'

'I'm probably going to make my dad a very happy man. And me too, all being well. But what about you, Mary? Do you think you could ever be happy loving a poor English student?'

It seemed as if the whole of Mary's face had become just one big, gorgeous smile. 'I think I could get used to it,' she said. 'But only if it's what you really want to do, though, Alastair.'

Alastair pulled her close and kissed her slowly, gently, for what felt like a very long time. Across the park the church bells began to ring out again, keener than ever.

'I really missed you when you were away,' Mary said, looking up into his eyes.

'I missed you too, Mary,' said Alastair. 'I missed you very much.'